THI

ABANDONED

Zoee Smith

Thank You Notes

For my amazing children, without you I am nothing <3

First of all I'd like to thank the following for keeping the faith and keeping me patient through writing the vicious stories of the Belmonte estate and of course giving me inspiration for my wonderful characters!; my amazing mother Joanne, you mean the world to me. You've lived the life a thousand times over and still you smile never change, I love you forever and a day. To my amazing boyfriend Lee, for mopping up the baby sick and washing the dishes while I lived my secret life of crime! Love you to the moon and back babe you're not only the father to my children but your my soul mate and the reason I get up every single morning with a smile on my face and love in my heart! You're the peas to my carrots, the Mickey to my Minnie.... and I wouldn't be without you for the world...

Stacey Rees, Jade Evans, Angharad Davies: Best friends, Always! No one will replace you girls! <3

To my amazing boys! The four of you have made me. You saved my life, without you I would literally be nothing. Thank you for the smiles, the laughs the tears, the amazing memories we have and will continue to have. I've watched you grow into such happy beautiful little boys and my heart bursts with pride at the mere thought of you! Love you all the moneys in the world, all the stars in the sky and all the fishes in the sea.

To my amazing stepson Luke- you complete me, you are the best big brother in the world, you're just the loveliest boy ever and I could never picture my life without you, you're going to capture the moment and make all your dreams come true. The world is yours babe shoot for the moon and grapple with the stars! Debbie&Gordon thank you for bringing him up so perfectly! He's a flipping credit to us!! Love you millions! My little Frankie-despite your lack of speech, you complete my world so much in so many other ways you're a little character! We'll get there in the end beautiful ☺ mammy loves you so much, your my first born, my world and you'll always have that special little place in my heart! Keep shining my star Love you little figs <3 Kalvin- well what can I say! You are my little comedian! Such a smart clever little boy! You're my best friend and I love you all the moneys baby boy!! Keep growing into that gorgeous little man I know you're going to be! You're my inspiration! My one in six billion I Love you peach! <3 Baby Brooklyn – you haven't been here for long but I already feel such an amazing connection to you! You've made me a proud mother to three handsome boys and you completed our little family!! You'll always be my baby!! That smiles a winner! Don't ever lose it! Mammy loves you <3 xxxx

To the most amazing writers who kept me sane growing up! Mandasue Heller. Jessie Keane, Kimberley Chambers and my absolute idol Martina Cole.... you took me to the depths, helped me through the toughest of times for that I will always be eternally grateful ☺

To Ami Jay- my sister from another Mr and of course my biggest fan ;) we may have been separated at birth, we may be cider drinking, shit talking, book reading Crazy kids but without your help and support this would have all still been just a dream... you're the peas to my carrots... Love ya ;) <3

To Cath- Your more than a sister, you're my truest most beautiful friend...and the person I trust implicitly I'm glad you followed your heart <3 Love you xxxxx

Last but not least I think I should say a quick thank you to the amazing artists and bands that helped me along the way! Second to writing, music is my passion! And I wouldn't have got through many a long night on the Belmonte without the help of my headphones and my favourites! Anyway guys enough of me rambling on I think I've had one too many wines! I hope you get as addicted to the Belmonte as I have! And hopefully this will be the first of many of our trips back there!!

Much love your all fucking perfect!

Enjoy!

Zoee x

Book One- The Belmonte.

When one lays down with the dogs

Then one should expect to catch the fleas.....

Chapter One

"Don't expect to see these fucking kids ever again Sammy, You've pissed on your fucking chips this time girl" Claire Horran called out down the stairs after her daughter, the door slammed shut and Claire breathed a sigh of relief. Sammy was hard work and yet again Claire found herself in the same old familiar situation where Sammy's latest Beau came before her two children Lily and Brogan. Both who were too young to understand their mother's abandonment but felt it all the same. Brogan being the eldest of the two kept questioning his Grandmother about his mother and why she never came home, a question Claire wasn't sure she could answer anymore with her usual story of "mummy's poorly" or "Mummy's not very well today" when describing Sammy's withdrawals from heroin or whatever drug she was flying off at the time weren't cutting it with him anymore. She hated lying to the children but she would never let them feel the pain she felt when she thought of how low her daughter had sunk. Claire felt nothing but hate for her daughter as she pounded down the stairs her anger so sever she was almost frothing at the mouth to see her grandchildren crying in the lounge her frown suddenly softened, as she took in their sad blue eyes red rimmed and full of hopeful tears that held on to the dream that mummy might just want to stay with them for the night. But the sadness that suddenly enveloped Claire's tired eyes showed the children what they had already knew. Mummy had left them Again.

A single tear rolled down Sammy Carters face as she reached the bottom foot well of the stairs to her mother's block of flats her emaciated body taking in the shrill icy wind as it wrapped itself around her, her whole body quivered as the cold enveloped her wrapping her up in its icy clutch. She was skeletal; her scarlet hair was tied scruffily on the top of her head in a topknot with an elastic band. The Adidas tracksuit she had borrowed from one of the men she was sleeping with on was easily four sizes too big and hung off her like a cloak making her seem all the more tiny. In her own warped way she did love the kids, she did, she just couldn't force herself to be a mother to them, and it was a burden she wasn't willing to carry. She wasn't responsible for her own actions never mind that of a two and a four year old. Her Lily was nothing but perfect, all blond hair and big blue eyes that shone like beacons on the dark winter sea, she was the prettiest little girl Sammy had ever laid eyes on, but Sammy was eaten with jealousy when people stopped to admire her pretty little daughter, she hated the attention little Lily received and so she had cast Lily aside like an unwanted toy. Her Brogan was the apple of his nannies eye, he was big for his four years with dark hair and emerald eyes, he was the spit from his father's mouth and Sammy couldn't even look at the child without wanting to vomit. She hated her son vehemently because he reminded her so much of her first and only love. Paul his name was, Brogans dad, she had only known him three weeks when she had fell pregnant with Brogan at the tender age of fifteen, all honeymoon period and no substance Paul was up and gone like a shot when he found out Sammy was pregnant, But as her mother had warned her those were the joys of fucking with married men, they took what they could and then they ran back home to their wives with their tails amply knocking their knees. Sammy had brought the boy into the world in an empty park on the estate surrounded by empty cans of beer and week old newspapers. Brogan never had a chance with the start he had in life and Sammy knew she would always owe the poor boy a mother. She was glad that her mother had agreed to be the kids legal guardian, it meant she could go out and act her age, get drunk, get wasted without guilt kicking in because no matter how hard she tried to block the fact out, she still gave birth to the kids so she would always feel like she had to at least think of them. Only the kids seemed to pop into her head at the most inconvenient of times, like when she'd smoked too much crack or drunk too much vodka, then Sammy tended to remember that she had birthed two children. Then guilt tended to fuck Sammy's head up all the more and she'd crave more drugs and more drink, just until her kids became just a distant memory and she would hit paradise and solace once more.

But for now Sammy needed a fix, she was starting to sweat, even though she was frozen and her head was starting to tick into overtime, she was agitated and the imaginary bugs that were scrabbling up and down her arms were starting to piss her off. She could see them she was convinced she could, her grubby nails scratching at her arms until the thin trail of blood started to run from the grazes but still they wouldn't piss off! Sammy knew she needed a hit, and fast, so she trudged in the direction of the other side of the Belmonte estate, in search of the only thing that would make the scurrying bugs and the static noise that filled her head settle. Heroin.

Leonora Powell or Leo as she was affectionately known to the druggies of the Belmonte opened her front door to a twitching Sammy and shook her head vehemently, the girl was a fucking mess of epic standard, her face probably once extremely pretty was now sucked in, her cheeks hollow and pasty and her eyes were grey and dead it was as if the life was literally being sucked out of the poor girl. Leo invited her in and sat her down in the living room on the shabby fabric sofa.

"And what can I get you then Sam?" she quizzed, her voice full of sarcasm as if she didn't already know the answer to her own question. She enjoyed seeing the girl squirm as she knew that she would be asking her for tick, Leo knew all of the local druggies giro days. It was her business after all. She smiled contently at Sammy, her face friendly and open, even though she couldn't wait to get this filthy creature out of her home. There was always something so dirty about having a drug addict in your home. Leonora wouldn't ever dream of touching drugs, she barely drank a drop of alcohol, but there was always money in the vulnerable drug addled no hopers of the Belmonte Estate, the place was a goldmine with the amount of crack heads and smack heads that swarmed the place in their drones. Sammy eyed Leonora shyly and handed her a crumpled up twenty pound note that she'd stolen from her mother's purse when she had been making the kids their dinner.

"Had a win on the scratch cards did you love?? Only your money don't go in till a Wednesday" Leo pointed out in an over exaggerated tone of voice, knowing that the girl had without a doubt been on the rob. When her reply was a half hearted shrug of the shoulders Leo knew it was time to hand over the goods and get this ungrateful little fucker out of her house. She handed over the two bags of heroin from a small purse tucked in her bra and shunted Sammy none too kindly out the front door. They were getting awful ungrateful to her lately she was starting to think she should give up dealing and start knitting; she let out a hearty laugh at her own wit! She could just see herself with a pair of knitting needles! What a hope.

Claire was sat at the kitchen table, her head in her hands, her eyes sad as she watched her grandchildren eating their tea, the house had been silent since Sammy had stormed out, each of them gathering their thoughts, and not one of them willing to share what was occupying their heads. She felt completely at a loss, she knew deep down that Sammy was a selfish horrid girl, who would never ever change for the sake of her kids, her heart though wanted to believe that Sammy was capable of change. Claire turned her attention back to the kids, they were such beautiful little people and they were so selfless and kind natured despite their rocky starts in life. Claire knew that she was doing an amazing job with these little mites. The same of course couldn't be said for her children. Sammy was hooked on whatever shit she could get her hands on and her Beautiful son Craig had died the year before last in a tragic unprovoked stabbing on the estate. He had been her world had Craig, he had made her the proudest mother on the planet when he had got his degree in English Literature at university at the beautiful age of twenty two. The other kids on the estate hated the fact that he was alien to them because he was successful, he loved to work and had never claimed a benefit from the social in his life. That was why he had been stabbed, because a gang of kids (the oldest member being only sixteen) attacked her boy because they accused him of "snubbing" them and being too snobby and stuck up to live on the

Belmonte. He had died at the scene of the stabbing and Claire could still here the resounding sounds of his body failing as she had held him in her arms sobbing her guts out willing him to live. She could hear his last words of "I Love you mum" echoing in her head every waking moment of the day. He had been perfection personified had her Craig, and she would give anything in the world, as much as she hated to admit it, even Sammy for him to be with her now. Maybe that was why Sammy was the way she was, because even Sammy knew that her mother worshipped Craig, Worshipped his memory and she hated the fact that Craig was gone and that Sammy was allowed to carry on living her sad little existence. It didn't seem fair to Claire somehow, it didn't seem very fair at all.

Chapter Two

Jenna Shearan sang along to the latest Celine Dion single as she attempted to conquer her pile of ironing, she was still in her pyjamas, her hair was all over the shop and she still had to get the baby out of bed. She gazed out of the kitchen window of her ground floor flat, someone was moving in opposite and she was desperate to check them out before she left for playgroup. It was paramount on the Belmonte that you knew who lived in the vicinity. Especially with the amount of druggies and criminals that the snobby bastards working for the council found necessary to just dump here. She lit herself a cigarette and held it between her teeth as she ironed the little pink flowery dress that her daughter Kiki loved so much. Jenna started humming along to the music as she spied the drop dead gorgeous man who had just jumped out of the removals van, all tight black t shirt, fitted jeans and short curly black hair that hung floppily on his forehead; he was just gorgeous like something straight from a movie scene. Jenna decided there and then that today was going to be a good day!

Jenna abandoned the ironing basket and shunted up the stairs to get herself ready "Kiki come on babe we're going to be late for playgroup" she called as she skipped past her daughter's bedroom. Entering her own room she pulled open the wardrobe doors and pulled out her tightest skinny jeans, the ones that made her ass look amazing! Jenna was a naturally beautiful girl, her hair was thick and glossy and fell down her back, she was slim with curves in every perfect place and she had a smile that could light up the darkest of rooms. She slipped into her jeans and pulled on her knee length leather boots. She left her hair out of its bobble and let it flow out in a big curly mass. Just as she was about to make a start on her face her mobile phone lit up on the bedside cabinet, it was Claire, Jenna quickly answered; a smile emerging on her face as she heard her panic stricken friend flapping about the gorgeous new neighbour that was moving in.

"Yes I know I've been watching him from the kitchen...Yeah he's gorgeous... Yeah I'm just getting dressed now.... pop down for a coffee before playgroup? Yeah I'm Going when Keeks decides gets out of bed... alright Hun see you then.... don't be long.... bye!" Jenna hung up and tossed the phone onto the bed before calling for her daughter again and returning to her makeup bag. As she applied thick lashings of mascara to her eyes she felt a twang of sadness as she thought of her Craig and how handsome he had been, they had been best friends since the age of four and she had loved him with all her being. They had been more like siblings and had never fallen out in all their years of friendship until the day he had been stabbed. It was a day that would haunt Jenna until the day she died, because she had told Craig the biggest secret that she could have ever kept from him and he hadn't taken to it well considering how close they had been. She just wished she had made a go of things with Craig. He had been the true love of her life and although they'd slept together on a few occasions he always said he saw her more like a sister than a girlfriend and he hadn't wanted to complicate they're friendship. As he had always told her "if it aint broke don't fix it Jen" She smiled thinking of his funny voice, he had always been so charming, so perfect. Kiki had loved him from day one, and he had loved her back, he was her favourite uncle "Craigy" he had been so good with her.

Jenna was suddenly snapped out of her trance by the sight of her gorgeous little girl standing in the doorway with her handbag over her shoulder, her crazy bed hair gathered around her face in a tangled mass, her pink ballet pumps on the wrong feet and her nighty tucked into her knickers;

"and where are you going young lady" Jenna giggled as her daughter sauntered into the bedroom, she was two going on twenty was Kiki, everyone who met her instantly took a shine to this truly beautiful little girl, she started giggled in delight as she ran to give her mother a huge good morning hug, Jenna held out her arms and caught the girl and sat her down on her lap attempting to sort out her messy mop of brown hair. "Claire's fetching Lily over now Keeks ready for playgroup" Jenna informed the little girl who was currently writhing on her lap through pure hatred of having her hair brushed.

The sound of the doorbell made Jenna jump up from the edge of the bed running down the stairs she shouted out "alright Claire don't be acting like you don't love being stood on my doorstep perving on the young new neighbours you old cougar you.... Oh hi" her face suddenly flushed crimson as she saw the handsome stranger from the removals van was stood on her doorstep.

"Hi" he smiled awkwardly "Uh I'm Dom Grey I'm just moving in opposite, I thought I'd come and introduce myself just in case you thought I was a weirdo or something. I know what these estates are like" he chuckled. Jenna nearly melted where she stood, he was absolutely fucking beautiful and here she was as red as a beetroot, her face half full of makeup and she'd made a complete twat of herself thinking he was Claire.

"Uh Jenna" she said offering her hand to him "Jenna Shearan. It's nice of you to come over and say hi" she replied trying to stop herself from stuttering. He was even more gorgeous close up his strong jaw, his straight, yet slight crooked nose which had obviously been broken at some point, rippled muscles underneath his tight t shirt and he smelled absolutely divine, she honestly thought she was going to die on the spot her heart was beating so fast. "Where have you moved from?" she questioned innocently trying her hardest to stem the crimson blush on her face and not make him feel any more awkward than what he already did.

"Well I'm originally from around here but I've moved out of town to Preston on business, only came back because my old mums been ill" he replied, showing those impeccably white teeth of his again, Jenna smiled as she saw Claire coming down the steps with Lily in tow thanking god silently that she no longer had to feel such a twat "This is Claire she lives upstairs" Jenna said as clearly as she could, her face still boiling hot with embarrassment.

"Uhhh the perving cougar" Dom chuckled offering his hand to Claire; whose face now equally resembled that of a garden tomato as she glanced back and forth from Dom to Jenna. Her mouth fell open, resembling that of a blow up sex doll as she shook his hand back confusedly. "Well I'll leave you two lovely ladies get on I've still got shit loads to do and the vans only mine for another two hours" he grinned as he walked off waving his goodbye before he entered flat number twenty four.

"What the fuck have you said now?" Claire chuckled as she bundled herself and Lily into Jenna's flat closing the door behind her.

"I'll get the kettle on, Lily, Keeks is upstairs in her room why don't you go and play while me and nanny have a cuppa" Jenna laughed as she began telling her friend the mornings events.

Chapter Three

Sammy awoke with the stale taste of sickly cheap cider on her breath, her mouth was sticky and her head was pounding so hard that it seemed to vibrate the floor, she didn't have a clue where she was, but she knew it wasn't her own flat; there was furniture here so it definitely wasn't her place. She sat up, praying her head would focus properly so that she could try and piece together the night's events. There were needles everywhere and tin foil scattered on the stained carpet with dirty black marks streaked on. The smell of sweat, piss and alcohol was overwhelming and Sammy coughed loudly as it hit the back of her throat, gagging slightly she covered her nose with the sleeve of her jacket. Only then did she realise that she had no trousers on and her underwear was scrunched in a ball in the corner of the room. She could smell herself then and she knew that she had slept with whoever was in this shit hole with her. She stretched her body out like a cat, her bones jutting out of her paper thin skin. Her whole body ached; she felt incredibly sore down below. Whoever this man was he must have a cock like a fucking anaconda she thought as she slowly got to her feet. The smell of the flat was fucking repulsive even by her standards and she knew that whoever lived here loved their drugs. It just looked like a junkie's paradise all hand me down furniture, dirty needles, even bed sheet curtains. The only source of light was coming from a grubby touch lamp in the corner. It was fucking filthy, but drugs were drugs in Sammy's eyes so as long as they kept supplying she'd learn to live in the dirt. She scuttled into the kitchen area the small pokey space was lit by a dim bulb in the ceiling; Sammy gagged at the smell coming from the blocked sink, the water so black and stagnant that she wondered how long it had been there. There were no cupboard doors, fag butts stubbed on the worktops and bits of decaying mouldy food in every orifice. The stench of the bin was so overpowering Sammy thought she would pass out, the contents had spewed out all over the greasy lino floor, grabbing a grease stained glass from the draining board Sammy poured a glass of water from the tap and gulped it down in one. Even the water tasted grubby. The sweat was pouring out of her pores and Sammy knew that she needed another fix, and soon. She spied the bedroom area and decided to go and venture and see if her friend, whoever he was, was still sleeping. She sauntered into the pitch black room, she started sexily swaying her nonexistent hips she got so lost in the moment that she stubbed her toe on the bedpost, grabbing her foot in her hands and hopping around painfully on one leg she quickly sat on the edge of the bed and soothed her injured toe. She reached over and shook the lump at the other end of the bed;

"Hey, Hey, wake up" she whispered to the lump in the threadbare quilt, she turned on the bedside lamp and attempted to again shake the stranger out of his drug fuelled sleep, Sammy took in her surroundings, just as she had imagined the bedroom was just as bad as the rest of the flat, in fact it was slightly worse. She leant over and touched his face, the panic sending her face deathly white as she realised, he was stone cold.

"Oh fuck no Leam!" she stuttered jumping off the bed in blind panic, she scrabbled back into the kitchen, hyperventilating as she stumbled over the litter ridden lino. Her eyes wide and the fear was making the sweat piss out of her, she was shaking so much she thought she'd be joining that poor bastard in the bedroom any second. She searched the kitchen high and low for a stash of some kind, she needed a hit now more than she ever did, just one hit and she'd be able to figure out what the fuck she was going to do.

Jenna and Claire had taken the kids out for a spot of lunch after playgroup and now they were sat outside their local sipping on a glass of wine each watching the girls playing diggers with a group of boys in the little park area. Claire was telling Jenna about her encounter with Sammy the day before, her words full of malice as she spoke about her daughter. Jenna could never warm to Sammy; she could never understand the girl or her actions especially towards her children. Sammy and her concepts on life were alien to Jenna, especially because Claire had always been an exceptional mother to Sammy and Craig. Neither had ever gone without and had always had the best of everything, especially when they were kids. Everyone always said about how much Claire had spoilt her children, dressing them in the smartest clothes, buying them all the top of the range toys. Their upbringing had been the complete opposite to Jenna's whose mother had been a raging violent drunk, who had suffered domestic violence all her life. Helen had turned to sleeping with the majority of the pub folk just so that she didn't have to spend the nights alone. Jenna didn't even know who her father was; her mother Helen had always referred to him affectionately as "That cunting sperm donor" Jenna had grown up willing that she would never ever turn out like her mother had. She had died of liver poisoning a few years back, and Jenna had never ever felt a relief like it in her life. Her mother dying was like balm to her, she knew that her mother was no longer suffering and now she could rest in paradise without her demons haunting her anymore. To Jenna there was nothing more satisfying than the thought of her old mum finally being at peace with herself. Her life had never been worth living in the first place, Jenna knew that her mother had just been surviving and in a selfish way Jenna was envious of the upbringing that Craig and Sammy had received. She would have given up anything as a child to have a mother like Claire. A mother who actually loved her children. Instead of a mother who depended on her children to care for her when she was pissed. She could slap Sammy right in her fucking arrogant face for the way she was treating Claire, Jenna really did love the bones of the woman. She had taken her in as a child; Claire's place had been Jenna's safe house growing up. It was where Craig was, it was where her happiness and her solace were and it would always be where her heart was. She sighed as she watched Kiki and Lily playing with the group of boys, the two girls were more like sisters and their bond was incredible despite their youth. Both girls loved each other unconditionally and Claire always affectionately commented on how the girls reminded her of how Jenna and Craig had once been

"What's up babe" Claire asked her voice full of concern, she could see Jenna was miles away.

"I can't stop thinking of him today Claire, it still hurts so much" she replied, her voice quivering, thick with sadness, the sad smile on her face made Jenna seem all the more beautiful. Claire held the girls hands, she would have given the earth for her Craig to have made an honest woman of Jenna, but he had always been scared of ruining their perfect friendship.

"Now missy, we'll have none of this" she smiled "He's always with you, he never left your side when he was alive, what makes you think he'd leave you now he's in spirit. He loved you so so much Jen" she smiled now a genuinely beautiful smile as she thought of how much her son really had loved his best friend. "Now then" she continued "Let's have another drink shall we? And maybe we'll have a little reminisce about our favourite boy" she winked at Jenna and went to fetch another round of wine. It was going to be a long afternoon, of that Jenna Shearan was certain.

Chapter Four

Jenna giggled as she lay under the covers propped up by the duck feather pillows of the bed.

"Wise men Say, only fooooools rush in, but I caaaaaant help falling in love with youuuuu" Craig was stood at the foot of the bed steaming drunk serenading her in his boxers. He was coming to the end of his strip tease and Jenna was flushed red and laughing her head off as he started flexing his muscles at her. He thrust his hips in her direction as he took another gutsy swig from his chilled can of Stella Artois. He had the body of a fucking god all muscles in the right places, naturally gorgeous and toned. He really was perfection. He dived on the bed grabbed her in his big embrace, his eyes locked on hers as he kissed her deeply, his tongue tracing her mouth so romantically. His body so close to hers she pulled him closer. She kissed him back, moaning in ecstasy as he traced her body with his gentle touch. Every single ounce of her ached for him, his steely eyes gazed at her with such affection and lust. He wanted her now, and despite every part of him screaming out that he shouldn't he had to have her. She was the only person who knew him, really knew him. And as he entered her, he knew that she would always be the one. Now as they made love for the first time and she had given herself to him he loved her even more. It wasn't awkward as he thought it would have been, there was nothing but their amazing bond and as he came inside her he whispered softly in her ear;

"I Love you Jen"

Chapter Five

Jenna awoke the following morning with a stinking hangover. She was in Claire's she knew that much, she could hear her singing along to UB40 downstairs. It was then that Jenna realised that she was in Craig's bed. She sat up and looked around the room lovingly rubbing her tired eyes; it was just as he had left it. The picture of the two of them in its pride of place on the bedside cabinet she smiled at how happy they had looked his big strong arms around her waist both grinning at the camera. She pulled the duvet up to her face inhaling deeply, hoping just to smell a trace of him. The musky scent of his Joop aftershave filled her nostrils and she knew that Claire must have been spraying his sheets with it just to feel he was still here. She sank her head into the quilt and sobbed uncontrollably, her whole body shuddering as the big fat salty tears rolled down her cheeks. She missed him so much. He should be here now cuddling up to her just as they had done for many nights growing up. He had been her absolute life; they had lived to love one another. There was no other way to describe their relationship; they were best mates, soul mates. Jenna pulled herself together, went over to the wardrobe and pulled out one of his favourite Adidas tracksuit jumpers. Pulling it on, it felt as though those big strong arms of his were around her once more and she felt as though she had come home. She opened the bedroom door and padded down the stairs; Claire was in the kitchen cooking the kids a cooked breakfast, the smell was enough to make Jenna feel nauseous. She leant on the doorframe and watched as her friend swayed her hips singing along to Craig's Ub40 CD. They had been his absolute guilty pleasure; everyone had taken the piss out of him whenever he used to play it. But now they treasured hearing his favourites. It gave them comfort.

"Oh babe I didn't see you there!" Claire exclaimed catching sight of her friend in the corner of her eye, she saw Jenna was wearing Craig's jumper and she smiled softly. "Haven't seen you in that one for a while" she giggled remembering how Jenna had always had this ritual of wearing one of Craig's shirts or jumpers for breakfast after they'd been caught after one of their many one night stands. It had been a household joke for years that if Jenna was in one of Craig's Jumpers in the morning then she'd been on the nest the night before. As the song changed to "Kingston town" Claire ran to turn the stereo up, it had been Craig's funeral song and his all time favourite. She closed her eyes and hummed along and Jenna knew that Claire was feeling the same stab of sadness that she did every time that she heard the song. Claire went back to her cooking, so that the kids didn't see the single tear that was rolling down her cheek.

"Thanks for having Keeks for me last night Hun, I feel like death this morning, now I know why I don't drink all that often" Jenna smiled as she spoke. She had never felt so shitty in all her life, her makeup had run down her face leaving big black streaks down her face. She smelt like a brewery and her stomach felt like her throat had been cut because it was so empty. Claire laughed placing a plate in front of her, a greasy breakfast was the last thing Jenna wanted to see but she knew if she didn't eat she'd probably faint.

"You look as bad as I feel" Claire replied placing the kids plates on the table before handing Jenna a big mug of tea and sitting down herself checking that each of the kids had their plates and cutlery and that none of them wanted anything else before she settled herself down.

"Nannies got Bad Head so shh" Lily commanded to her brother who was sat opposite her, his egg running down his chin as he gobbled his breakfast down in huge forkfuls. For a four year old Brogan had an amazing appetite and it always left Jenna in awe how quickly he could polish off such huge portions in his little body. He was like a little piglet shovelling his fork in his mouth and making his usual funny grunting noises as he ate. Lily's face was etched with disgust as she watched her brother, her eyes wide like saucers in pure amazement; she was a funny little girl. Her humour left them all in stitches. Brogan nodded and grunted, not even taking his eyes away from his plate which led to lily shaking her head and daintily picking up her knife and fork to begin her breakfast. Claire and Jenna both sat there smiling to themselves pushing the grease laden breakfast around they're plates. The smell of stale alcohol and lard was eminent and they both felt like complete shit! Jenna picked up a small piece of sausage on her fork and attempted to bring it to her lips before placing the knife and fork back on the plate again. She couldn't stomach it, just yet.

As soon as the kids had finished they're breakfast Claire ordered they go and get changed out of their pyjamas whilst her and Jenna cleaned the breakfast plates away.

"Keeks when you're dressed we'll go home yeah? Mummy's got to clean the flat babe. But we'll come and see Lily and Claire later okay?" Jenna explained kissing he daughter affectionately on the top of her head before she bounded out the door after Lily.

Chapter Six

It was about half twelve in the afternoon when Jenna finally managed to get back to the flat, Kiki had demanded to stay with Claire and they had agreed that she would go back up at four to pick her up. She had just walked in through the door and turned the radio on when there was a knocking from outside. Jenna peeped through the spy hole curiously she wasn't expecting anyone so it must have been one of the neighbours; she was surprised to see Dom standing on her doorstep. She opened the door and greeted him with a great big waft of her drunken breath as she muttered an almost inaudible hello.

"Oh someone had a rough night" he chuckled catching sight of her unwashed face and her scraped back hair; she was still fucking gorgeous though. "I was wondering whether you had the number for the housing association, the gas metre is playing up and I haven't got any hot water for a bloody shower" he smiled

"Come in" she smiled; She barely knew the guy but she had found herself trusting him enough to invite him into her home.

"I'm pretty sure it's in my mobile, You'll probably be told to ring the gas supplier though because I don't think it comes under housing association maintenance thingy's" she said grabbing her mobile of the mantelpiece and offering him a seat on the leather sofa.

"Boyfriend?" Dom quizzed innocently, nodding toward one of the many pictures of Craig and Jenna that were lovingly placed around the lounge. She smiled sadly before replying;

"No he was, well is my best friend"

"Wouldn't like to get on the wrong side of him, he's huge" Dom chuckled taking in the muscles on the stranger in the pictures.

"He died last year..." Jenna's voice trailed off as the sickness that came with admitting Craig was gone enveloped her. Dom could see the poor girl's sadness and his heart went out to her. She was clearly devastated and the guy in the photos had obviously meant a lot to her.

"What happened if you don't mind me asking?" he quizzed

"He was stabbed" the bitterness in her voice didn't go unnoticed as she scribbled down the number for Dom she noticed his discomfort.

"Sorry" she said her voice was soft again now "It's just since Craig died, I can't stand this fucking shit hole and the drugged up cunts that live here. But like Claire I need to be surrounded by him, by his stuff, by his friends, by his family you know? It helps that I know he's still here as long as we're all here too." She spoke of him with nothing but pride lacing her voice and Dom knew that this Craig had been someone very special indeed. "I tell you what" Jenna added "why don't we have a housewarming party to invite you to the estate? I'll invite Lee and his girlfriend Lisa from across the hall and Claire's neighbour Tracey will come, at least then you'll get to know everyone" she said in an excited tone, she had got an idea stuck in her head and now she would make sure that she followed it through. She could do with a good party, and seems as the one year anniversary of Craig's death was coming up it would take their minds off everything.

"That's a nice idea thanks Jen. How about Saturday?" Dom replied

"Saturdays good with me!" she squealed excitedly, taking the notepaper from Jenna, Dom said his goodbyes and made his way home to ring the gas people.

Chapter Seven

Jenna pulled on her tight black dress and pouted her lips at the mirror, she looked absolutely beautiful her long dark hair was curled tightly and flowed like a veil down her back, her eyes were a Smokey black and thick with mascara and her red lipstick gave her outfit a sultry pop of colour. The sound of Ke\$ha blaring from the radio getting her well into party mode and the bottle of white wine and pink lemonade she'd already drunk had gone straight to her head. Tonight she was going to get absolutely mortal in the memory of her best friend, a whole year had passed already. The pain was still so raw. She zipped up her knee high leather heels and checked herself over once more, tousling her hair and applying one more coat of lippy before heading downstairs to wait for her guests to arrive. She turned the stereo up a little louder and poured herself another glass of wine, she was quite excited for tonight actually. Everyone had decided to have a little drink in hers before going out into town for the night. Hearing the thumping at the door she quickly slapped her flashiest smile on and opened the door to Dom who looked absolutely breathtaking in his half open shirt and tight fitting jeans, his hair was tousled neatly and he smelt absolutely delectable. Jenna hugged him a welcome and handed him over a beer before inviting him into the lounge.

"Ooh don't you look handsome" she laughed cheekily showing all her beautifully straight white teeth as she sat down next to him on the sofa before pulling a little bag out of her bra. He knew instantly it was cocaine; she tipped a small amount onto the back of her mobile phone and expertly snorted it off the back with a cut off straw.

"Want one?" she quizzed her voice thick with phlegm as she drew back the rest of the coke from her nose. She instantly went back to looking like normal Jenna again. He could tell this wasn't a regular occurrence with her. She was obviously on a mission tonight, and who was he to judge her. He quickly nodded his head and took the small bag from her. He knew that tonight was going to get very messy indeed. The sound of the door going sent Jenna into a sudden panic "Quick sniff that!" she giggled like a naughty school girl as she stuffed the bag back into her bra "Claire doesn't know I'm sniffing so get it gone quick!" she smiled as she sauntered off to answer the door. Dom couldn't help but watch her cute little ass wiggle out of the room. She was looking fucking smoking there was no denying that, and he'd give his left bollock just to get an in with Jenna, she was just absolutely fucking perfect. He had to laugh at her hypocriticalness mind. It was the only the other day she was saying she hated drugs and now here she was with a gram stuffed in her tits.

Jenna returned with a group of girls and probably the hardest looking man that Dom had ever seen. He was fucking huge with rippling muscles that stuck out vividly under his tight black jumper.

"Right Dom, this is Sarah, Becky and Emma, they all live upstairs, this is Vick she lives next door to you and this is Lee and Lisa they live next door to me" she explained pointing to each person as she named them, Dom hugged each girl in turn and offered his hand to the huge man who hung over him like a giant. He returned the shake his huge meaty hand almost crushing Dom's. He was obviously a face and obviously not one to be fucked with. Jenna went about her duties handing everyone drinks and offering small talk with the other girls whilst Lee and his girlfriend Lisa went through to the kitchen to have a quick line before Claire arrived. Jenna followed them out dragging Dom with her.

"How are you doing babe?" Jenna asked her face etched with an air of sadness as she gave Lee a real hug this time, he held her close to him the tears in his eyes imminent as he nodded his reply.

"Lee was Craig's best boy mate" Jenna explained to Dom before going off to answer the door for the third time.

"It's Claire!" they heard the girls screeching in the living room and Lee started laughing as he put his bag of drugs back in his pocket "Now the party really fucking starts" he chortled going off to join the rest of them he turned to Dom, "Best of luck living round here mate their fucking animals. Now come on are we welcoming you to the Belmonte or what!" he half shouted, half laughed as he wrapped his arm around Dom's shoulder and led him out to the party.

Chapter Eight

Town was absolutely buzzing and Jenna Shearan was incredibly drunk, incredibly drunk and absolutely off her fucking face. She was currently up on the DJ's stage in the Red Lounge dancing her head off with Claire. The music was thumping and the girls were in fits of giggles having a dance off which Jenna was winning by miles. But Claire didn't seem to care at all. She didn't even know what twerking fucking was but attempted to join in all the same! The drinks were flowing and the gang were having a fabulous time welcoming Dom to the estate. He had made some new acquaintances in his neighbours and was glad that he finally had some "friends" in his new surroundings. He ordered another round of drinks and went to join Lee who was sat at a VIP table in the corner handing out coke like it was sherbet to any Tom Dick or Harry that would have a line with him. Turned out that Lee was everyone's best friend, he seemed to know every single person in the club and they were all too willing to lick his arsehole just to be seen with him. He was currently in conversation with one of the promoters for the club, her tiny frame encased in a see through lace body stocking, her nipples jutting out like two little peas on her chest, Dom had to laugh because despite Lisa sitting right next to him with her arms folded across her chest Lee's eyes were still fixed firmly on the girls tits. Dom on the other hand had his eyes set on a much more worthy prize. That prize was currently attempting to pole dance on Claire, writhing like a twisted cat on Claire's leg whilst Claire was practically pissing herself with laughter. She looked so carefree, so fucking beautiful and Dom wanted her. Dom needed her. And he would get her, if it was the last thing he ever did. She really was stunning and Dom was pretty sure that right now she had the eyes of every man in the club on her. As she gyrated on the stage with Claire he could see every gorgeous curve of her body and he craved her, craved her on him.

Jenna went over to the DJ booth and asked him for one very special request before going back to the VIP with Claire. At first the DJ had point blank refused to play the song she had requested, but had been forced into reconsidering when Jenna explained what it was for. She was all danced out and was looking forward to getting home, her feet were killing her and she wanted to get her head down for a few hours before she went to pick Kiki up in the morning. She came and sat right next to Dom and waited for her song to come on. The opening to UB40's "Rat in me kitchen" had everyone in hysterics, it had been Craig's karaoke song and had left the all in stitches every time he had sang the "I'm gunna fix that rat that's what I'm gunna do I'm gunna fix that rat!" chorus in his put on Jamaican accent. There wasn't a dry eye at the VIP table as they all sang their hearts out and raised a glass to their beloved Craig and the life that got so viciously snatched from him.

Chapter Nine

Craig was sat on Jen's sofa with his head in his hands. He had never thought she would ever sleep with anyone else, they had never felt the need to as far as had been concerned. They had been each other's firsts and as far as he was aware he had been her only partner up until right now. Jenna sat crying big fat tears as she showed him the pregnancy test that was in her hands.

"What am I gunna do Craig? It was a mistake a stupid fucking mistake and now look at me!" she shrieked "Fucking pregnant by some cunt whose name I can't even fucking remember!" Her sobs were stifling and she was shaking violently. Craig held her to him, his big strong arms enveloping her

"Shhhh" he whispered taking in the scent of her hair and kissing her head softly "We'll be okay, I'll look after you babe, and mum; you know she thinks the bloody world of you. You're not alone I promise" his voice was so soft and calming. Jen had never felt so scared in her life but Craig made her feel so safe and she knew that he would be there for her and the baby even if he thought it wasn't his.

Of course Craig would never admit how genuinely hurt he was with Jens betrayal. He knew he would never abandon her. He just wished that it could have been their baby. He wished that he could have been the baby's daddy and he wished that he could make a future with Jen... but he'd never ever risk their friendship... no matter what the cost was.

Chapter Ten

It was gone three in the morning when the gang got back to the estate. Claire went straight home; Lee and Lisa had walked her to the front door and made sure that she got to bed safely before calling it a night themselves. Being the gentleman that he was Dom was half carrying, half dragging Jen to her front door. She was steaming drunk and hadn't stopped crying since they'd played Craig's song in the club. She was slurring something about seeing Kiki but Dom who was also pretty intoxicated himself was barely listening anymore. He had got to the point where he was just agreeing every now and then so she thought she still had his attention. They cut across the car park and made it to the front of their block of flats, she was laughing hysterically now as she stumbled to the floor her heel buckled and snapped off her shoe causing her laughter to ricochet around the estate. Dom picked her up gently and helped her to the front door;

"Where's your key babe?" he quizzed propping her up against the doorframe, trying to keep himself balanced. Her head flopped onto his shoulder as he patted her down looking for her key, it was then that she grabbed his hands and pulled him into her. He looked into her eyes that even though they were like fucking saucers dancing about in her head they had the power to posses him, pull him in. She trailed soft little kisses up his neck, each sending shivers down his spine. He was tingling sensationally as finally her lips locked his and suddenly in that moment he was addicted to this beautiful girl. She kissed him harder and he reciprocated, thrusting himself against her so she could feel his erection nearly bursting out of his boxers. She pulled him closer wrapping her legs around his waist as he pinned her to the door his tongue evading her mouth in long passionate strokes, he nuzzled into her neck and ran his hands against her thighs, she pulled him closer moaning quietly into his ear as he kissed across the top of her breasts.

"Keys?" he repeated gruffly, his hands slipping her dress up around her waist exposing her black silky underwear. She fumbled in her bra before dropping her door key into his palm. He scrabbled with the lock, too over excited to get the door open. She continued to kiss him as he fumbled about with the door lock tugging at the buttons of his shirt almost ripping them clean off. Such was her need to feel him on her. He finally managed to get the door open, carrying her over the threshold he kicked the door shut casually behind him. Dropping her none too gently on the couch she started tugging at the belt of his jeans. Her eyes manic as she yanked it open, she was licking her full lips as she eased his jeans down. Exposing his rock hard penis, she took him into her mouth and sucked hard. He was breathless wrapping his hands around her hair and forcing himself into her mouth further. He pulled her dress up over her head and smiled broadly as he took in her gorgeous body, her shapely thighs, gorgeous pert breasts that despite her having a child were still firm on her chest. She was just fucking beautiful. Even know as she was sucking him off, with her mascara running and her lipstick smudged all over her face, he wanted her. He eased her head away from his throbbing member and scooped her into his strong arms before carrying her through to the bedroom kissing her harder with every step he took. He slung her onto the bed he started clawing at her underwear tearing them off within seconds. He was just about to enter her when he could hear that she was crying, small stifled sobs and he quickly jumped off her bed, his face etched with confusion.

"What's wrong?" he asked, his voice quivering now as she was really crying hard, he automatically assumed that he had hurt her.

"Get out! She screamed clutching the sheets to her naked body. She was hysterical now her face was contorted; she looked like she was ready to claw his fucking face off. Dom instantaneously grabbed his boxers from the floor and quickly dragged them on; he was angrily going through the motions. He was trying to make out what he could possibly have done to her. He hadn't said anything to her, he hadn't handled her too roughly, and he was fucking confused alright. He grabbed his shirt off the sofa and pulled on his shoes before slipping out of the front door, slamming it shut behind him. He needed to calm down. He rushed across to his flat glad to be in comfort of his own home, surrounded by his stuff and where there weren't any crazy fucking women! Jen had really scared him and he wondered what the fuck he had even done to upset her so much. He eventually put it down to too much drink and too much fucking coke! He sat up until the small hours playing the nights events over and over in his head. Little did he realise that Jenna was lying in bed doing exactly the same thing. Dom had been so nice to her, so loving, it hadn't been anything he had done as such and she knew that he would probably never want to speak to her ever again. It was Craig, he was etched in her head and she couldn't dream of going with another man, knowing that Craig had been the last man to touch her, to make love to her. It felt wrong somehow, as though she was deceiving him. As much as she knew it was stupid and as much as she hated feeling so disconnected from the reality that Craig was never ever coming back to her. She still tried her hardest to convince herself that he would walk through the door any second and whisk her and Kiki away from this horrible place. She missed him so fucking much and all she could do was carrying on surviving despite the ever growing need to be with him that was forever grasping hold of her. Why couldn't it have been one of the fucking junkies that had been stabbed? Why didn't he fight back more? He was a big man capable of anything yet he had succumbed to a bunch of kids! And that was all Johnny Fenton had been was a kid. Jenna knew she was being selfish but she couldn't help the way she felt, and as sleep enveloped her. So did the nightmares that crept up on her every time she closed her eyes.

Chapter Eleven

It was another three weeks before the body of Leam Reynolds was found, his decaying corpse had been found after the postman started smelling a peculiar odour every time he was delivering to his address. The police had done their door to door enquiries and if they were honest the boy would not be missed. What they did know though is that whoever had been in the flat with him at the time of his death had cleaned him out. His drug stash under the floor boards had been disturbed and his wallet had been emptied. That being without whatever else they had taken with them. Scum. That was the only words to describe the junkies of the Belmonte Estate. You'd think with them all being needle pushers they would have stuck together, But no, these lot were of a different fucking breed round here. They were animals. The police had come to the conclusion that he had died of an accidental overdose of heroin and the case was wrapped up within a week. The police had no time for the drug moguls around here. The big mystery was who was the brazen fucker who had robbed the poor bastard blind? And where were they now?

Chapter twelve

Lee had just finished fucking his latest conquest. He never usually brought his girls to the home he shared with Lisa. But he was feeling brave today and couldn't be arsed to make the drive to Sasha's house which was over the other end of town. She was a classy bird, all high end dinners and fucking church going parents and she had completely freaked out coming to the estate. Lee had pissed himself when she turned up as white as a sheet because she'd never "ventured to these parts before" as she had so quaintly put it. He liked her though because she knew she wasn't his only woman. She wasn't delusional either; some of them got too attached and started threatening to tell Lisa if he didn't leave her. Sasha though used him just as he used her, she had a husband and they had been happily married for years. But he was a lot older than her thirty years at seventy seven and so the sex life had all but fizzled out. She still loved her husband to death but she missed the attention and affection that he had once lavished on her. Lee lit himself a cigarette and settled himself back against the headboard. He hated being unfaithful to Lisa but he couldn't help it; he simply couldn't keep it in his trousers.

Lisa knew that he slept around, but she wouldn't accept a permanent fixture, she loved Lee too much to let him succumb to some slut who would try and flounce into her mans bed and into his wallet! The thing with Lee was that he liked to please people, constantly handing out his money or his drugs; it was easy for girls to take advantage of his kind nature. It wasn't that Lee didn't feel guilty for cheating on Lisa he really did love her; she was his stability, the only woman in his life that he really had given himself to one hundred percent. He would have given Lisa the world if she asked for it, but he would never stay faithful, he just didn't have it in him. He lit himself the joint that sat in the ashtray, inhaling the thick hazy smoke he laid back in the bed and cuddled into Sasha who had fallen asleep beside him. She was snoring softly her head bobbing up and down as his chest rose and fell. Lee finished his joint and drifted off to sleep himself. It was only eleven thirty in the morning and Lisa was in town shopping with her mother so she wasn't due back for hours yet. It gave him enough time to have an hour or two with Sasha before he carted her out. It was probably the worst mistake he would make in his life. Ever.

Jenna was sat out on Claire's veranda sipping a hot mug of coffee, the winter winds were starting to chill the air and the skinny jumper she was wearing was doing nothing to keep her warm. She may as well have been sitting there bollock naked. She still hadn't spoken to Dom and had avoided him like the plague ever since their little encounter. The thought made Jenna sad, because despite everything that had happened between them both she knew she had over reacted. Craig would have wanted her to be happy, not shuddering every time she thought of another man. She had to face up to the reality that Craig was never coming home. No amount of tears that she cried, or how hard she wished it not to be true, he was dead and sooner or later they'd all have to get back to normal. It was hard there was no denying that, but keeping his memory alive was even harder when everyone acted as though he would walk through the door any second with his big grin and his cheeky eyes. Life was a bastard sometimes. It really fucking was. Claire had pulled out the family photo album again and Jen really wasn't in the mood for a trip down memory lane, it was bad enough already without having Claire sobbing to her before twelve in the afternoon. So she faked a headache, deciding that she and Kiki were going to go home, have a bath, put their pyjamas on and have a film day. She needed to be with her daughter today, just to chill out and do girly things with her, she had been so wrapped up in herself lately and her own drama that she hadn't batted an eyelid over little Kiki who had taken it all in her stride despite her tender age.

She put the little girls coat on and said her goodbye to Claire, it was fucking freezing out and she was glad she'd put the heating on before coming out otherwise the flat would have been like the fucking arctic when she got in. As she came down the stairwell she spotted Dom putting his rubbish out, it was too late to go back up the steps either because he had already spotted her. He smiled an awkward smile and Jens heart went out to the poor guy, he was so bloody lovely. If the shoe had been on the other foot she would have fucking slapped him. He turned to walk back into his flat when she called his name, she didn't even know why and regretted it instantly but she had to sort things out with him, they lived across the hall from one another, they had the same friends. They couldn't exactly avoid each other could they?

"Uhhh Hey Jen" he replied clearing his throat, turning round to face her now. She came down the rest of the steps and stood in front of him the look of curiosity in his eyes was evident and Jenna could kick herself for what she had done to him.

"I know you probably think I'm a right twat" she whispered "but I really am sorry about what happened....." she trailed off on a tangent, her voice thick with embarrassment.

"Well I know not to ask you to suck me off again" he chuckled his voice jovial and he quite enjoyed watching her squirm at the mention of what had happened. Her face was turning that ever so lovely beetroot colour again. "Forget it" he laughed before playfully punching her arm and she could see by the kindness in his eyes that he truly did mean it.

"You got time for a coffee?" she asked him subtly her kind eyes flickering to and forth from him to Kiki "Mummy makes a mean hot chocolate doesn't she Keeks?" she smiled at the gorgeous little girl who was nodding frantically in her arms "Call it my way of saying thanks for not being a dick" she added looking back at Dom

"Now what man would I be if I said no to hot chocolate with two gorgeous girls such as yourselves" he replied, his eyes twinkling as he linked arms with Jen before signalling for her to lead the way. It wasn't until she gave his bum a cheeky pinch that he realised that maybe, just maybe, they could still be more than "just friends".

Claire Horran was busy tackling the massive basket of ironing that had accumulated under her nose when she heard a massive thumping at the front door. The kids were upstairs so she knew it wasn't them. She crept down the passage, trying to keep her ears alert for clues as to who was on the other side of the door.

"Who is it?" she called, voice trembling with fear as the thumping became louder. She turned the key in the lock each movement she heard from the other side of the door making her heart palpitate quicker and quicker, she yanked the door open to find an extremely drugged up Sammy raising her fist for another crack at the door.

"Where's me kids" she slurred, she was absolutely reeking of booze and she looked fucking filthy and Claire noticed immediately that she was missing a front tooth. She was unwashed and Claire could smell the distinct smell of sex pouring of her polecat daughter in waves. Trying to hold in her sheer disgust of this animal that she had raised Claire smiled quaintly before dismissing Sammy away from her doorstep;

"You think you're so fucking high and mighty don't you, you vicious Cunt!!" Sammy's voice laced with malice as she took a swing for her mother, Claire dived out of the way and watched as her daughter landed in a heap on the concrete veranda, her skeletal body cracking as she awkwardly hit the ground. She started laughing then an evil deep laugh and her face twisted as she spat a thick glob of green phlegm vehemently in her mother's direction.

"If only you knew the fucking truth, you wouldn't be so fucking quick to fuck with me then you jumped up cunt!" her words thick with pure hatred and for a moment Claire Horran was genuinely scared of her daughter, Sammy was definitely not of sane mind at the best of times, but now there was something pure evil about her daughters distorted face. She was fucking crazy there was no denying that.

"What the fuck are you on about?" Claire replied her voice full of bravado as she folded her arms across her chest, in truth she was acting braver than she felt, she had no idea what her daughter was capable of. Getting to her feet suddenly, Sammy stumbled off pointing at her mother she started making a weird stabbing motion with her hands before screaming the words that would haunt Claire for the rest of her life….."You're Next".

Chapter Twelve

Jenna and Dom had just sat down with a bottle of wine when they heard the commotion outside the flats front door; getting up to investigate she ordered him to stay put and listen out for Kiki. Who she hadn't long put to bed, opening the front door she met the sight of Lisa dragging a stark naked girl out of her flat by her blonde hair extensions and dragging her out into the corridor that separated Jenna's flat and Dom's, Lisa was shrieking obscenities at the top of her voice as she ripped out a clump of hair from the girls head. Jenna could see that the girl was bleeding heavily from the nose so she guessed Lisa had clumped her one. The girl was crying her eyes out, choking on her words as she attempted to cough out an apology, this like a red rag to Lisa who punched the girl square in the mouth and watched as she crumpled to the floor.

"Sorry! Fucking Sorry! Weren't so fucking Sorry when you were riding my fella's cock just now were you sweet fucking heart" Lisa shrieked, raining hard blows down on the girls head. She stopped suddenly when she caught sight of Jenna in her doorway;

"Alright Hun, not keeping the baby awake am I?" she asked calmly before sticking her boot into the girls ribs. Jenna looked at her friend as though she had grown an extra head. She had never seen her acting up so much in her entire life. She hoped to god that the poor girl on the floor didn't die from the beating that she was being handed to her.

"No Kiki's in bed, Dom's keeping an ear out for her." Jenna replied closing the door behind her before stepping into the hallway that separated her flat from Dom's. It was then that Jenna heard Lee pounding about in his flat, he was punching doors, shouting at the top of his voice. He resembled a caged fucking animal.

"So what's happened then?" Jenna asked innocently, although she had already put two and two together and came up with four she wanted to hear it from the horse's mouth.

"I'll tell you exactly what happened" Lisa replied sarcastically, kicking the naked heap in front of her in the small of her back. "This dirty little fucking trollop thinks it's ok to shag my boyfriend in MY bed, in my fucking house.... it's a fucking liberty Jen!" Lisa's sarcasm wasn't lost on any of them and she began laughing hysterically as the girl tried to stem the bleeding that was leaking from her nose. Jenna knew that at this point it was time to get back in the flat, she would put money on one of the nosey bastards upstairs phoning the police and she didn't fancy playing witness tonight. She waved her good bye to Lisa who had started dragging the girl out to the car park. Shutting the door behind her as she went back inside she was surprised to see Dom hovering behind her, a cheeky grin plastered on his face as he asked courtly "Are all you girls of the Belmonte psycho or is it just the ones in this block?" his finger pointing at the door as he spoke and Jenna couldn't help but laugh at him.

"She caught Lee shagging some bird, fucking mess on her now mind" Jenna replied ushering him back into the lounge. She was hoping to god the police wouldn't turn up at hers demanding to know the ins and outs of what had happened between Lisa and Lee. She loved both of them and would never ever speak ill of either of them to the police. Grassing wasn't known on this estate. Anyone who went against the rules of the Belmonte was kidding themselves if they thought they would get away with it. The Belmonte Estate was a place where crime was normality and if you weren't in to violence or drugs, you just weren't welcome. It was a jungle filled with people of all walks of life but they all had one thing in common on the Belmonte, they had all lived the life. A life where you didn't live.... you just merely survived.

Chapter Thirteen

Lisa had never been so fucking angry in all her life. She felt like going back to the flat and chopping that cheating cunts balls off and wearing them as earrings. The few days she had spent at her mother's house had been a real eye opener to how much she had loved Lee. She had been utterly crushed when she had caught him in bed with that fucking tart, it had been the straw that had broke the camel's back so to speak and she knew that she could never take him back now. She had given him the world, loved him with every ounce of love she had in her body and it still had never been enough. She glanced out of the bedroom window, the view from her mother's little country cottage was breathtakingly beautiful, all green shrubbery, perfectly shaped hedges and gorgeous flowerbeds filled with a multitude of vibrant colours which her father nurtured just like he had nurtured his children; with sheer love and tenderness. She loved staying here it was her little safe haven, her little slice of paradise and she knew her mother secretly loved having her home despite the amount of excuses that she had conjured up for Lee and his actions. Lisa's mother was a beautiful person both inside and out, her kind nature shone through within minutes of meeting her, she was polite, kind and saw the good in everybody despite their flaws. Donna Dawson was an impeccable mother and Lisa loved her with all her heart. She was one of life's good people, nobody on earth could ever say anything bad about Donna, and she didn't have a bad bone in her body. She was still a looker even though she was nearly sixty years old, all thick black hair peppered with thin white streaks, deep green eyes which were mesmerizing and intense and could still attract the eyes of any man despite her years, her curvy fuller figure suited her perfectly she didn't have a bump out of place. Lisa watched out of the window as her mother and father sat together out in the garden eating sandwiches out of a little picnic hamper, just basking in each other's company. Lisa's father had his hand tenderly placed on his wife's knee and they were happily chatting to one another, Lisa was intoxicated watching them, they had made their lives so perfect and she felt so half hearted knowing that she lived in such a shit hole, with a failed marriage behind her and a cheating fiancée who had given her nothing but hell for five years, constantly coming home smelling of other women, expecting her to sleep with him knowing that he had been elsewhere first, taking what little money she had to squander on coke or pay back his drug debts. She knew she had let Lee walk all over because she was scared of losing him like she had lost her first husband. When Lisa thought of Lewis she had to fight back the tears, like Lee, Lewis had been a ladies' man completely gorgeous with long bleach blonde hair, twinkling blue eyes and the body of a fucking Adonis, he had been her very first love and he would probably be her only true love. He had accidentally killed himself in an insurance scam gone wrong Lisa still had nightmares of the night that she had drove home from work to find their home ablaze, their bathroom doors lock had been faulty and would only lock from the outside; he had set fire to a rag in the lounge and had attempted to escape through the bathroom window, he had accidentally locked himself in the bathroom and had forgotten to take the key for the toilet window with him and had been burnt to death. It had been the most stupid mistake he could have ever made and it had cost him his young life. It wasn't like they had even needed the money, but Lewis had thrived on greed and to him it had seemed like such easy cash, not even he could have predicted how it would have ended. She could still hear her screaming gut wrenching sobs as the fire fighters had bought his charred body out of the wreckage. His gorgeous blonde hair singed to his scalp and crusted with blood, his skin was reduced to looking like melted plastic all glossy and oily looking. He was distorted and unrecognisable as the gorgeous man she had married. Lisa had never in her life felt pain like that in her life, Losing Lewis had broken her both physically and emotionally, before he died she had had everything, a gorgeous modern mid town penthouse, a flashy sports car, high paid job and friends who had appreciated the finer things in life. Dinner parties and social gatherings had been their life then, and Lewis had been the life and soul of every single party they attended. The stress of losing Lewis had also caused her to miscarry their unborn child at seven months pregnant; the little girl who she had called Louise had been absolutely gorgeous despite her prematurity and Lisa had loved her from her very first breath to her very last and even now she craved for the daughter she had lost. It had been since then that her life had taken a dreaded downward spiral and she had started taking drugs and drinking heavily to try and numb the pain of losing every piece of normality that she had ever known, stripping her of every moral value that she had ever been taught. She had lived on the streets for six months, working in strip clubs to keep her nose white and to try and keep a roof over her unstable head. She had overcome a crippling cocaine addiction and even though she still did the drug recreationally she would never ever go back to being a dependant. She ran her fingers over her tattoo of Louise's name, the tears began to sting her eyes as the pain, still so raw cursed through her body, she had craved nothing more than to be a mother and it had been so cruelly snatched from her, she hadn't even been left with enough money to give her daughter a proper headstone. The bog standard council cross she had covered in pink ribbon and her dad had planted flowers around the graveside but it hadn't been enough for Lisa, Her little angel deserved the best in the world, and she had failed her as much in death as she had in life. The tears came then thick and fast etching her pretty face in sadness, Lisa had led a dog's life, despite having the unconditional love of her parents she had still turned into the bad apple and she knew her parents were secretly disappointed in her. They had never showed it, or spoke of it directly to her, but she could feel it, and she knew that if she had been her own daughter, then she would be equally disappointed. As she gazed out at her parents sitting in the garden of their beautiful home, the love between them so evident and so pure Lisa felt an overwhelming sadness envelope her because she knew, she had failed them both, they deserved so much more than her and her self pity. She was their only child, of course not by choice, Lisa's mother had become victim to ovarian cysts a few years after Lisa had been born and was advised to have a full hysterectomy because the cells on her ovaries were pre cancerous, so to limit her risks her mother had given the ultimate sacrifice and had her womb removed, it had killed Lisa's mother to know that she and her husband would never parent more children but that had been the cards that life had handed them and even now they were so in love and so content with each other's company that Lisa hoped and prayed that one day she too would find that unmistakable bond with someone special. Until then though she would have to watch from afar at her parents fairytale marriage and wonder whether hers would have ever ended up the same way had Lewis not been snatched away from her so viciously. She closed her eyes and succumbed to her memories of her old life the tears rolling down her face a reminder that she would never ever get it back no matter how hard she tried.

Chapter Fourteen

Sammy Carter was sat in the community gardens of the Belmonte Estate, the cold wind billowing around her, her teeth chattering loudly in her head as she waited for her dealer to arrive, she had already been to see Leonora Powell but she had refused to serve her because she still owed her tick money, so Sammy had to wait around on one of the local junkies Kevin O'Brian to deliver the goods. Kevin was homeless Irish traveller who scrounged off anyone and everyone who had a ten pound wrap in their pocket, he was a lanky string of piss with a massive ginger beard and a shock of long ginger hair which stood crazily up on end, he looked a right fucking weirdo but he pushed the heroin around the estate like he ran the local sweet shop and Sammy had taken a liking to playing with the dirty Irish bastard for free drugs, all it took was a flash of her toothless smile and he was like putty in her skeletal hands. In a way they were perfect for each other, they were both disgusting dirty junkies, both had absolutely no moral values what so ever and both had lost their kids through drugs. Kevin's three children had been separated by the care system. His daughter and son from his first marriage to a gypsy woman called Eve were both adopted out because of the pairs use of heroin and other narcotics and his third child who had been the result of a drunken one night stand with his step daughter who was twelve at the time of conception had been adopted to a family with three special needs children, the child had been severely deformed because of drug and alcohol misuse throughout the pregnancy and had been taken straight into care because of the incestuous relationship between Kevin and his then daughter. Not that he cared of course he still went day to day stabbing whatever drugs he could manage into his abused veins without even a little bit of shame. He of course had been glad to escape the clutches of the Irish gypsy camp he had lived on, when the town's people had found out of his sexual acts with a girl of his own family circle there had been riots and he had been outcast from his people. Of course no one on the Belmonte knew he was a registered sex offender, but what they didn't know wouldn't hurt them.

As Kevin O'Brian approached Sammy, she immediately caught sight of his green teeth bulging out from in between his bulbous lips and she almost vomited in her mouth a little, he truly was gruesome. Between his green teeth and his ginger hair he resembled a box of fucking tic tacs, but drugs were drugs in Sammy's eyes so she plastered her toothless smile on her face and attempted to flirt her way to a free bag of heroin and quick shag in between the bins. It was in that crystal clear moment of clarity Sammy Carter realised she and Kevin O'Brian weren't so different after all. They were both just as scummy as each other.

Chapter Fifteen

Claire was nursing a glass of whiskey and her beloved photo album, it was eleven in the morning and she was having one of her off days. Craig's death was swimming around in her head and for the life of her she couldn't shake the stinking mood that she had woken up in. Ub40 was on repeat and she was feeling at a loss, her whole head drowning in memories of her precious boy, he had always been her favourite ever since the day he had been born, he resembled nothing to his sister who had been a sickly horrid baby, he had always been so content, so happy, he had been the apple of Claire's eye. She would have done anything on this earth for Craig, he had been her world, he had always been such a smart, well mannered child and she could never fathom why he had been taken away from her so soon. She flicked through his baby pictures in floods of tears, her beautiful boy who had the whole world at his feet had been snatched away from her. She felt so suffocated as she remembered his first steps, first word, first football game... it all seemed such a distant memory to her now and she would kill just to have those little moments back right now. As she came across his graduation pictures her heart burst with pride, he looked so fucking handsome in his robes, his hair all shaved to perfection and his big muscular arms cloaking her as they posed against the university backdrop. She had been so proud of him that day, he had been the most handsome of all the boys who had graduated the English Literature course that day, her Craig had always had a passion for writing, ever since he had first held a pen in his pudgy hands she knew he had a flair for writing. She still had his first ever story that he had written at the tender age of seven tucked away in his memory box, it was all about how he and his sister had gone to a goldmine and robbed the mean old gold merchant of hundreds of pounds. Craig had worshipped his younger sister all his life. She had been his one and only comfort as a child, as long as he loved Sammy then Craig had been complete. Even when Sammy was being a complete nuisance to all around her Craig still made excuses for her, still stuck his neck out on the line for her, Sammy had been his world, until he had met a little girl called Jenna Shearan.

Craig had been four when Jenna and her mother had moved to the estate, the beautiful black haired princess had knocked Craig off his pudgy little feet and he had fallen head over heels in love with her instantaneously and from that moment him and little Jenna had been inseparable. He had loved Jenna with a passion that was unknown to Claire. They had a bond that could never ever be separated and Claire knew that Jenna Shearan had been the key to her son's heart. As much as Craig had played it down and acted as though he and Jenna were just "best friends" Claire had always known that the girl held a special place in her son's heart. Even when Jenna had announced she was pregnant with some no name, Craig had been there, He had even watched little Kiki come into the world, sang the beautiful little girl nursery rhymes and cradled her in his strong arms until she fell asleep. He had been Jenna's best friend and Claire still cursed the fact that her son had never made an honest woman of the girl. Claire could still picture the day that the two had met, Craig had been dressed in a pair of denim dungarees and Jenna had been in a little Barbie T-shirt and a pair of knickers, it was summer and Claire had been having a little get together with a few of the neighbours; Helen Shearan and her daughter hadn't long moved to the estate and Craig had gone into their garden as bold as brass and asked if they had wanted to come to his mothers party. And from that day her Craig had been mesmerised by the little girl in flat thirty seven despite her mother's ill will. Everything her Craig had done or said since that point had been about Jenna. Jenna did this and Jenna did that, but Claire had loved the little girl as much as her son had and despite her awful start in life with her alcoholic mother Claire had tried her very best to raise the little girl as her own. That was why Claire felt so guilty, because Sammy had always came second place to Craig despite the girls best efforts to remain on her mother's good side, Claire had always found the worst in Sammy.

Yet now as Claire looked through the pictures she had hoarded of Craig she felt an awkward sadness because she wasn't looking at pictures of Sammy, she wished more than life its self that she was grieving for Sammy instead of Craig. She had always despised Sammy since birth the girl had caused her nothing but trouble; she had been born breech and was the sickest baby God had ever laid on this earth, constantly she had cried for hours on end and Claire had slowly sank into a deep depression. It had taken her years to even allow herself to even like her daughter. Claire had taken so many years trying to build a bond with Sammy but her daughter had never been the easiest of children, it wasn't that she had been naughty or that she had been a gobby little mare, she had been neither, but her mother just couldn't take to her. It was as though something in Sammy didn't sit well with Claire, unlike Craig who had been so delicate and so loving towards his mother. He had been such a happy gorgeous little boy and Claire would never ever fully recover from his death. Claire's tears stung in her heavy eyes as she glanced at the photos of her and her son, the smiles on their faces so prominent. The photo had been taken on his twenty first birthday, Claire could still picture his face as she had bought out his cake which she had made herself shaped like a woman's bust. He had burst out laughing; his face had flushed red as he had made a joke about him hoping the bust had not been made with her boobs as inspiration his twinkling blue eyes winking at her cheekily and his infectious chuckle reverberating off the walls. He had always been such a comedian and Claire Horran would honestly give her very last breath to hear him crack one last joke. Sammy hadn't been the same since her brother's death; she had always dabbled in drugs ever since the tender age of twelve when Claire had caught her with a spliff hanging out of her gob down the bus stop waiting for the school bus. Claire had gone ballistic and the girl had been grounded for a month and it had gradually worsened over the years. But drugs had always been Sammy's forte, her biggest weakness had always been heroin, but these days Claire barely recognised the girl she had bought into this world, she was scruffy, unkempt and Claire would love nothing more than to catch hold of the little toe rag and chuck her in the bloody bath with some good old fashioned soap and elbow grease. Claire knew Sammy's demise had been nothing to do with her, she had always been a brilliant mother to her two kids and she continued to do her motherly duties to Sammy's two children, Claire had hoped so much that having children of her own would have curbed her daughters erratic behaviour, but if anything it had made her worse. Both the kids had come out addicted to drugs, Brogan had severe learning difficulties and had suffered with ADHD since the age of sixteen months, Both children meant the world to Claire and she really did love the bones of them both despite their problems, her grandchildren were her second chance and Claire thanked God every single day that these children had been given to her instead of the care system.

It was almost three in the morning when Claire finally called it a night; she was incredibly drunk and extremely emotional and had spent most of the night crying her eyes out, her heaving sobs echoed around the dark kitchen walls, Claire had never felt so lonely in her life. She stumbled up the stairs all that buzzed around in her confused drunken mind were Sammy's words to her, it wasn't so much what she had said , it had been the stabbing motion she had done with her hands. It had really spooked Claire and now her head was working over time trying to figure out what it had meant. She stared at her reflection in the bathroom mirror and for the first time in her life, she felt old, old and haggard, age was slowly creeping up on her and the sleepless nights were starting to take their toll, her skin had lost its youthful glow and despite using endless supplies of anti wrinkle cream, the crows feet and fine lines that crisscrossed her smooth complexion told the true story of a mother who despite her best efforts, was still struggling to hold onto her past and the memories that now seemed so far away. She felt so disconnected, so distant from herself and it hurt her to know that she was still here, still breathing, still living, when her baby was stone dead and buried six feet under the round. He had so much life left in him, so much he wanted to do, he had wanted to write a book based on his sisters life, he had wanted to become a journalist, which juxtaposed so much against his athletic physique and his tracksuits and trainers. He had been a real diamond had her Craig, and she would have sold her grannies knickers if it meant just one moment with him, one last kiss goodnight, one last tender hug in his monstrous arms, one last chance to tell him she loved him, one last chance to cook him his favourite lasagne and chips, it was the simple things like that, that so many took for granted that Claire would kill for. That night Claire went to sleep with a heavy head and an even heavier heart and as she had done every night for the last year, cried herself into a deep and troubled sleep, one from which she dreamed she would never wake from such was her undying need to be reunited with her son once more.

Chapter Sixteen

Sammy awoke from her drug induced coma, surrounded by the familiar sights of the Belmonte Estate community gardens, she was soaked through to her threadbare knickers from the heavy downpour that must have occurred in the night, her head was pounding and her she could barely open her left eye. The last thing that Sammy remembered from the night before was being chased by Leonora Powell and her fucking mob and being battered by the group over Sammy pick pocketing one of Leonora's mobs purse. The girl Vikki Hadley a drugged up prostitute from out of town was an ex champion boxer and had smoked Sammy to within an inch of her life, in fact the gang had all assumed that Sammy was dead so they had left her in a heap in the gardens before fleeing in fear of the police catching hold of them. Sammy clung to the bench that was next to her but her legs were like jelly and wouldn't hold her weight so she kept tumbling back to the floor every time she attempted to move. Her whole body ached viciously and she was missing at least two teeth from what she could feel as she traced her furry tongue around her phlegm ridden mouth. She sat up awkwardly, propping herself up against the bench, she reached into her pockets, rummaging for her heroin wrap but it was long gone, Sammy held her battered head in her bloody hands and cried violently into her sleeve, she was completely broken, completely battered and she was flooded with over whelming self pity. She closed her eyes and urged her mind to picture her handsome brother, the tears were really rolling now as she remembered how he used to stick up for her when they had been kids, he had been her hero and she would have done anything in the world for him. He was like a big huge teddy bear and Sammy had always felt so safe when Craig had been alive, he had always protected her, despite when she owed money for drugs or she had slept with some crazy bitches husband, Craig had always been there to diffuse the situation and he had always sorted things out for her regardless of whether he had agreed with her choices or not, he never judged her decisions, he had just understood them, accepted them and still loved her regardless. And now here she was, twenty one years old with a raging heroin habit, hardly any teeth left in her drug rotten mouth, the apparent mother to two children who she couldn't even bring herself to love, she had bought nothing but shame to her mother and she would never ever forgive herself for the horrible secret that she harboured constantly in her heart. That she herself had been responsible for the death of her brother.

Chapter Seventeen

The soft and sultry tones of Michael Jackson's "You are not alone" played in the background as Craig Carter held Jenna in his big strong arms gliding her across his bedroom floor, her head firmly placed on his shoulder as they swayed along gently to the music, he could feel the baby in her stomach moving and kicking around and he could almost burst with pride if it hadn't been for his hidden sadness of the fact that the child was not his own. He ran his fingers down the small of her back, pulling her in closer, taking in every single breathtaking moment. She nuzzled into his bare chest and wrapped her slender arms around his neck, her swelling baby bump pressing firmly against his stomach, he could feel every single kick the baby made, his body drank in every single beautiful movement, he couldn't help his head feeling so conflicted between happiness and sadness and sometimes he wondered how he would cope when the child was actually born, he didn't want to hate the child, but he was unsure of whether he could ever love it either. He softly kissed the top of her glossy hair and smiled as the familiar scent of coconut conditioner and hairspray filled his nostrils, her skin felt so natural against his and he wished he could fight the feelings he had for this beautiful girl, nothing compared to the love he had for Jenna Shearan, nothing ever had and nothing ever would, ever since their first meeting all those years before Craig had known that she was the one. Her beauty was incomparable to anything he had ever seen and she had a personality that could light up a million night skies, she truly was perfect and Craig wished with all his heart that she would find happiness just to stop the pain of knowing he would never take her for himself despite every single fibre of his body screaming out to do so. Even now as he gazed down into her unsure eyes he felt the desire to reassure her that everything was going to be alright, that he would love her and the baby more than words could ever say, that he would always protect them and cherish them until the end of time....but his mouth couldn't bring the words out and his heart couldn't cope with what would happen if it didn't work out, their beautiful friendship would be ruined, That was a risk Craig Carter could never ever take. It just didn't bare thinking about. She kissed him tenderly on the lips, her caress sending his head spiralling and as she settled her head on his chest once more; Craig Carter knew he would have to let her go, let her be free, let her be alone, if he had any chance of saving his own sanity, he just didn't know if he could stay away from the temptation of the bewitching Jenna Shearan and her unborn child.

Chapter Eighteen

Emma Fenton pushed her twin buggy into the Belmonte Estate and prepared herself for the torrents of abuse that she knew would soon be bestowed upon her, at twenty three she was the mother of two gorgeous little boys called Toby and Josh who were just turning three and she led what other people would see as a pretty normal life on the Belmonte, council flat, hire purchase furniture that she would never actually own and knock off clothes from the Tuesday market. She had lived on the Belmonte all of her young life and all her family had all still lived nearby. Until the family had been turfed off the estate by the local residents because it had been her brother Johnny who had been the leader of the gang that had murdered Craig Carter. Johnny Fenton was only eighteen and was now serving a life sentence for the killing, who had thought it was funny to take the piss out of Craig because he worked hard to walk around in his posh tracksuits and trainers and Johnny and his mates were still stuck hanging around in their cheap outfits bought out of mammy's giro. It had seemed like such a jealous callous attack and Emma hated what her younger brother had done but it was her husband Freddie who hated him the most, she herself had always like Craig , he had been a good man, drop dead gorgeous kind and loving and he had always been polite and respectful to Emma and her family. Now though things were different and Emma still suffered the vicious stares and nasty comments from all around her because her Scummy cunt brother and his mates had killed Craig. What hurt Emma the most was that she had to face the nasty tongue of Craig's poor mother every single day at playgroup, every time she turned up with the boys she was given the evil eye and referred to as the "murdering cunts sister" by all the other mothers and as a result her boys had been out casted by all of the other children. That was without the abuse she suffered at home at the hands of her violent husband. As she pushed the buggy into the gardens of the Belmonte she spotted a girl crying on the ground, her soaking wet tracksuit clung to her skeletal body as the hacking sobs reverberated from the skinny body, Sammy put the brake on the buggy and went over to investigate, the stench coming of the emaciated body before her was absolutely mortifying and Emma had to stop herself with all her might from vomiting all over the girls dishevelled head. She tapped the girls shoulders and murmured a silent "are you alright love?" before stepping back slightly, it wasn't until the girl looked up, and Emma really focused beyond the black eyes and the blood splattered face, did Emma realise that it was indeed Sammy Carter who was in front of her, she stumbled a little taken aback by the girls almost feral appearance, raising her hand to her mouth when Sammy gave her a demented grin from her toothless mouth.

"Oh Sammy who did this to you?" she winced as she spoke, her voice trembling as she placed a hand on the girls bony shoulders attempting to pull her up trying her hardest not to hurt the poor girl. She spied the girls two missing teeth not too far from where she was stood and Emma's heart sank, Sammy had once been such a beautiful girl, all bouncy hair, flawless skin and hips that even Audrey Hepburn would have envied. But as Emma looked at the unrecognisable girl before she felt an overwhelming sadness for her. She managed to get Sammy up onto the bench and sat her in a little more comfortable position. Emma sat beside Sammy looking at the nasty lacerations in her hollow cheeks, Emma was sure she had been slashed with a blade or something similar, the gashes were starting to scab over with dried blood but Emma could see plain that they were fresh cuts. Sammy pulled her tracksuit jacket around her, her remaining teeth were dancing around in her head and her whole body was shivering, whether it was through craving drugs or the sheer coldness outside she wasn't entirely sure but all she did know was that she was in some serious pain.

"Look Em" she forced "I don't need no sympathy from no one I did this to me self" her face grimaced as a vicious pain shot up her body, she held her ribs tightly as she coughed harshly, trying to catch her breath she continued to ramble on about thieving a purse or something for drugs, Emma wasn't especially paying attention to the girls excuses, it was only when she started mentioning her brother did Emma's ears suddenly prick up, Sammy was droning about how Craig's death was her fault, the girl was crying again, loud holing wails that seemed nonexistent in such a tiny body. Emma frowned as Sammy continued to repeat "It was me I killed him" continuously, she didn't know if the girl was taking the fucking piss or she was so loony on drugs that she didn't even know what she was saying, but something in her gut told Emma that Sammy Carter knew a lot more about her brother's death than she had let on. As they both sat there in silence on the garden bench Emma took in the girls words, her brother had been caught with the knife that had killed Craig, his gang of friends had been seen on CCTV near the scene of the stabbing not fifteen minutes before the crime had occurred, the finger had automatically been pointed at Johnny and his mates, Johnny had even owned up to killing Craig in court. So Emma couldn't piece together what the fuck Sammy was on about, but she made a mental note there and then that she would find out what happened that fateful day, even if it killed her. She made up a story of having to get the boys home for their dinner, gave Sammy a quick half hearted goodbye before departing in the direction of her block of flats. She was really spooked by what Sammy had said and would be phoning her mother as soon as she stepped through the door to tell her the morning's strange events.

Chapter Nineteen

Donna Dawson had just finished making a massive pot of her famous chicken broth when Lisa arrived back home from town, she had been visiting and old friend and Donna smiled as Lisa flounced into the kitchen with a huge smile on her face and a spring in her step, it had been nearly a month since she had left Lee and she was finally starting to get her head back on track. Lisa had spent the first two weeks trying to suppress the horrible rages of anger that she displayed over the horrid betrayal Lee had bestowed upon her. She had since learnt that the little posh trollop he had been fucking had been found out to be a secret call girl who was working under a pimp who ran his business from abroad. Kenny Kingston was a big name in these parts, but he was nothing but a fucking filthy disgusting pervert and the girls who worked for him were barely out of nappies when they fell for his gentlemanly charm and his bewitching good looks. Lisa hoped Lee caught a bad dose of the clap, sticking his dirty fucking dick in prostitutes, she felt so worthless and used but she had learnt now to laugh it off in front of everyone else. It didn't stop the hurting, but it made the pain more bearable. She plonked her bag down on the table and grabbed two wine glasses from the cupboard before grabbing a bottle of red wine out of her carrier bag;

"Want one mum?" she quizzed pouring herself a large measure of wine and gulping the majority of the contents down in one mouthful. Pouring herself another immediately and pouring a smaller measure in the second glass she handed Donna one without giving her a chance to reply. Her Lisa was a beautiful girl, all curves and bouncy hair and she looked so trendy dressed in her little ankle boots and skinny jeans, her dark eyes encased in a smoky violet pencil, she looked immaculate and Donna was so proud of how well Lisa was coping. She knew her daughter could be a handful when angry and Donna had been worried when Lisa had first turned up on her doorstep in floods of tears with her suitcase. But Donna had come to realise how much she had missed her daughters company.

"So how were the lovely Kyle and Marissa?" Donna asked her daughter flittingly, stirring the contents of the saucepan on the stove whilst taking small swigs from her wineglass. She took a mental note of the twinkle in her daughter's eye as she began to tell her of what a great afternoon she had had shopping and lunching with her old friends. Kyle and Marissa Marsden were twin brother and sister and had been Lisa's best friends for as long as Donna could remember, Kyle was a hairdresser and was as camp as the proverbial Christmas but he had the most bubbliest personality that Donna had ever encountered with his painted on jeans and floppy hair, he truly was a quirky little diamond and Donna loved him to pieces, whereas Marissa was a swimsuit model who adored nothing more than flashing her fake assets and showing off her goddess body in the tightest dresses but she had the shyness and innocence of a little girl. They both were chalk and cheese but they were the loveliest people that Donna had ever met in her life and had always classed the pair as family rather than her daughter's school friends. Donna thanked the lord that her beautiful daughter was away from that shithole estate and the rats who occupied the place, she had heard some none to pleasant stories of the Belmonte and its residents, all of whom appeared were all criminals or on drugs of some sort, oh no Donna Dawson could never fathom her daughter living in a place like that, and she would rest assured that her daughter would never step a perfectly manicured foot on that estate ever again, even if she had to commit murders to keep Lisa away, she would, she loved her daughter too much to let her girl return to the life she had wandered into and she had worked too fucking hard to see her go back there now. Lisa needed her independence, Donna understood that but she would never let her go back to the negative influences of the Belmonte Estate. For the first time in months, Donna Dawson got a glint of the old Lisa coming back to life she looked healthy, happy and Donna would do anything on this earth to reignite that flame that she had thought had long died out, she would get her daughter back, even if it killed her.

Chapter Twenty

Jenna Shearan was sat in bed reading Kiki her favourite book, it was late, around midnight and the little girl had been wound up like a top all afternoon, Jenna's flat was an absolute bombsite, there were clothes emptied out of every cupboard, a vase had been smashed and Jenna's most beloved canvas picture of her and Craig that had taken pride of place on her living room wall was now covered in crayon due to her daughters new habit of climbing on the back of the sofa, Jenna was completely exhausted and had spent the afternoon alternating between shouting at the girl and crying at the devastation she had left in her little path. She was absolutely gutted that her canvas had been ruined, it had been a present off Claire for her birthday and she had treasured receiving such a lovely gift off Craig's mother. It had been taken on Halloween; they had gone to a fancy dress party dressed as a bondage dominatrix and a kinky cat. She had been so embarrassed as they had strutted through town barely dressed, arm in arm swigging from cheap cans of Tesco cider. The photo had been taken at the start of the night; they both had the biggest smiles on their faces, Craig's arm wrapped around her slender waist as they both posed for the camera. They had looked so happy, they had been so happy and it made Jenna sad that they would never be like that again. She glanced down and realised that Kiki had fallen asleep, laying her down onto the pillow Jenna got up to turn the bedroom light off, she looked out of the bedroom window and noticed that Dom's lights were all on in the flat opposite. Jenna sat back on the bed and tapped vigorously on her phones keypad, her fingers hanging over the send button, closing her eyes tightly; she threw the phone back onto the bed. She just couldn't bring herself to ask him over, she couldn't do it to Craig.

Across the Belmonte, The dish water had long gone cold, but still Emma Fenton's hands lay placed in the sink. Her sad eyes staring wide out of the window over the estate, the melancholy sadness of Karen Carpenter hummed quietly from the radio. The silence which she craved so much these days making her relax into herself the twins had been in bed for hours and she was glad of the peace, her filthy pyjama nighty hung off her tiny frame, her lank jet back hair was scraped back into a topknot on her head. The thick purple bruises that trailed her emaciated body a constant reminder that he was in control, he would always be in control..... She glanced around the kitchen, the smoke stained walls splattered with tonight's dinner, the smashed china that was scattered around the floor and the blood, her blood that snaked into the grooves of the cheap lino tiles. She promised herself silently that this would be the last time, the last beating, the last time she was made to feel so worthless, so run into the ground. She was tired, tired of Freddie, tired of this house, tired of life. As the final drones of The Carpenters faded out on the radio, the sound of the front door brought Emma back to reality with an icy shudder. She knew it was Freddie and she knew he was drunk, just by the way the front door had bounced off the walls on his entry. The muffled sounds of Freddie's muscular frame stumbling through the hall, the sound of his steel capped boots thudding on the carpet, suddenly the room felt claustrophobic as if the walls were closing in on Emma, she could smell him, the whisky that laced his breath, the clinging familiar smell of cigarettes that hung on his clothes, she daren't move, fear seeping out of every single pore. She didn't even turn to greet him, just kept her hands in the freezing dish water, her body rigid she could smell the anxiety on her skin, taste the dry saltiness of her mouth her tongue like sandpaper, her heartbeat thudding in her chest. He was by the door now, his steely blue eyes burning holes into her back, Emma tensed further her breathing was laboured and reserved, trying to remain as calm as she physically could she turned slowly around to face her husband, he was leaning against the doorframe, trying as best as he could to keep himself in a standing position.

"Where you been?" she croaked, her voice barely audible, she felt weakened by how quietly she spoke.

Freddie ignored her question and tumbled over to the fridge, on inspection he took out the carton of orange juice and took a long deep slug, the liquid quenching his thirst only momentarily. He could feel the mother of all hangovers creeping upon him and he'd only finished drinking an hour ago, he felt remorseful as he stared at his Emma all busted up and scared. He knew he had done this to her but he couldn't help but feel she looked pathetic just standing there all stiff and wide eyed as though his sheer presence was enough to make her go into cardiac arrest. He shot her a glance and smiled one of his ruthless grins that had stolen her heart all those years ago, when they were happy, and they had been happy once.

"Nowhere that you need to know about" he slurred, his eyes dancing around in their sockets. He took a few steps forward and jenny found herself leaning back into the sink, it wasn't until she could feel his breath hitting her nostrils that she realised how close he was, she closed her eyes tightly, wincing as he stepped towards her, the menace in her eyes evident as he began rambling on about her brother Johnny.

"Mugging me off they were down The Crown, won't even speak to me now because I'm associated with that murdering cunt! How do you think I feel aye? Losing me mates over scum like your brother" he slurred, his voice laced with malice and thick drunken spittle that spilled out of the corners of his chapped sticky lips. He was close now; his eyes bore into her as he slapped her face, the blows that followed came thick and furious and Emma tried her hardest to keep silent for the sake of her boys. He dragged her across the kitchen, pushing her to the lino floor he tugged at her knickers, pushing himself harder against her slim body, his disgusting drunken breath eroding on her skin as he forced himself into her, his weighty body crushing Emma's as she felt the cold of the lino floor creeping up her naked back, even though this hadn't been the first time he had raped her, the pain and shame continued to flow in abundance and for the first time since they had been together she felt scared of her Freddie, as the tears rolled down her face, she silently prayed that she would die soon, just to stop the nightmare life she and her boys had to live behind closed doors.

Chapter Twenty One

Little Kiki Shearan was playing out the front of her block of the Belmonte flats, her glossy hair tied in a neat ponytail on her head and her gorgeous powder blue paisley dress blew elegantly in the breeze, she sat on a little mat playing with her two favourite Barbie dolls, engrossed in her own little world. She was brushing Barbie's long blonde hair and chattering along to herself engrossed in making up a whole fantasy world for her dolls. She was happy, she could hear her mummy and Dom laughing in the flat at one of Dom's silly jokes, he was always here lately and Kiki loved how happy he made her mummy. He reminded her of her uncle Craigy Bear, he wasn't quite the same as him of course, and Craigy bear was special. He was her angel now. Despite her young years Kiki understood that uncle Craig was gone to heaven and that he would never be coming back, as her little thoughts drifted off to uncle Craigy and how fun he had been, his big special laugh, his special cuddles and his funny jokes that had Kiki in fits of laughter. Suddenly she felt the dirty rag over her tiny little face, the horrid chemical smell filled her nostrils, she felt the hot fat tears roll down her face as she struggled silently and then she was asleep. All that remained when Jenna Shearan went to check on her little girl was Barbie and her brush.......

Chapter Twenty Two

The hysterical screams of Jenna Shearan echoed out over the estate, she was inconsolable as she scrabbled about looking for her daughter, her eyes manic and hungry for any single glance of her little girl. Her whole body aching just to see that Kiki was safe, she had only turned her back for a second, or so she had thought it was a second, she was convincing herself it wasn't longer than a minute, she'd only gone in to check on their dinner, but Dom had grabbed her, kissed her, distracted her, how long had she been inside? How long had Kiki been gone? Where had she gone? The questions whizzed around in Jenna's head as though they were in a blender, her whole head was banging, and she was confused, her whole body felt tense with fear, the sweat dripped from her brow as she ran into the car park, searching in between the bins all the while screaming her daughter's name. She hugged the Barbie doll close to her, smelling the familiar scent of Kiki her beautiful baby scent mixed with Fairy fabric softener. Her eyes were wild as they bounced around her surroundings, her heart was pounding hard and fast her chest felt as though it would explode. She eyed the flats opposite, nothing. She ran further into the Belmonte estate, her hands clutching the Barbie doll as though her life literally depended on it all the while screaming Kiki's name at the top of her voice, her tears rolling down her cheeks, mascara running in tracks across her ghost white face. She felt as though the life had literally been sucked out of her, she tried reasoning with herself that Kiki couldn't have gone far; she was only two for fuck sake. She glanced around her eyes manic with fear, but her daughter was gone, had vanished into thin air, Dom ran behind her panting his hands on his knees as he caught his breath, he placed his hand on her shoulder before declaring that he had called the police. He held Jenna close, feeling every hurried breath escaping her lean body, she was shuddering with fear, her racking sobs jerking her whole body with undeniable force, In that moment alone Dom had never felt so useless in all his life, he wanted nothing more than to take this grief away from her, to find Kiki safe and sound as he hoped they still would, As she turned away from Dom and threw her guts up onto the pavement, her hacking coughs echoing around the car park, there were people out on their doorsteps, watching the young girls anguish as the dark haired man rubbed her back lovingly telling her, assuring her everything would be okay, although the notes in his voice were filled with uncertainty, he didn't believe his own words... so why would she?

As the police squad cars surrounded the estate and closed in on the car park where they were stood, Jenna held Dom's hand quaking as she led them into the flat, tears rolling down her scarlet cheeks, she had aged a lifetime in the last hour, her complexion was ghostly white, despite the crimson flushes on her cheeks from crying so much, thick black mascara streaks ran in tracks down her face, she ushered the police into the flat, she seemed calmer now, shock had set in and she was finding it hard to function, to communicate, she sat down on the couch and stared blankly at the wall, the whole room was spinning but she felt as though it was in slow motion, she could hear the police woman's voice but she couldn't quite register what she was saying, it sounded slurred, incomprehensible, Jenna's eyes remained fixed on a photo on the wall of Kiki and Craig, her pupils in full dilation as she focused in on her daughters beautiful face, she was only a baby, why would anyone take her? The tears came again as did this incoherent noise and for a second Jenna didn't realise that the noise was coming from her, she clung to Dom desperately holding his shirt as she shrieked mournfully it was a full guttural noise and everyone in the room recoiled as it filtered in their eardrums. It was then that one of the young officers called for a paramedic to come and sedate the poor cow, she was a mother herself so could understand the girls pain, When the paramedic arrived she took Dom out into the kitchen area and took some notes from him, the girls description, what she was wearing and all the necessary information they needed to start their enquiries, Dom explained as best as he could what had happened and gave the police a photo of Kiki from the mantelpiece.

"This is a pretty recent one, she still looks very much identical to this" he added handing the young PC the photograph. The young PC looked at the picture and smiled a solemn smile as she tucked the photo into her notebook and signalled for the other PC's to start scanning the area, it was then that a buxom red faced Claire Horan burst in through the front door, breathless and shouting "Where is She? What's happened?" at the top of her voice, she flung the living room door open and glanced around at the bewildered scene before her, there were four police officers in the room, the two paramedics, Jenna was KO'd on the sofa and Dom who was being questioned in the kitchen, her eyes filled with fear as she took in the scene before her, she looked almost feral such was the wild glint in her eye. She had seen the police cars screeching onto the estate and had automatically thought that it was one of the druggies playing up as usual, she had been in the bath when her neighbour Dolly had banged the living fuck out of the door and nearly given Claire a heart attack! The nosey old bastard had gabbled breathlessly something about Kiki being snatched and Claire had instantaneously dropped her towel to her ankles and ran up the stairs to get dressed, and here she was now, hair dripping in tendrils on her face, her cheeks an angry red from the rush of getting herself down here and her eyes manic with fear for her friend and her little darling Kiki. The Young PC bid Dom a quick goodnight and promised she would be in touch when they had some news and would be back in the morning to take a statement from Jenna. In the meantime she begged him not to panic and not to let Jenna get flustered and try to take the situation into her own hands, she promised that the police would be doing all they could and he thanked her in abundance before showing them all out, he told Claire to stick the kettle on and he would come and explain everything to her. He stood on the doorstep and waved a sorrow goodbye to the police officers, he saw the vast number of neighbours out on their doorsteps, all gossiping, all eyes on him as the police left, the car park was swarming with a sea of crime tape and high visibility jackets, scouring for any bits of information, the door to door enquiries had been started and Dom could hear various neighbours above being knocked up and quizzed about what they had heard or seen in the course of the afternoon. He pushed the door quietly as he re-entered the flat, he turned to find Claire Horran in his face, arms folded over her chest, her usually neat ginger red bob was starting to frizz as it dried slightly making her looked like a deranged clown.

"What the fucks happened Dom?" she quizzed, her voice was loud, full of authority.

"Come through" he started, offering her into the living room as though he actually lived here, Claire had to laugh at the boy's gumption he'd only lived here five minutes and here he was playing martyr in her friend's home. She took his invitation into the living room and stood by the fireplace; her arms bolted to her chest as he sat down and began to explain what had happened.

"And where the fuck was you two when little Keeks was being pinched off the doorstep then aye?" Claire added sternly when he had finished, his head in his hands as he relayed the little girl's disappearance in his mind, he was clearly upset, Claire could see that plain, but in all honesty she didn't give a fuck, Jenna knew how dangerous the estate could be and she couldn't believe that her friend had let her guard down so stupidly and left her two year old daughter outside the flat alone, even if it was for "two minutes" as Dom had so convincingly reiterated that it was. Claire wasn't convinced though, people around here were always in their windows, it was a curtain twitchers haven was the Belmonte, Claire didn't believe for a second that the gorgeous little girl could be taken from outside her home, so silently, so sneakily without anyone noticing and when Jenna came to Claire was going to give her the biggest tongue lashing of her life!

Chapter Twenty Three

It was dark, stifling hot and the little girl was hungry, famished in fact, her little belly ached for food, she didn't know how long she had been in this dark room, the one with the dirty mattress and the smelly little cloth cot sheet that was used as a blanket. The dark was unwelcoming, fearsome and the little girl had cried nonstop all the way here, the nasty woman with the green eyes and the big strong man who both wore a mask on their faces, scary masks that were made from potato sacks, with gaping holes for the eyes, like an old executioners mask. The room in which she was kept was small, incredibly small, with no windows only a door that was bolted from the outside, she thought she was underground, in a basement maybe, she was scared, extremely scared and she hoped that mummy would come soon and take her home. She missed her mummy, she wished mummy would just come and get her now, she promised to herself that she would be a good girl now, and make mummy happy, she would never be naughty again when mummy came to get her. She sniffled as she sobbed, pulling her little dress over her knees, hugging them tightly to her little chest, she had to stay quiet or the nasty man would get angry and shout at her and put that horrible smelling hanky over her nose, the one that made her sleepy, the one that made her so groggy and lifeless. Kiki went over the small water bowl that was on the filth strewn floor, only to remember that she had drunk it dry hours ago, her little mouth was as dry as sandpaper and she would kill for her dummy and bottle of milk right now..... Where was mummy? Why couldn't she hear mummy coming yet? She could hear the nasty man and the nasty woman's feet shuffling above her, their voices raised, they were shouting, she heard plates smashing, more shouting, then silence, She curled up into a ball on the piss soaked mattress and drifted off into a deep restless sleep, sleep was her friend, it kept the hunger from her belly and it kept her mummy with her, she dreamt of her beautiful mummy giving her hugs and pushing her on the swings, and playing their special games of hide and seek like uncle Craig used to, but never ever getting it right, she was a silly mummy, but Kiki Shearan loved her ever so much and would give all the toys in the world to have her mummy with her now, But little did Kiki Shearan know it would be a while before she would see her mummy again....

Chapter Twenty Four

Jenna was on her third bottle of wine, the liaison officer had come by this morning and informed her that nothing new had come of the case to find her daughter, it was as though Kiki had just vanished off the face of the earth, it had been a month, a horrible torturous four weeks and still there had been no contact from the kidnappers, apparently this was unusual, but Jenna didn't understand the gangster world, it was something from gritty books and films to her. She didn't know about ransoms and potential paedophile rings and all the mean nasty people of this world who went around snatching little girls for money, she was shot to pieces, her nerves were all but dead and she was struggling, really struggling to maintain a level head. The was stick thin, her skin was sallow and pale and her usually curvy size ten frame had emaciated so much that she could swear her and Kiki were the same size in clothes, she polished off the rest of her glass and swiftly topped it up again, Dom was on the front door smoking his cigarette, the smell emitted throughout the flat, she welcomed it into her nostrils, the familiarity of it, mixed with his smell, she couldn't put a name to it but it was Dom's smell and right now it felt like home to Jenna. She was sick of hearing the gossips every time she stood out on the doorstep, so she had retreated to hiding away indoors, drinking herself into oblivion, nursing away the days so that pain didn't seem so real. She had lost her baby girl, she was God knows where, she might have even been dead for all Jenna knew. The thought often plagued Jenna, Dom had taken every nasty snarling drunken fight she had instigated on the chin and held her as she bawled her eyes out, crying for her baby, he had held her in his strong arms, stroked her face, kissed her hair, promised her that he would protect her, that Kiki would be found, alive and well. It wasn't a promise Dom could keep she knew this but she took some comfort in the thought anyway. He had been her rock these last few weeks and she had grown used to having him with her, had craved him being here, even when he just took her to bed to hold her, kiss her, show her that even though everyone else had turned their backs on her and got back to their daily business that he hadn't, he was still here. He was an amazing friend and Jenna would never forget how lovely he had been to her. He walked back into the living room, the cold evening air blasting in behind him he rubbed his hands together coldly, he could see Jenna had been crying again, he walked over to her and pulled her up from the chair, holding her in his strong arms, he could smell the rose that laced her breath, but he didn't care, he understood, he wouldn't allow her to drink anymore though, she had to do a TV appeal in the morning and she would need a clear head and drinking wine from the bucket load certainly wasn't helping. She hugged him tight, smelling his intoxicating aroma, taking him in, he was absolutely gorgeous, inside and out and he had the tendency to just make her smile, despite how heartbroken she was over Kiki, just being with Dom made the days more bearable. None of her other friends had come close to how amazing he had been, he was a constant support to her, and even when she had got so drunk that she started blaming him for Kiki going missing he was still there, holding her hand, picking her up as she fell deeper and deeper into depression, telling her everything was going to be okay and that he would do whatever it took to make sure Kiki was coming home safely. She knew that he and Lee had been scouring the estate for information, he'd roughed up the druggies but they all for now were keeping schtum. He'd even gone around to mad Kenny Kreegan's knocking shop on the other side of the estate and paid him a considerable amount of money to keep him in the loop if he heard or saw anything. Kenny himself had two daughters and despite being in the business of prostituting women out to whatever scabby punters he could, he felt for the poor girl who had lost her daughter and had wisely promised to keep his ears to the ground, he dealt with all sorts here and it would only be time before someone heard something of the little girls whereabouts. Besides he like Dominic, he seemed like an impressionable young man, Kenny had been around the block a few times and knew that private, trustworthy men like Dom were hard to come by and he wished for the love of god that one of his daughters would find a man like him quick sharp instead of the usual steroid abusing self absorbed muscle men that his daughters seemed to go for, men who would be all coy and charming on first sight, but would beat them to a pulp without a seconds thought if they didn't play by the rules.

Jenna polished off another glass of wine before stumbling over to Dom who was sitting on the couch flicking through the channels on the television, she sat herself down on his lap and nuzzled into his neck, wrapping her fingers in his and kissing his neck lovingly, he reciprocated with a small peck on the top of her glossy head. Her eyes were glazed over, her eyelids hooded, half open drunkenly she gazed at him, he smiled uneasily at her, cuddling her skeletal frame close to him, he could feel her aching body ease into his, she felt so fragile, as though she would inevitably shatter if he mishandled her in any way. He held her there in the silence, just looking at her, staring into her beautiful troublesome eyes, she was shattered, he could see the dread of sleep lingering there, the nightmares had become so severe now that he had started to sleep with her in his arms, clutching her so tightly so she didn't wake up flailing, screaming, aching for her daughter, the nightmares were by far the worst thing to come from this ordeal, Jenna had the most awful nightmares about her daughter, many a night since her disappearance had Dom woke to find her screaming at the top of her lungs, flailing in her sleep, clutching her face in sheer agony as the relief washed over her and she woke to find it was all a dream. She couldn't tell him exactly what happened, it was too painful for her he understood that, but he knew they were dark, horrid dreams that haunted her even more when she was awake than when she was asleep. She was plagued with the horrid images of her daughter, dead, suffering at the hands of the monsters that had snatched her. He had found her one night in Kiki's bedroom, steaming drunk crying into the little girls bedding, smelling her cute little baby smell, the talcum powder, the fairy fabric softener that she used religiously on Kiki's clothes now the only comfort that she had, the only homely reminder of her baby girl, all her toys were still strewn about the flat but all the childlike humour had been sucked from the place and the whole home and a feeling of mourning leaking from its pores. He placed his arm tenderly around her tiny child like waist and bought her closer to him, he kissed her slowly, passionately his tongue skating in her mouth, he held her, nothing more, and kissed her so lovingly, she felt so safe with Dom, she knew that she was falling head over heels for him and there was nothing she could do to stop her emotions running wild as she kissed him back, slowly at first lapping her tongue with his, feeling so close to him, so entwined with him, so disconnected from her emotions as he just cuddled her close breathing ever so slightly heavier than normal, his heart beating like a drum in his chest as she placed her head there, running her hand down his chest, her fingers trailing the open buttons of his shirt before resting her arm over his lean muscular stomach, nuzzling her head into him, smelling his scent, breathing him in, loving every single delicious note that bounced from his skin, he really was a remarkable man and in that moment she truly loved him.

Chapter Twenty Five

The man and the woman talked in hushed notes, they had drugged the girl again this afternoon and were now on the understanding that they were surviving on borrowed time, they had to move on, further away, abroad maybe, the police were trawling the streets looking for the girl. The woman sat at the grubby kitchen table watching the news feed transfixed, there had been no new developments in the case and there had been no mention of the police getting any closer to finding the kidnappers. As the TV appeal was shown at the end of the news reading the woman saw in stunning clarity the little girl's mother. She was beautiful, much more beautiful than herself, she was stunning in fact, absolutely flawless the lucky bitch, she was crying her eyes out on the television, praying the safe return of her little girl. Even the word kidnapper bought the woman near enough to tears, she had never wanted this, she had never signed up for this, she knew her boyfriend had gone crazy when he had formulated the plot to steal the little girl, she herself had no children, so didn't understand the sheer pain that the girl's mother was emitting on the screen her skin tight black playsuit kissing every curve on her body deliciously, the subtly applied makeup although slightly run with her tears still illuminating her skin. The woman was jealous, there was jealousy written all over her face, she wasn't ugly by any stretch of the imagination, but she was no match for the little girl's mother. In an instant the woman took dislike to the girl's mother. The man entered the dimly lit kitchen swigging his can of lager, she hated it when he was drinking, he was horrible to her, compared her to the girl's mother, how fat and ugly she was compared to the beauty of her love rival. Yes she hated him drinking, she absolutely hated it. When sober he was a doting, loving man who treated her with respect and lust, she wouldn't ever go as far as to say he loved her, she knew he didn't, but lust was enough for now. After this, after she had proven her worth by snatching the little girl away, he would love her now, she was sure of it, as he slouched in the chair opposite her swigging another large mouthful from the can and burping loudly after he had swallowed, he noted the look in her eyes as she stared at the television screen almost in awe of the other woman, he laughed at her then a deep dark chortling laugh that resounded around the kitchen in a haunting echo. She had quite taken to watching every single news report that was on the TV in case the kidnap came up on the agenda, he was cool and calm as he stood up and calmly struck her hard across the face, the blow knocking her sideways off the chair that she was constantly perched on, he returned quietly to his beer, kicking his feet up onto the table, watching as his girlfriend writhed on the floor clutching her cheek, tears rolling down her face as she called him "nothing but a horrible cunt" he laughed again as he took another deep swig from his can before shooting an icy glance at her with his vicious steely eyes. Soon they would all know he was back and boy he couldn't wait for the shit to hit the fucking fan.....

Chapter Twenty six

Jenna was at her wits end, Lee had been here for all of an hour and already she was tempted to stick a brick over his head. He had never been good with words in all the years she had known him, but right at this moment she couldn't shut the cunt up, he kept on and on about Kiki, thinking the worst, speaking out of turn and generally pissing Jenna off, she slammed her glass down on the table and cut him an evil glance that told him instantly that she was annoyed. He apologised under his breath and the room instantaneously fell into an awkward silence, Jenna knew Lee had meant well coming round to see how she was, but in all honesty she couldn't be any less bothered with him if she tried. The search for her daughter had gone all but dry, whisper on the street had fallen silent and the police had been as much use as a nun in a brothel, it had been six weeks and in all honesty she was starting to lose hope in ever having her little girl return home unharmed. She hugged her cardigan around her thin body, trying to mask out the icy chill in the air, she was constantly cold lately, she knew it was from all the weight she had lost, but food physically choked her, she could barely manage to think straight never mind make a meal for herself. She stared around the room awkwardly, Lee sat opposite her fiddling with the skin on his fingernails, she exhaled wearily filling her glass back up from the bottle of Rose that occupied the table, she offered Lee a glass but he respectfully declined stating it was "Too Early" for him, the pompous arsehole Jenna thought as she downed the contents in one sour mouthful, the urge to vomit was evident in her face as she swallowed down hard. Since the TV appeal a fortnight ago she had heard nothing from the police other than "they had a few leads they were trailing" which of course was no good to Jenna, she had been to the depths this past month, one minute she was seething angry ready to commit murder on the cunts who had her baby, the next she was in floods of tears drinking herself into a stupor wishing she was dead. She had hit a point now where she was just stuck going through the motions, trying to stay positive, she had stopped listening to the gossips of the estate as Dom had advised her to, let them think as they wanted, as he had said, people would always have a negative opinion regardless of how well you did. Jenna looked at Lee, her eyes glazed over from the drink, she was a little tipsy despite it being only eleven in the morning, she was an ugly drunk lee thought instantly taking a dislike to what his poor friend had become, and God was he glad he didn't have kids.

"Heard from Lisa?" she slurred grabbing the wine bottle and sloshing some more wine in her glass, again she offered the bottle to Lee and again he declined. She shrugged her shoulders in disinterest and knocked back the glass in one go, Lee stood up and grabbed his jacket which was hanging on the kitchen door.

"I'll catch you later Jen, you want to stop pissing getting in this fucking state! I can't deal with you like this" he gave her a swift hug before leaving, slamming the door shut behind him, Jenna hung her head in her hands and sobbed bitterly, the dry spittle in her mouth rimmed the corners of her lips as her salty fat tears rolled down her face, she sank to the floor hugging her knees to her chest crying into the dirty blue pyjama bottoms that she'd had on for at least a week, or was it more, she couldn't remember, she tugged violently at her long cobby hair, she could swear she could hear her daughters voice in her mind, so sweet and innocent, but she knew it was just her fucked up head playing tricks on her, Kiki was gone, and unless a miracle happened soon she was gone for good. Jenna stood up and scuttled over to the kitchen drawers, she opened it slowly and gulped as she saw the set of knives glistening up at her, she took one from the drawer and slid it back into place, she let herself fall to the floor, running the knife over her arms, slicing carefully at the skin, watching as the blood bloomed like dirty red roses on her arm, she gazed in wonder as it dripped and zigzagged in between the grooves of the lino tiles, she had never felt so helpless, so angry in all her life, she rocked back and forth slowly caressing the scars on her arm with her fingers, the pain was so effortless now, she was sick of feeling hurt, and for a moment she felt nothing, empty, defeated, she felt absolutely useless. She knew Dom would be coming over soon, he always popped in around lunchtime to try and coax her into eating shit she didn't even want, she just needed more wine and she would be fine. Her arm was bleeding quite profusely now, the little sprays coming from it were starting to frighten her a little, her heart was beating so fast but she couldn't react, couldn't move, she was so in the moment, lost in her own despair but loving the feeling of finally being in control of something, even if it was her own pain. She laughed then at the irony of it all, here she was pissed as a fucking fart on a Tuesday morning, or was it Wednesday? She couldn't even remember. Suddenly she started to feel numb, and then her world turned black.....

Chapter Twenty Seven

Jenna awoke with a banging headache, she could barely opened her eyes, it took a while for her to recognise the fact that she was in hospital, her arms were aching, tingling she saw the heavy bandages that encased them and suddenly it came back to her, the self harm, the kitchen, Lee, Kiki all of it came flooding back in stunning clarity, she was groggy, her mouth pasty and dry, she looked around wearily, Dom was sat beside her smiling sadly at her, his hand was wrapped in hers tightly and he was rubbing her fingers ever so gently with his own, his touch was electric and she felt a sensuous shiver tingling her spine, tantalising her teasing her, he was disappointed, this was evident by the saddened look on his face, his gorgeous smooth face, he looked tired though, worried and it didn't suit him one bit, she knew she was the cause of this and she could have very easily have kicked herself. She smiled at him, she was absolutely gutted that she had acted like a complete twat, and here he was still showing her this overwhelming kindness that he had, showing her that despite everything she still had a friend, she loved Dom so much, he really was an amazing guy. She knew that the feeling was mutual too, he had a big space in his heart for this single mother who had just paraded into his life with all her baggage. She knew nothing about him, yet she felt she had known him a lifetime. He was kind, trusting and handsome. He had the most beautiful personality of anyone she had ever met. He leant in a planted a soft kiss on her forehead, there were no words, just that single gorgeous display of his affection for her. Jenna raised her hand and stroked his baby soft cheek, smiling weakly at him, she mouthed a silent apology, he kissed her fingertips, holding her hand to his face, relishing in the fact that she was awake, that she was okay. He promised himself there and then that when all this was over, and Kiki was home and safe that he and Jenna would make a proper go of things, go on dates, he would spoil her, treat her like a princess, above all he promised to himself there and then that he would love her above anything and everything. Now he had to up his game, he had contacts all over London, he would keep his ears open for anything now, absolutely anything that would lead him to little Kiki, he promised there and then that even if it meant busting a few kneecaps and paying a few sweeteners he would bring her home. The room was silent, it was easier that way, he wanted to bloody slap her hard in the face for scaring him as much as she had, she wanted to scream how scared she was for her daughter, for her own sanity, but they both knew that it could wait, because in that moment, they were finally on the same page.

Chapter Twenty Eight

Claire Horran was busy attempting to clean up after the kids, she had heard about Jenna's apparent suicide attempt through nosey Dolly next door, she felt bad for not being a better friend to the poor girl, but she was hurting herself, Kiki had been the light in Claire's life since Craig's death, she was like another grandchild to Claire, she had grown extremely fond of Jenna's gorgeous little girl, and she prayed each and every night for the girls safe return. She sighed as she flopped onto one of her kitchen stools and lit up the remainder of her cigarette that she had placed in the ash tray earlier on that morning, the kids were out with one of Claire's friends for a birthday party so she was home alone. She could feel Craig's presence today, with a heavy heart she wondered what life was like on the other side, if there was of course another side to life. She wondered if he was happy, if he was watching her, missing her just as she missed him. Her son had been her life, everyone had known how much she had loved Craig he had been her rock through her turbulent life he remained the most constant thing in her life, he had loved his old mum, he would have moved heaven and earth for her. She smoked the rest of her cigarette in peace, enjoying the silence, as much as she loved her grandchildren being here it was hard work, she knew she had to soldier on for the kids sake but in all honest she just felt like saying fuck it all. She was too fucking old for this shit, she'd spent her younger days up to her arm pits in nappies and she never ever dreamt in a million years that she would be forced to do it all again for her grandchildren. She had known from the beginning that Sammy had not a single maternal bone in her body and she had sometimes wished that Sammy had done them all a favour and aborted the children, she knew it was selfish thinking such things but, she knew deep down it was how she truly felt, Sammy had not only snatched the lives of her children away but she had also snatched Claire's away too. Claire thought instantly of the kids father, Kev had been the love of her life, had swept her clean off her feet from the tender age of fifteen, they had gone all the way through school together, were childhood sweethearts, got married at young and had both of their children in quick concession, it was only after Sammy had been born had things started to go horribly wrong, Kev had hidden a secret addiction to prescription drugs from her for numerous years and finally under her constant suspicion he eventually left her because he had been so far sucked into the drug lifestyle, he had become homeless virtually overnight, scruffy and unkempt had started using heroin and had died with a needle in his arm in a squat in East London. She had loved that man with a passion so strong that it had killed her when he died; it was as though a part of her had been taken to the grave with him. The kids had taken the news with a shrug of their shoulders and a sad "well mum we knew it was gunna happen". But Claire found it so unfair that he had been taken away from her snatched from life so cruelly. He had never been into hard drugs, he had worked all his adult life and provided for his family well, the flat that they owned had been their first home together and Claire held so many wonderful memories there. Their children being born, their children growing up, their children having to deal with all the horrible and life changing things that come with adulthood. Claire loved both her children immensely but the decisions that they had both made had proved to be the wrong ones in the end. Her children were gone they were no longer the loving gorgeous children she had nursed and natured, Craig had been stabbed to death and Sammy may as well join him all the good her life was worth. She lit up a cigarette on the butt of her previous one sucking in the intoxicating smoke into her lungs, filling her with the seemingly instantaneous euphoric high she craved before it quickly faded again and she was left sucking away at the cigarette deep in thought, high off her minds almost idyllic images of how she had pictured her life turning out, she wouldn't let reality hit her just yet, her dreams were solace, even if they were short lived.

Chapter Twenty Nine

The man's fingers trailed his naked flesh, every pore of him tensed as he ran his fingers over the thick hot red flesh wound, the scarring was fading slowly but the horrific vivid lacerations all over his strong muscular body were a reminder just how lucky he had been. His fingers traced the grooves between the scars, like Braille to his fingertips, each one telling a different tale, each one grimmer than the last. He looked at his reflection in the full length mirror, glancing painfully at his once Adonis like frame, now ugly and horrific to look at. He winced, having to look away before he got angry and started smashing this shit hole up, he had already scared the girl again this morning with his bear like gruffness and his boiling temper which he had been trying so fucking hard to contain. He reached over and grabbed his T-shirt from the bed, pulling it on, the smirk on his lips evident as he finally hid the evidence of any misdemeanours. He ran his fingers over his grisly military precise cut hair, he was still unsure what he was doing, he still didn't know exactly why had taken the girl, he had no real use for her she wasn't a bargaining tool of sorts. Again his attention returned to the mirror, he felt shy, he could no longer face looking at his own handsome face without feeling the uncontrollable tension bubbling in his gut, that pure, sheer feeling of sickness that came with fear, he felt unhinged, in fear of himself because he was unsure how long he could possibly keep his control. The crazy cunt he'd found himself lumbered with called it "PTSD" or some shit, but he wasn't quite so convinced, he was just a crazy cunt in his own humble opinion. Taking a deep slug from the can of Stella Artois that was sitting on the bedside cabinet he grimaced at the memories that he held drinking this shit, the smile emerged on his lips then, that fucking beautiful heartbreaking smile so bright that it could light up a million seas, the smile that had captured many a young girls affections, he knocked his head back now laughing in a high pitched drawling laugh that was neither false nor believable.... oh yes they would soon fucking see he thought taking another deep drink, dead man walking he thought the laughter now reaching a deafening crescendo ..... Dead man walking indeed.

Chapter Thirty

Jenna found herself waking with her arms hugging around Dom's naked waist, she snuggled into his neck, basking in his scent, drowning in his simple deliciousness. She kissed him softly on the neck light puckering kisses which sent his body into a flurry of goose bumps that dimpled his pale baby soft skin. She smiled gently as he turned his head into hers and kissed her on the lips. She stroked his cheek taking in every breathtaking feature on his beautiful face a seductive little smile snaked across his lips as he turned over and held her in his muscular arms. He gazed into her tired eyes, she was truly beautiful even in her despair, even now in the early morning she was still completely stunning, her skin was luminous, bright and milky which contrasted against her long black hair and her beautiful emerald eyes in such a picturesque way. Even though the last few weeks had been really hard on Jenna and she had literally been to the depths, she had her good days where she felt super positive and Dom could see a slight spark back in her gorgeous eyes, and she had her horrible bad days where he thought she would never ever smile again. Kiki's disappearance had hit her hard, more than hard but he was determined to help her through it. He nuzzled against her fragile body, ever since Kiki had gone missing the weight had literally peeled off Jenna, her once curvy hips and thighs now resembled matchsticks and her once toned tight stomach literally sucked in now at the ribs making it look like she was constantly struggling for breath, Even her breasts had deflated from a once comfy D cup to a nonexistent A, she hated how her body looked and she hated being undressed around Dom, it made her feel worthless knowing that despite having the body of a pubescent boy he still found her insatiable. It made her uncomfortable when he called her beautiful, because she knew herself that they were just words and words meant nothing when she knew herself that she was a complete shadow of her usual self. She glanced over at the bedside clock, 6:30am, she had been sleeping since two o clock the previous afternoon and had felt physically better after a good night's rest. She cocked her legs over the side of the bed and raised herself up, stretching out in a cat like pose, yawning loudly as she pulled on her pyjama bottoms that hung like bags from her tiny waist, she rolled them under at least four times to get a better fit. She caught Dom's dark eyes skimming over her tiny frame, she saw him gulping back the tears, placing his arm over his face to cover his distain, the upset written vividly on his handsome face. She pulled on her dressing gown which too swamped her and suddenly she exited the room without a second glance. The evident hot flush that spread across her face indicating her embarrassment, the tears that trickled down her face silently threatening to tear her apart, she really liked Dom, but every time he looked at her, held her, kissed her she could help but compare him with Craig. She had tried her hardest not to, but every time she closed her eyes she could feel herself pretending that it was Craig's kiss that lingered on her lips and that to Dom was unfair of her. She hated the thought of losing him, he had been her rock throughout all of this but she hated the thought of moving on from Craig so soon. The police were due to call this morning and if she was honest to herself, her flat was an absolute fucking tip. The wine bottles that littered the units her evidence of how much the pain of losing her daughter hurt her inside, the dirty slime covered dishes showing the pure neglect that she had shown her home. Then there was her physical appearance to contend with, she felt ugly, unattractive and for the first time in her entire life she felt she had aged a decade overnight. She turned to the sink, rolled up her sleeves and fished her hands around in the murky water, digging around for the plug, her face grimacing as she felt the grime under her fingertips, she had never felt so fucking filthy in all her days and in the hazy clear light of day did she realise that she had to up her game, buck her ideas up for the sake of her daughters safety. She couldn't be dealing with moping around the flat day in day out drinking herself into a steady oblivion, she didn't want to look like an emaciated fucking creature anymore. She needed to get herself fit and healthy ready for Kiki to come home, which of course she was coming home, eventually. Maybe. She ran a fresh load of water into the dirty sink and began to scrub the life out of the stiff food that was glued to her plates her heart not fully in the effort.

She leant over turning on the stereo and putting on her favourite CD that Craig had made her for her birthday three years previously, she couldn't quite understand how he had claimed it was her gift when it was full of his favourite songs, but she had loved it all the same, and now she treasured every single memory that came with the music of their youth. She wondered intently whether Craig and Dom would have been friends, whether he would have allowed Dom to be part of their special little clique, she highly doubted it, they had FOREVER been a duo. Craig had hated her having other male friends, not that he ever made it obvious to her, it had been okay for him to flirt obliviously with any bit of fluff that had passed his nose, he had been a fucking charmer alright, Jenna giggled at the memory of her best friend. A part of her had gone to the grave with Craig, she would never ever meet another man who had melted her heart the way he had. Sure Dom came a very close second, she had fallen for him in a school girl way but of course that's all he ever would be, second place to a fucking dead man. The thought upset Jenna more than it pleased her, but Craig had been irreplaceable in life, so he always would be irreplaceable in death too. She missed him so much that it physically hurt to think of him, but if she didn't have him in her thoughts then she felt as though she had abandoned him. It was nothing but a bittersweet situation one that Jenna hoped would ease with time, and it was time alone that would decide whether or not Jenna would fully heal from the scars of losing her soul mate.

Chapter Thirty One

Sammy tightened the dressing gown rope around her arm, pulling tightly as she tried to trace her battered veins for a good one to plunge the needle into, the dirty track marks that etched her arm like some crazy dot to dot pattern a clear indication of how bad her drug habit had become. She held the needle carefully between her teeth as she pulled the tourniquet tighter around her upper arm, still nothing. She growled angrily through her gritted teeth getting frustrated with herself for not being able to find a good enough vein, she was sweating profusely, shaking uncontrollably, she yanked the dressing gown rope from around her arm and dropped her trousers, lifting her leg up onto the filthy toilet seat and inspected her groin her bony fingers tracing every inch of her paper thin flesh, she was correct in guessing that she had also fucked that option too, she needed this hit fast, she was starting to feel desperate. The kind of deathly desperate that only a junkie felt and understood completely, the kind of desperate that drove you slightly deluded. She spotted up the large oval mirror from the corner of the room and instantaneously positioned herself down in front of it, gazing at her reflection she craned her head towards the mirror, showing her skinny neck, she allowed her fingers to feel the little ridges and dips of the veins in her neck before concentrating really hard on one vein in particular, she pulled the needle away from her dry lips and locked one eye shut tight while watching intently with the other as she sank the needle deep into the flesh in her neck. Shuddering as there was a spurt of blood that splattered onto the threadbare carpet, screeching a little as she pushed the plunger down, as the heroin entered her system she let out the sweetest moan of ecstasy that she had ever experienced, the hit calming her instantly soothing her battered nerves, kissing caressing her insides so she felt nothing but pure sweet haven. She flopped down onto the carpet barely able to move, the blood rushed to her ears and the only thing reminding her that she was still alive was the faint heartbeat that drummed in her chest.

Kingston Marshall was walking back up to his flat on the Belmonte, the thick black dreadlocks hung heavily down to his waist his skin as black as ash wrinkled like an old potato sack, his thick beard peppered with white whispers of hair, he stood at just under seven foot tall and worked as a doorman over in Kenny Kreegan's "Women's house" which of course was his gentleman's term for a fucking brothel. Kinny as he was lovingly known to all the brasses as loved his job, despite all the girls being mardy middle aged old trollops who still thought they had the looks and charms that they had once possessed at eighteen, he loved them all, even the new foreign ones. Kinny himself was of heavy Jamaican descent and everything about him echoed his heritage, even his thick Jamaican accent which he spoke in such a polite velvet tone. The girls loved him, the sheer size on the fucker was evidence enough that no punter would even attempt to give them any grief, he was built like the proverbial brick shithouse and could put the shits up the toughest of gangsters and mobsters in reality he was as soft as a teddy bear, a polite well spoken, well educated man, he was wise and kind and treated everyone with the utmost respect despite many of them not giving his the same grandeur. He had put Sammy Carter up out of the goodness of his heart and as a favour to young Emma who lived in his block, she had found the girl battered out in the communal garden and had asked Kingston to take the girl under his wing. Despite being a complete pain in the fucking arse Sammy was proving to be quite the house guest and he found himself warming to the troubled young sole. He hated the fact that she was on the gear, he himself could smoke weed until the cows came home, but he was extremely against any of the street drugs that so freely bounced around this estate. He had finished work early today, business was slow and Kingston knew it was the run up to Christmas that was killing them, and the usual married executives and the posh banker types that normally frequented Kenny's were too busy with their families trying to at least make the effort for the one day a year where they could all pretend to be happy with their fat overweight wives and their miserable snotty nosed kids. Kingston himself had only been married once, in the old country, to his little Dolly, she had died a few years prior to him coming to London and finding himself in the security business as one of the henchmen for one of the undergrounds most notorious gangsters. Kenny was old school, he didn't deal drugs. He worked in protection, loan sharking and prostitution. Each of his girls were preened to within an inch of their lives, perfect hair and makeup perfect personal image and hygiene and each were tested once a month for any fatalities. It was the safest whore house in London. The madam who ran the place under Kenny's command was a gorgeous leggy blonde called Cathy, or Curvy Cath as she was known at work. She was an absolute bombshell, hot as fire cool as ice and everyone treated her with the utmost respect. Kingston was hired as her personal bodyguard when he wasn't running the doors of the brothel. This suited him perfectly of course. He cut across the Belmonte over to his block, trudging up the stone steps which stank heavily of piss and stale neglect, coming out onto his veranda he strutted down the corridor whistling through his teeth, he pushed his over sized hands into his trench coat pocket and dug around amongst his tobacco tin and spare change for his house key. He fumbled with dainty key in his pudgy fingers before pushing the door open, it was deathly silent and the air stank of unwashed bodies and cannabis, if that little fuckers been at my weed again, he thought as he crossed the threshold he called out in his thick accent Sammy's name, still silence. He wandered into the living room, the smell of drugs was definitely coming from here, he noticed the dirty foil decks strewn on the floor and the joint stubs in the overflowing ashtray. Then he noticed the dirty looking naked body that was laying in front of his mother's ancient antique mirror draped in nothing but a scratchy, dry old bath towel, the needle that had been stuck in her neck now entwined in her spindle like fingers. She was breathing, but it was shallow, unsteady and out of rhythm. He leaped over to the other side of the room and held Sammy's body in his huge hands, she had choked on her own vomit, the puddle of curdled mess and congealed blood that lingered at his knees almost killing him with its odour he had to hold his breath tightly. He nursed her head in his hands all the while repeating her name with feeble attempts to resuscitate her out of her drug addled stupor. Pulling his mobile phone out of his pocket he dialled 999 and slurred hurriedly at the operator that he needed an ambulance immediately, he gave her his address and slammed the phone down hard. He dropped Sammy down onto the carpet, she couldn't be seen in here, he had Kenny's stash of money in the bathroom behind the sink and that was without the shit load of weed in the bedroom. No she definitely couldn't be seen here. He went back over to Sammy's limp body and heaved her up in one effortless swoop, hauling her through the passage to the front door he traipsed her down the corridor and dumped her on the end of the veranda a few doors down. He swivelled around and headed back to his flat to get rid of any trace that Sammy had been staying at his, she had barely any possessions so he guessed it wouldn't be hard to dispose of her. He grabbed his spliff box off the top of the cheap box back television set and sat himself down on the tatty fabric couch to roll himself a joint. He was feeling anxious and he hoped to fuck that the plod wouldn't come sniffing around his gaff for info because he had been the one who phoned the bloody ambulance, he toked on his joint rapidly, allowing the hazy smoke to circulate his lungs before billowing it out in a thick cloud of smoke, his mind boggling as to how he was going to get out of this mess, god help his good nature! He could punch himself square in the face for being so thick as to take a junkie into his home. He could hear the sirens outside a few minutes later, he stepped out into the corridor about to relay his story to the paramedics of how he found the poor drugged up girl out of her head outside his flat. He had to take a second glance as he reached the far end of the veranda.

Where the fuck was she?

Chapter Thirty Two

Craig handed the large envelope over to the lanky teenage boy before him, it was stuffed with crisp twenty pound notes and the boy looked like he was about to come in his pants as his crystal blue eyes popped out of his skull;

"You sure you know what you're doing now dopey cunt?" Craig asked sarcastically, the boy nodded his head briskly, for years he had wanted to be in Craig's gang, he was like a fucking Don to him, he was a successful business man despite his young age, oh sure he went to college to study writing or whatever it was but all that was just a facade surely, just a smoke and mirrors thing to keep his foghorn mother off his back. Craig took a big gulp out of his can of Stella, thinking for a long moment before he spoke again;

"I don't want Jen involved, not yet anyway, she'll know why I'm doing this eventually. I can't stay here and watch her bring up another man's kid you know, it kills me" he looked straight into the boy's eyes as he spoke "You'll only get a few years in borstal I'll set you up in a cushy little set up, see you right" he continued taking a fat wad of cash from his pocket and counting out a hundred pounds in crisp notes and handing them to the boy. "Get a decent knife, one that will make a good fucking wound, I want this to be as believable as possible, I need to be dead to them. I'll sort it out from the hospital I've got Daniel Owens doing me a death certificate and he's getting me some of that shit that slows your pulse down so that your practically dead anyway" he added taking another deep drink from his can. The boy nodded again, words unable to exit his mouth. He couldn't believe that he was going to be the one to inevitably help Craig Carter fake his own fucking death. They had been planning this for weeks and now the time was here Johnny Fenton was officially cacking himself. He knew that Craig had already planned his own funeral, he had paid the undertaker well to allow him to stay in the mortuary if his mother wanted to come and pay her respects, which of course the loud mouthed cunt would, he was being cremated, well obviously he wasn't but the poor fucker in his place was and he was flying out to Spain under the name Levi Bourne to spend a few months lying low.

"Make fucking sure you and them soppy fucking mates of yours doing fuck this up Johnny boy" Craig exclaimed crushing his empty can in his hands and tossing it aside. "When I come back and I start the clubs up there'll be plenty more fucking jobs for you my son" he added smiling that devilishly handsome smile of his. He was a cunning cunt when the feeling took him, and now he was ready to make his mark on the criminal underworld.

Whether dead or very much alive....

Chapter Thirty Three

The man brushed his hands through the woman's thick blonde hair, they had been shagging practically all day and she was starting to get tired, but he was buzzing from the gram of coke that he'd bunged up his nose earlier on in the morning. His steely blue eyes blazing wild as he ripped at her knickers, she was wriggling beneath him begging him to stop, but he refused to hear her between her continuous whinging and carried on regardless. There was no fucking way was she not shagging him now, he was rock hard and ready to just glide into her, but here she was again making it difficult the fat fucking pig that she was. He leapt off her, grabbing the small pocket mirror and the rolled up twenty off the sideboard and manically snorted the fat line off the surface hocking his throat as the coke hit the back of his nostrils.

"Get the fuck up you pathetic fat cunt and get the fuck out of my sight!" he screamed, ripping on his boxers, his throbbing erection still showing plainly through the thin cotton of his briefs. He licked his dry lips manically before heaving her off the bed and slinging her against the wall. Her head thudding hard against the plasterboard, she was crying now, hysterical as he mauled her now batting her head with his meaty fists. She tried shielding her head with the duvet that was wrapped around her but he whipped it off her in an instant. He was in her face now, strong hands gripped tightly on her hair as he yanked her up to face him

"Jenna was twice the shag you are, it's like fucking a fucking rhino you sweaty fucking mess" he spoke through firmly gritted teeth, his angry eyes wandering over her size fourteen ample body in sheer disgust. He knew he was hurting her, but in all honesty he couldn't give a flying fuck. Merely the sight of her was starting to fuck him off. The punch landed squarely on her jaw and when it landed her jawbone popped beneath the blow;

"Craig I'm pregnant" she screamed; regretting it the second the words had escaped her mouth. She threw her hand over her face as he leapt back from her. That was it the girl could hear them from the room next door, she would now know who her captor was, and he couldn't risk anyone finding out he'd got this fucking twat up the stuff! He began a vicious assault on the woman all the while yelling about how much of a fucking stupid cunt she was. He was fucking furious, she had known from the very fucking beginning none of their names were to be used and even worse she had told him she was on the fucking pill so that mounted to twice she had deceived him the fucking tramp. Well she wouldn't survive this there was no fucking chance. he started to slam his can of Stella over her stupid fucking head, all the while screaming out obscenities until she no longer struggled and there was nothing but calm, he stepped away from her mutilated body blood sprayed the walls in a crimson mist and her fleshy face hung from her neck, it was brutal, disgusting to look at and he knew right then that he had to get out of here. He grabbed his phone from the bedside cabinet and punched the keys until he found the number he wanted, he held the phone to his ear, his teeth grinding wildly in his head, his jaw swinging from too much coke.

"Davey you cunt. You better find me a new place to stay… I've made a bit of a fucking mess here…. yeah ill meet you tonight…. ill torch it…. yeah no evidence then is there? Alright fella I'll see you later." He disconnected the call and slumped back on the bed, his hands tugging his boxers down, fuck it he thought, may as well finish myself off he thought chuckling sadistically. He was away with the fairies tugging at his throbbing member when he heard a little tap on the wall, he stopped, glaring at the blank space between him and the girl. His heart leapt into his mouth as he heard the cutest little voice in the world saying….

"Uncle Craigy Bear is that you?"

Chapter Thirty Four

Claire Horran sat at her daughters bedside willing for her never to wake up, she had never been so fucking angry in her life and she hoped against hope that Sammy would just fucking die so that she could stop worrying every night whether she would get the call saying her daughter had finally killed herself through drugs. Claire was tired, run down, her whole body ached from the bitter insomnia that plagued her every single night she just wanted this nightmare to be over, it had been terrible when Craig had died, but with her daughter she wished it would hurry up and happen. She looked at Sammy, she was like a fucking corpse, her ghostly white paper thin skin barely covering her skinny body, her arms and thighs covered in track marks from years of drug abuse, her hair was lank and thin, roots showing a vague hint of her dark natural colouring, her eyes were dead blackened holes in her face, her lips twisted in some sort of wired grin, she was sickening to look at. Claire was just glad her fucking mouth was shut so she couldn't see those disgusting black gums that Sammy had, and the dirty decayed holes where her stunning white teeth had once sat neatly. She still hadn't come to and Claire was starting to wish that she wouldn't, the doctors had told her something about severe brain damage, that Sammy may never be able to speak or do anything for herself again because it wasn't normal for someone who had taken an overdose to be out for the count this long, it had been three weeks since Sammy had made the stupid decision to inject heroin into her neck and the doctors were puzzled as to why she hadn't woken up yet. They had run countless tests, continuous brain scans; she had gone under twice but had been bought back to the brink by the skin of her teeth, it had been touch and go for about a week now, she was still in a coma, still hooked up to all these tubes, still being kept alive by the puffing of the life support and the oxygen tank. The doctor had been earlier to have a chat with her, and she had been sat there ever since, staring into the blank space on the wall. Craig had been bought to the very same intensive care unit when he had been stabbed, all Claire could think about was that fateful day when her boy got snatched away, fuck the fact Sammy was laying here fighting for her life, even in death Craig still cast a huge shadow over his family. Claire remembered that final goodbye she shared with her son, she had kissed his beautiful face as his favourite ub40 song played in the background. She had held his frightfully cold hands, hugged into his tracksuit jumper and just prayed the moment could last forever. Despite having his guts spewed all over the Belmonte estate he was just as stunning in death as he had been in life, he was tranquil, calm, breathtaking. Claire had loved him so much; he had definitely lived up to the stereotype of mummy's favourite boy. She had nurtured him, loved him watch him grow into the beautiful intelligent man that he had become, She knew he had loved his coke, she knew he drank like a fish and she knew he had had a dark persona behind all that confident front but he had been her everything and she would give her very last breath just to tell him that she loved him one last time. He was so vivid and fresh in her mind's eye, he could have just waltzed through the door right at that moment and it would be like he had never left, how Claire wished that would happen. She closed her eyes as a single tear rolled down her cheek and dripped onto the crisp white hospital sheets. He had been one in a million had Craig. Now she was faced with an agonising decision, did she turn off Sammy's life support or did she wait and face the rest of her life caring for a paraplegic. Life was so fucking cruel and now Claire Horran had to sign her own daughter's death warrant, yet either way whether she turned the machine off or not she still had lost both her children. Both gripped by their own choice of drugs, both in with the "Wrong crowd". There was nothing more Claire could do, it seemed that her children hadn't been so different after all. She called the nurse and revealed to her, her final decision.

Chapter Thirty Five

Claire left the hospital that evening with a heavy heart, she had cried nonstop for the past hour and now she was outside she finally felt a serene calm wash over her tired body, she had made peace with the fact that Sammy was no longer in pain and would no longer have to fight her addictions every single day as she had done for years now. She had kissed her daughters grubby cheek and gave her a solemn heartfelt goodbye. But it didn't feel like she was mourning Sammy, it was though she had finally given her the chance to be free she had said goodbye to the girl Sammy had been as a child, that carefree gorgeous little madam who had stolen Claire and Kevin's heart from the moment she had been born. She had completed their family at one point, and now she had torn it apart. She was just glad that the kids were still too young to understand that their mummy had gone away. Claire would sit them down tomorrow and try to explain it as best she could. She hailed a taxi down and told him with a heavy sigh that she was going to the Belmonte Estate. She stared out of the window all of the way there, barely noticing that there was a new night club being built in the town centre. The bright neon display that flashed outside read opening soon, The Mamma Rouge gentleman's club and bar. Claire's head was a whirlwind and as she passed through the bright lights of the town centre in a flurried blur, she settled into her seat in the back of the cab hugging her coat around her tightly, she was now the carer of her two grandchildren solely, she was now completely alone in life, her husband was dead, her son was dead and now so was her fucking daughter her druggie smacked up daughter. Claire couldn't cry, she felt that if she did, she wouldn't ever be able to stop. She stared up at the dark night sky and said a silent goodbye to her two babies, she hoped that they would keep each other safe and of course look after their silly old dad up there.

As the taxi pulled into the estate Claire realised that she owed it to her children's memory to make something of her and her grandchildren's lives she had to take charge and make something of herself, get back into work, get out more and make more precious memories with the kids. They were wonderful children and Claire promised herself there and then that those two wouldn't turn out like her two children had. They would grow into successful happy adults and they would always above everything know that they were loved unconditionally by Claire. There was so much skating around in her head, Claire couldn't wait to get in and drown her sorrows in a bottle or two of strong wine, and grieve in the secret solace of her own home in her own room simply alone.

Chapter Thirty Six

Kiki Shearan giggled loudly as the swings went higher and higher, she was wearing her pretty new dress and coat that Craig had bought her and for the first time since being taken from her mummy's house she didn't think about her mummy at all. She didn't really know why her mummy hadn't come back to get her, but she was glad that uncle Craigy had come back to get her. Now that he had got rid of the nasty lady he didn't shout at her anymore, they went outside together to the park almost every day and he bought her some new toys to play with so she didn't get bored anymore. Today he'd promised to take her to McDonalds for lunch after their visit to the park, he was nice to her now instead of shouting at her all the time and calling her nasty names. Kiki loved him he was her idol again.

"C'mon Tiger lets go get some dinner shall we?" he called to her, stopping the swings slowly so that he could lift her out gently, he cuddled her close to him and kissed her on her forehead, taking in the soft scent of her freshly washed hair and her distinct baby smell that she still carried despite being almost three. She squealed in delight as he tickled her lightly by her ribs sending her into fits of hysteria, she truly was a beautiful child and Craig felt guilty for taking her hostage and treating her as he had done. But now he could spend all his time with her, love her, care for her like he should have all along. Like he had promised Jenna so many times that he would provide and care for them both over anything else in the world. He buttoned up his suit jacket and strolled down the little path that separated the park from the main road holding the little girls tiny hand and chatting away like nothing bad had ever happened between them.

Jenna was having a mad tap on the stout little police officer who stood before her, arms folded over her ample chest as she asked Jenna for what felt like the millionth time for the information on her little girl's father, she had continuously avoided the polices questions about Kiki's dad and now she felt as though the net was slowly closing in on her;

"I fucking told you lot before he's just some bloke I met at a club" she shouted, her voice reaching an agonising crescendo.

"Not what you told us in your initial interview Miss Shearan" she policewoman added her lips pursed tightly as she sneered at Jenna with her beady little piggy eyes. Jenna had told the police at first that the baby's father was a man she used to work with whom conveniently she didn't have a name for. Dom stared at Jenna from the sofa his eyes willing her to tell the police the truth, he had already guessed who Keek's father was and he was betting a pound to a penny to a pinch of shit he had been right. He had known from the moment he had seen the photos of a heavily pregnant Jenna in her photo albums where the father lovingly placed kisses on her rounded stomach. He had known the minute he clapped eyes on little Kiki Shearan and he was quite surprised that no one else had made the same connection. It was blatantly obvious, the two were like peas in a pod. Dom glared at Jenna knowing that she wouldn't admit her sordid secret out loud because if she didn't believe it then it wasn't real.

"He's dead" Dom piped in over the stout policewoman who too was starting to grate on his last nerve, everyone's attention was suddenly turned to him and Jenna gasped in disapproval of Dom and his big fucking mouth, her hand reaching up to clasp her mouth as she realised that Dom had known her dirty little secret all along. When she had convinced so many others that it wasn't true. There had been no other man, no man from work, no one night stands Craig had been her first, her last her only lover; he was indeed her daughter's father.

Jenna stared at Dom as though he had grown another head, she shook her own in sheer shock that he had known all this time. The policewoman shot a stern glance between the two of them, her face suddenly etched with a look of confusion, she asked again, her voice full of conviction as she said

"Jenna ill ask you again, who is Kiki's father? it could relate to the case significantly" she stated pulling her notepad and pencil from her pocket; Jenna slumped down onto the sofa, her head in her hands the tears streaming down her face making her mascara smudge thick shadows under her eyes;

"It's Craig Carter" she whispered through the torrents of tears than down her cheeks, Dom sucked in his breath in mock surprise as he placed a supporting arm over her shoulders and hugged her close to his chest, whispering sweet nothings to her as the policewoman recorded notes in her little book. The police woman's eyes turned pitiful, they had all heard the sorry story of poor Craig Carter being stabbed on the Belmonte because of his success in college and because he didn't cause riots like the rest of the horrid little bastards who occupied this shithole estate. He had been an A level English literature student, had earned all of his GCSE's at B grade and above and he had never once been in trouble with the plod. Unlike his younger sister of course. The stout policeman had been on the receiving end of many of Sammy Carter's foul mouthed assaults in the past she'd locked her up numerous times for drugs, shoplifting and other offences in between. The policewoman took any extra information she needed, not that there was much more to go on, the girl's father was dead so that instantly ruled him out as a suspect in their enquiries. Dom ushered her out of the flat and closed the door quietly behind him, Jenna was still sobbing in the living room. He knew that this had been hard on her, what confused him the most was that nobody had put two and two together with Jenna and Craig. He had done so from day one, he knew that they had been more than just "friends" the minute he saw the photos that were lovingly placed around Jenna's, the proud smiles on both faces as he held her pert little bump, the face of a proud father, not that of a best friend. The smiles in their eyes as they posed so seductively for pictures as thought there were nobody else in the room but them, the private little glances between them in each and every single photograph that captured their treasured relationship so perfectly. Dom suddenly felt sickly, jealous even, because even though he had always guessed Kiki had been Craig's daughter, now he knew that he indeed was the girl's father he felt the sly pangs of jealousy hitting him, his ego dented slightly. In all honesty he thought he might have preferred the previous story of Keek's being some no names child. Now as he glanced around Jenna's living room and caught the sly grin of Craig's in each picture as if to say "Haa gotcha you cunt" he turned away reluctantly from Jenna when she went to try and comfort him. He was a sucker for tragedy alright, he pushed Jenna away from him lightly, she was sobbing now, heartbreaking sobs that shook her whole body the words I'm sorry tumbling out of her mouth meaning nothing to Dom, he turned abruptly and walked away silently, slamming the door behind him, she was alone, completely heartbroken. She slid down the front door, hugging her knees to her tightly, she couldn't risk this getting out. She hoped against hope that he wouldn't go and do something stupid and tell Claire. She crumpled to the floor, the tears rolling down her cheeks, she had finally admitted it out loud that Craig was Kiki's father and the reality hit her like a train, her beautiful daughter would never ever know her daddy, she would never share that beautiful bond between father and daughter. Jenna was devastated, she had held on that perfect little secret for so long and now she knew that it would explode straight back into her face. Craig was dead; she had wanted everyone to believe that Kiki was some random child because she didn't want to share the last final thing that connected her to Craig with anyone. She was hers and Craig's precious little angel and she didn't want anyone stepping in on that, didn't want anyone knowing that against all odds, they had finally committed the truth to each other for him to be snatched away the very same day. She had loved the bones of that man and there would never be another, she hugged herself tightly willing for the pain to be taken from her, she didn't even want to live anymore, where was the fucking point? Dom hated her, Craig was dead and Kiki was fuck knows where, all her so called friends now looked at her with sympathy and tip toed around her like she was some sort of fucking grenade or something. She hated it. She let the feeling of pure self despair wash over her, she had never felt so low in her entire life, she wiped the snot and tears from her face with the back of her jumper sleeve, she was so overwhelmed and scared all at once and she couldn't quite deal with how fucked her head felt. She laid her head in her hands and sobbed herself to sleep, right there by the front door.

Chapter Thirty Seven

"Jenna, Jenna I swear to fuck you better open this door or ill boot it down and drag you out here by that fucking bedraggled mane of yours you little cunt!" Claire's bell in every tooth voice echoed from beyond the other side of the door, she was evidently pissed her voice was barely recognisable and she had more than obviously bumped into Dom. She was angry that much was evident and Jenna could bet a pound to a penny to a pinch of shit that Claire was stood outside with smoke coming out of her ears such was the malice in her voice. Jenna darted into the living room, she glanced up at the clock, it was three in the fucking morning and Claire was this drunk? Where were the kids? Jenna thought as she tiptoed to the front door, the pounding of Claire's meaty fist on the door literally made her jump out of her skin. She looked through the little peephole and saw that Claire was right on the threshold of the door and Lee and Dom were behind her trying to pull her away. Jenna turned the key in the lock and pulled open the door, the slap hit her hard, sharp and quick and she lunged back recoiling in shock. She held her cheek, Claire was as red as a tomato, not a good look against her copper hair, She was screaming, inaudible babble that was spewing out of her mouth in a torrent of drink fuelled insults coupled with manic hand movements that made her look slightly fucking crazed. Jenna stood back a few steps, looking out at the scene before her, like something out of a soap opera, Lee was trying his hardest to restrain Claire, but it was useless, like waving a red rag to a bull, she pulled hard against his restraints all the while screeching at the top of her voice.

"You vicious little bitch" Claire seethed through gritted teeth, her buxom frame pushing heavily against Dom and Lee as they tried they're hardest to pull her away from Jenna's doorstep.

"I'm so so sorry Claire" Jenna replied timidly, hand still stuck to her cheek. Her pathetic voice making Claire even more eager to get her hands on the smarmy little bitch, Jenna could smell the mixture of stale scotch and cigarette smoke on her breath and she could see from the fact that the two men were literally holding her up that she was fucking legless. Jenna stepped out onto the doorstep her bare feet touching the icy concrete sending shivers through her skinny body; she looked Claire straight in the eyes before clearing her throat, she didn't expect the globule of spittle that came flying out of Claire's mouth as it hit her square on the cheek, she looked at her former friend in disgust;

"Fucking finished?" she remarked, wiping the spit from her cheek with the back of her sleeve; if it was one thing she hated more than anything in the world it was spitting, she wanted to ram her fist into the fat fuckers smug face but no, she was angry and Jenna owed it to her to tell her the truth from her own mouth instead of the mouth of Dom, the two faced cunt. She respectfully told the two men to leave Claire go; Dom immediately declined making Jenna almost want to punch him with rage;

"I fucking said Let her go!" she protested grabbing Lee's arm firm until he left Claire go, there was no fight from Claire as Jenna knew there wouldn't have been, not now Jenna had stepped outside and confronted her. This was all bravado, a show for the neighbours benefit; Jenna squared up to Claire, her face literally touching the older woman's, her eyes strayed to Dom's face she smiled sadly as her gaze met his, her eyes returning to Claire's, her breathing was laboured, fast and furious and Jenna smirked as she stepped aside, offering the woman into her home.

"Instead of shouting your big mouth off out here, go in and I'll speak to you properly, ill even invite your two gofers in" she smirked sarcastically as she spoke, her eyes reverting to Dom when she made the referral looking him snidely up and down. Lee didn't need telling twice and he strutted in through the front door, taking a fag out of his tin and lighting it in the passage as he went. Claire hung her head as she sulkily walked into the flat, Jenna closed the door quietly behind her, she focused her attention on Dom, who was stood there with his hands in his pockets, his face on the floor like a naughty school boy, Jenna felt nothing for him at this moment in time, she wished he'd kept his fucking big nose out of her business.

"You had no fucking right Dom" she spat angrily, grabbing his arm so he was forced to look at her. His dark eyes bore into her, his gaze steely, piercing, his thick lashes framing them so beautifully she knew instantly from the huge dilated pupils that he was on something.

"I had to, it didn't feel right Jen, Sammy died this afternoon. Kiki's her granddaughter remember? And she's on the missing list. So don't you dare tell me about right from wrong when you clearly don't know the meaning of it yourself." He retorted angrily, his off his head eyes bulging, the sweat pouring off his brow in floods. He looked evil; Jenna barely recognised this creature before her, she sighed angrily and turned away from him before storming inside, she left the door wide open so he could help himself, but he didn't have the heart to follow her, so he turned on his heel and headed home. He had fucked it good and proper this time. He could happily kick himself at this precise moment, he felt more than stupid for interfering but he knew how he would feel in the situation and he reasoned that he would want to know the truth. Fuck it all he thought grabbing his phone out of his pocket and rang his dealer for another gram, he wasn't going to be doing much sleeping tonight anyway so he may as well end the night getting high as a fucking kite.

****

Jenna closed the door behind her as she stepped in the living room, Claire was engrossed in a picture of Craig holding Kiki as a baby, a single tear trickled down her face, a slight smile edged on the corner of her mouth, placing it back on the mantle, she turned to Jenna;

"Did he know?" she whispered, her voice tiny in the airspace between them, Jenna nodded slowly, stepping closer to Claire, she laid her hand on her friends arm, Claire winced slightly at the girls touch. Jenna ordered Lee to grab them a glass of wine from the fridge as she sat Claire down on the couch, taking the seat opposite her she sucked in a breath through her teeth before she spoke.

"Yeah he knew, I told him the day he died" she said flatly "He had been going on at me for weeks to tell him who the father was so that he could go and give him a piece of his mind you know what he was like" she smiled sadly at the thought of the man that she had loved so whole heartedly, she saw her memory mirrored in Claire's face as the woman grinned slightly, the thought of her son 'giving a piece of his mind' to some down and out over paternity of the little girl he had worshipped tickled her slightly. Jenna continued "Well he wouldn't stop going on and on about how Keek's deserved better and we got into a huge fight over it" she paused as she remembered one of the first horrific arguments that had ever occurred between them. The way Craig had lunged at her pinning her to the wall as he called her nothing but a stupid selfish cunt for not putting Kiki first; "he was screaming at me, he was so nasty Claire, he was calling me a slut and all sorts, so I told him that he'd never find the other man because there was no other fucking man" she recoiled her hand from Claire's arm momentarily to take the wine glass that Lee handed her, taking a deep drink, her thoughts pondering in her mind.

"What did he say?" Claire murmured, her voice thick with the tears that threatened to pour from her eyes.

Jenna took another gulp from her glass before she cleared her throat, "He called me a liar at first" she continued "but then he knew the second I swore on Kiki's life that I was telling the truth. Craig was the only man I've ever slept with Claire, even to this day he's still the only man I've ever slept with." Her voice was thick with honestly and Claire knew instantaneously that the girl was telling the truth despite how much Claire didn't want to believe it for a second. Her face was pale and deathly white and she felt as though she would pass out any second all this stress was clouding her mind and she was starting to feel that she would soon have a heart attack if this lot didn't stop with their stories.

"Why didn't you tell me Jen, you knew you could have come to me" her eyes glistened as she murmured softly, Lee placed his hand on her knee, he was no good at this lovey dovey shit, he stared awkwardly around the room before fixing his eyes at the wall, hoping that he would at some point become relevant to the conversation because at this particular moment he felt about as useful as a bacon sandwich in a synagogue.

Jenna took another deep swig from her glass her eyes twinkling as she looked at the photos of Craig that occupied every corner of her living room.

"He made me swear that I wouldn't Claire we had to protect Kiki, he didn't want her coming to any harm" her voice trailed off at the end of the sentence, Claire knew that whatever was coming next she wasn't going to like it, she tensed her whole body preparing herself for the worst as she urged Jenna to continue.

Jenna sat further back in her seat pouring herself another large glass of wine from the bottle on the table, hugging her knees tight to her chest her eyes still firmly fixed on the picture on the wall, she gulped hard, all confidence gone from her voice as she stated

"Right..I'll start it from the very beginning........"

Part Two-Twenty Months Previously .....

Redemption that is all we need.

Anon

Chapter Thirty nine

"You owe me money boy, a lot of fucking money and it's about high time you started coughing up" Kenny Kreegan's eyes bore into Craig, the boy shuffled uneasily in his chair, for a big man he looked somewhat pathetic under Kenny's electric gaze. His heavy muscular shoulders slumped, his head down glaring at the floor. Kenny cleared his throat in mock contempt and started as Craig Carters eyes met his own, she steely gaze of someone who knew they were fucked. Kenny's smile beamed from ear to ear the sarcasm dripping in his voice as he added;

"Well Mr Carter you young boys will try to play with the big boy's wont you?" he laughed at his own wit slightly, tossing his head back to emphasise his delight in the boy's discomfort. Craig huffed angrily it was a slightly childish mannerism of his and he could have slapped himself for being so fucking stupid as to dabble in drugs from Kenny Kreegan. Sure it was all well and good when Kenny was handing the coke out like sherbet on tick to all and sundry, but when it came to this, being thousands of pounds in debt and his dealer wanted repayment did Craig realise how much shit he truly was in.

"Look Kenny" he sighed scrunching his hands together on the desk before him "I don't have your money, you know I haven't. I've been helping Jen out with getting stuff for the baby and if I'm honest mate I'm broke. Can't I just keep working? I'll do extra shifts" the embarrassment in his voice was evident; Kenny thrived on the boy's weakness. Craig sat back in the small plastic chair, his shoulders too wide for the bowing chair back, so he had to return to his slumped position. He huffed again, making gestures with his hands as he explained himself to Kenny, but Kenny had never been one for sympathy.

"No you can't, breaking knee caps isn't making me any money Mr Carter. I need something more" there was a long pause "productive"

Craig's mouth was dry, he was slightly confused, if Kenny didn't want him out sharking anymore then what had he intended for Craig to do? They sat there in a slightly awkward silence for a while, Kenny deep in thought, Craig couldn't think of a single thing to say, he was anxious now, he hated not knowing where he stood in the means of business. Of Course he wished now that he had never got involved with this pompous old cunt. His eyes scanned the room awkwardly, he wished the batty old bastard would say something, anything just so that Craig could hurry up and get the fuck out of here. Kenny's brothel wasn't a place he frequented regularly, and now he knew why, the smell of stale unwashed bodies and the distinct scent of heavy dirty sex hung in the air like dense smog. The red cheeked sounds of women moaning in delight and the bang bang bang of headboards against walls was just sheer embarrassing and Craig wondered why any man would be seen dead in a place like this. It was sad, really sad, half Kenny's dolly birds couldn't speak a word of fucking English and they'd all come over here in the hopes that the lovely Mr Kreegan would give them better opportunities in life. The charming old bastard. Craig scratched his head and smirked ever so slightly as he heard one of the punters in one of the other room screeching for one of the girls to "stop chewing on his cock and suck it tidy" Yes this was a strange old place indeed he thought, hiding his smirk with his fingertips.

A wry smile glittered on Kenny's lips as he spoke

"Pretty Girl that Jenna, seems like a dirty bitch too, could do with a girl like that on my payroll." Kenny chuckled, licking his thin lips in a seductive manner, the sick glisten in his pale eyes told Craig exactly what they old bastard had on his mind. Craig had to do a double take to check that he was serious and for a moment he was truly rendered speechless;

"What?" Kenny continued "didn't think I'd noticed your little piece of pussy did you boy" he was laughing at Craig now a hearty gut wrenching laugh, his face screwed up like a ball of paper, his eyes evil, delicious with malice as he slammed his fist down on the table, the hysterics making him resemble a cackling hyena. Craig glared at him his eyes crazy as he lunged over the table at the man, Kenny stood and caught Craig square in the jaw with a flying uppercut. "You vicious old Cunt!" Craig screamed at the top of his lungs grabbing Kenny by the throat and pinning him to the wall. His face inches away from Kenny's, his eyes raging in their sockets from the sheer amount of Coke and rage that ran in his system. The man before him just exhumed disgust and Craig could see the sleaziness of him oozing from every pore. Kenny was chortling at him now, sniggering beneath his baited breath. Craig slapped him hard in the face;

"Oh what Mr Carter, Hit a nerve have we?" Kenny laughed sarcastically as he spoke. Craig threw him back onto the desk;

"Fuck you Kenny the deals off" he stood up and backed away to the door, he left Kenny's office. He caught the glance of the big black motherfucker that Kenny had on his door, Craig shoved past and headed for the front door. As soon as he got outside he sucked in the fresh air, kissing his lungs, that place was a fucking dive, and Kenny Kreegan could come and suck him off before he coughed up a fucking penny now. He didn't care if Kenny beat him senseless; shot him in the fucking head even.... he wasn't getting his dirty hands on Jenna.

Kenny sat back at his desk, the smile still vivid on his lips as Kingston Marshall entered his tiny office, Kenny looked up at his most trusted henchman and laughed sarcastically as he offered the much larger man a seat on one of his plastic chairs, respectfully the offer was declined. Kenny stood up so that he was almost on a more even level with the man as he said quietly.

"I want that cunt dead, Get Fenton on the blower tell him I want a fucking meet. Today."

******

Craig walked into his mothers and slammed the door shut, the smell of home suddenly filled his nostrils and for a second he felt so much calmer. He could hear his mother bustling about in the kitchen, the pots and pans clanging about as Claire fished around for her slow cooker. She glanced over her shoulder and saw her little treasure stood in the doorway, instantly she stopped what she was doing and ran to hold him in a loving embrace, he held her close basking in the smell of home, he loved his mum so fucking much, he would do anything on this planet to make sure Claire was happy.

"I've only gone and lost me fucking slow cooker" she said sulkily as Craig looked down at her, a cheeky grin on his face which soon turned to a high pitched cackle. Only his batty mother could lose a massive slow cooker in her piss poor space she called a kitchen.

"Losing your fucking marbles you are girl" he stated matter of factly as he sat at the table, watching in awe as his mum instantly went to the kettle to fix him a cuppa, it was their little thing and he loved her for it. She was perfect in every single way, they might not have much but without a doubt they always had each other. She patted Craig's hand gently, she could see by his face her had been on something his eyes were bulging, it broke her heart in two but he was an adult now so there was nothing she could do. She couldn't baby him forever.

"Want to talk about it?" she quizzed going back to their tea, swirling the spoon in the cups and placing his in front of him, she joined him back at the table her face full of concern, as usual he shut her out dismissing it as nothing but she knew Craig like she knew the back of her hand. She wouldn't push the issue though, she knew when Craig was like this he had a vicious temper, she just hoped he looked a little more respectable when he went to Jen's scan with her later, poor cow had no one else to go with her but she could hardly rock up there with Craig in this fucking state could she? Claire sat beside him and lit herself a cigarette, offering Craig the packet, he slid one out and clamped it between his teeth as Claire gave him a light, they both sat in an uncomfortable silence nursing their teas and smoking their cigarettes, every now and again glancing at each other nervously awaiting for someone to break the tension.

"Fucking lost the slow cooker" Craig muttered between the thick billows of smoke, a smile appearing on his beautiful face. Chuckling now as he took another deep drag of his cigarette. Claire's nostrils flared as she huffed sulkily; and she knew then that the awkwardness that was between them had all but disappeared.

"It's not fucking funny Craig I was gunna make a bloody stew tonight!" she was clearly fuming, but Craig couldn't help but laugh at her. She was a sweetheart in every single way and he adored her. "Why don't you go and have a lie down babe, make sure you're at your best for Jen's scan later yeah" she suggested handing him a few Paracetamol from the medicine cupboard. Craig looked at her, a confused look on his face,

"Is it that obvious?" he asked, his finger instantly reaching to check his nostrils were clear and none of the cocaine residue had been left behind. Claire nodded her disapproval and gave him a sad look that made him know she was upset with him;

"Unfortunately Craig yes it is obvious to someone who knows you as well as I do, don't even try and deny it" she tutted scooping up they're cups and bunging them none to gently into the sink. She turned away from him briskly, plunging her hands into the scalding water and completely blanking him out now. Craig cautiously left the room silently without another word and made his way up the stairs to his bedroom. He closed the door quietly behind him kicked off his trainers and jeans and spread himself on the bed, his head was throbbing, his nose was running constantly and he was sick of blowing it now, the sweat that was pouring off his body in waves making him feel sticky and damp. He closed his eyes trying his hardest to stop his mind from ticking into overdrive. He knew it had been a stupid decision having a fat line after leaving Kenny's but he had needed a pick me up, badly. His head felt fuzzy and the morning's events had knocked him aback somewhat. Who the fuck did Kenny cunting Kreegan think he was? Making sick jokes about his pregnant best friend like that. He was fucking furious! Craig knew he had to get his own back on the dodgy old bastard but how the fuck was he supposed to strike while iron was hot without any cold hard cash to back him up. He leant his arm over his head and closed his eyes, his whole body was twitching violently from too much coke and all he could do was fidget like a little kid who had ants in his pants. He turned over and flicked on his CD player, the sound of his favourites Ub40 filled his ears and he laid back the feeling of bliss envelope him. He leant over and grabbed his half a spliff out of the ashtray and lit it, toking it slowly, taking down the vicious hazy smoke, feeling his mind balance out a bit and the twitchy feeling in his legs started to subside. In its place came the inevitable laziness that came with being stoned, he lay back on the pillows after he'd smoked his Joint as the soft melodic notes of red red wine filled the room he relaxed... Within ten minutes he was out cold.

Chapter Forty

The feel of soft bare lips kissing his made him wake with a start, Jenna was sat beside him wearing a tight white vest and a pair of knickers staring at him with her intense green eyes, he smiled and pulled her closer hugging her too him and planting soft butterfly kisses on her neck, she shivered as he placed his hands on her swollen belly still kissing her so softly, she was still so gorgeous despite being six months pregnant, there wasn't an ounce of fat on her taut tight thighs, she was beautifully curved and her little bump made her all the more alluring. She nestled against his chest as he stroked her stomach with his long fingers hugging her in his strong loving embrace.

"Your mum said you were a bit upset earlier" she whispered holding his hand in hers, his eyes still locked on hers, those crazy manic eyes that she loved so much, the lashes long and thick framing them so beautifully, he had the most addictive eyes she had ever seen in her life, she could have happily sat here all day staring into them. He pulled her up gently now and pulled her leg over his waist so that she was straddling his hips she smirked as he cupped her swollen breasts in his hands winking at her cheekily.

"With you here gorgeous a man like me could never be upset" he giggled softly cupping her face with his hands and pulling her in for a deep long passionate kiss. She laughed heartily at him; he was such a flashy bastard when the feeling took him but she loved him all the more for his outspoken ways.

"Mr Carter" she whispered softly against his lips "we have a scan to get to" she could feel his bulging erection underneath her arse and couldn't help but smile knowing he was so aroused by her despite him clearly being off his head. He pulled her closer his tongue skating in and out of her mouth as he pushed his erection deeper against her, she rubbed herself against him slowly as his hands fumbled at her vest top, he yanked it over her head burying his face into her breasts as he unclipped her bra behind her back, he let it drop onto the bedspread, her gloriously naked flesh puckering beneath his touch he took her breast to his mouth and tantalisingly lapped at her nipple, caressing her other breast with his fingers. She yanked his boxers down just enough to unleash his throbbing cock, she smiled at him coyly as she rubbed it against the cotton of her knickers, the tip was soft and teasing, she yanked her knickers to the side and felt his cock rubbing against her naked wetness, she was soaking for him, she eased her hips down onto him, he filled her perfectly each and every solid inch that he eased into her making her shiver with delight. He kissed her mouth hard as he thrust himself hard into her, she was so wet, she gasped as he fucked her harder and harder, each thrust taking her to the brink of ecstasy, he could feel she was about to come, so he slowed himself down teasing her, making her surrender to him, he kissed her again she rode him so softly shuddering with each delicious stroke his cock made inside her, she moaned quietly against his lips, she was breathless, he grabbed her hips and guided her down onto him, setting his pace, he could feel he was so close to coming inside her he sped up again, pumping away at her briskly she clutched at his shoulders as an electrifying orgasm rocked her, she moaned loudly as she felt his hot semen squirting inside her, he throbbed delightfully underneath her, his eyes locked on hers as she panted against his face, he kissed her again as they're pleasure subsided, he loved the feeling of her after he'd come inside her even though they'd been here a million times before it never got old, he pulled her against his chest feeling himself slipping out of her dripping wetness kissing her glossy dark hair he whispered "Love you Jen" softly against her ear.

They laid there for almost an hour, just kissing and holding each other. Her bump neatly snuggled against his rippling muscles he felt the baby kicking and he closed his eyes tightly savouring every little movement, there was a little life growing inside her and he was so proud that he was around to be a part of it. He knew the baby wasn't his but he was going to be the best father figure he could possibly be. He stroked her naked back hugging her close to him. She had never looked so beautiful, her hair all puffed up and fluffy from rolling around in his bed sheets. He felt the same old pangs of guilt rack his body as he gently reminded himself that the baby wasn't his child, he couldn't ever be satisfied with that knowledge that she had deceived him and slept with someone else. Not that they had ever been exclusive of course to everyone else they were just "best friends" but he knew there was more than that to whatever it was they were. He loved Jenna she was his whole world, he would go to the ends of the earth and back again for this beautiful girl but he couldn't bring himself to try just in case they ended up spoiling their amazing friendship. Jenna knew instantly what Craig was thinking and she held his gaze as she ran her fingers through his short hair, she cupped his gorgeous face in her hands and for just a moment drank in his stunning features, his beautiful soft skin, little dimpled cheeks, and the steeliest ice blue eyes she had ever encountered. She gave him a sad half smile, she knew this little haven they'd built would again be destroyed the moment she opened her mouth;

"I love you too Craig, I really do." She whispered lovingly;

He was up and off the bed in seconds, yanking up his boxers and pulling on his jeans, she looked dumbstruck as he threw her clothes at her, his face was sad and she could see yet again she had told him what he hadn't wanted to here. They had being doing this for years now and she shouldn't have been surprised, but it didn't make the pain ease every single time he just rejected her. She felt as though he had just slapped her clean in the face, he pulled a clean t shirt out of the wardrobe and threw it on, before looking at her briefly and quickly exiting the room to no doubt go and scrub her scent off him.

Chapter Forty One

The air was tense in the hospitals ultrasound suite; the pretty mousy haired ultrasound technician who announced herself as Helen had noted the awkward silence between the young couple before her the instant they strolled into cubicle number four. She asked the girl politely to lie down on the bed and explained the procedure beforehand. As she swiped the scanner over the young girls bloated stomach, she noticed that she had looked away from her partner in disgust and focused all her attention on the little monitor beside her, the boy sat there with his head in his hands staring at the floor, an angry red flush on his stunningly handsome face. She smiled awkwardly as she asked them politely if they would like to know the sex, to which both replied in a bitter tone that they did. The girl took in each little feature of the grainy image on the screen, her eyes glistened with happy tears girls appreciated these things so much more than the men did. Helen finished off her checks, she was happy that the baby was growing lovely and was healthy, she turned to Craig and Jenna as and announced proudly that they were expecting a perfect little baby girl. Craig's face turned almost purple with rage as he fled from the room slamming the door furiously behind him. Jenna's bottom lip started to quiver violently as she heard him growling out in the waiting room, he was fucking livid. She grabbed her bag and her coat gratefully accepted her scan picture and mouthed a silent apology to the poor woman before her and left the scanning room her beautiful face tomato red with embarrassment. She walked straight past Craig who was in the car park smoking a skin tight roll up, his hands shaking as he blew an angry cloud of smoke out through his nose into the crisp winter air, he hear the clatter of Jenna's high heeled boots on the kerbstones beside him and he looked up to see her darting across the car park. Her dark hair flailing wildly behind her the collar of her parka coat pulled up tightly to her face, her arms folded neatly over her chest as she walked toward the bus stop. Craig stood up from the wall on which he was sat and flicked his cigarette to the ground. His eyes followed her to the bus stop at the far end of the car park; she sat down on the small bench pulling her coat tighter around her, she was staring at the scan picture that she was clutching in her hands, every now and then he noticed she was swiping tears from her eyes with back of her sleeve. He could fucking kick himself he really could. He was devastated, that stupid fucking ultrasound woman with her stupid "oh and is dad excited" comments on their arrival, he couldn't pretend anymore that he was going to be a dad to this kid, she kept dragging him along to all the scans and antenatal stuff and they all instantly put two and two together and came up with ten and now trying to lie his way through these appointments was getting embarrassing. He looked at his phone, he had a text off his mother. He opened it and smiled as her read "Let me know how it goes I'm so proud of you! Mum x" he wrote a quick reply and put his phone back in his pocket. He made his way across the car park the icy wind whipping at his face, his eyes streaming from the bitter cold; he zigzagged through the minefield of parked cars until he stood faithfully at her side. She looked up as he sat down beside her, he peered over at the crumpled picture in her hands, the grainy little bean he had seen at the first scan was now a fully formed tiny baby girl, he could see her little features plain in the photograph, the cute little button nose the tiny delicate face, his heart lurched as he beamed with pride. He laid his hand gently on her stomach and rubbed it slowly. He hated it when they fought like this it was so fucking pointless. He turned to Jenna and attempted a heartfelt apology. She just stared into the blank space before her, taking in none of his bullshit words, because that's all they were in the midst of it all were just pathetic words. He had promised her that he would be there for her, but she had known all along that he would cop out last minute hence the pathetic lie she'd told over the baby's paternity. She swore to herself in that solitary moment that he would indeed find out when the time was right, but for now he was too immature to even think about being a father let alone actually step into the role. She stood up, she dropped the grainy little scan photo onto his lap and slowly walked away, there was nothing more she wanted to say to him.

Chapter Forty Two

Kenny Kreegan sat opposite the gangly teenage boy before him and smiled his most knock em dead smile, He was happy that the boy had agreed to meet him despite his reservations at first, Kenny had put his plans into motion, this would take months of careful planning and hard work from both parties but he was more than determined to get it done. Craig Carter would pay for double crossing him the slimy little coke head cunt. But first Kenny would make the boy think all was forgiven, well he was even thinking of giving him his job back. He was good at busting the cunts up who didn't pay their way. Then when he was trusting again, Kenny would fuck his little dolly bird as he sliced her fucking throat because one thing Kenny didn't do was forgive and he sure as hell did NOT forget. He lit himself a cigarette and slid the packet across the table to the boy sitting opposite him, of course the boy took one out of respect and lit it up, all the while staring at the ugly old cunt across the desk with his cheap shirt and trousers his ugly screwed up old face scarred with thick layers of acne, he looked and acted like a fucking toad and a cheap one at that. Despite throwing the drugs about like sweets at a kids party and running the Belmonte estates one and only knocking shop he surely was fucking rancid, and he certainly didn't act like he was in the money, but he could smell it seeping out of Kenny's wretched pores that he was one loaded cunt. Ever since his wife had been carted off to the funny farm, Kenny had seriously lost the plot. The boy took a long drawl on his cigarette it was a gesture of boredom more than anything else and he could wait to get out of this bloody shit hole. The eerie shrill moans of the women who occupied the surrounding rooms and he was starting to get the creeps, at first he'd thought it was quite funny, but now it seemed never ending and he wasn't so sure that half the women here were enjoying their work, there was something not quite right about the place. From the big black fucker on the door to the big titted blonde madam that sat beside him, preening over some papers, chest spewing out of her skin tight purple skirt suit, the makeup that she had literally plastered on her face dark and smoky, the liner in her waterline giving her a cat like appearance. She was undeniably stunning and Johnny had a little boy crush on her, Kenny obviously liked his girls young which made Johnny a little sick to the stomach. His thoughts were broken by a little rapping noise on the heavy door, Kenny ordered for whomever it was to enter, Johnny gasped as big tits sexily strode in, her porcelain white heels clattering on the dark oak floor, she tossed her hair over her shoulder and perked her curvaceous backside on the edge of the desk, her hips wide and sensuous the fabric on her skirt stretched to the limit as she sat down and Johnny was sure she was about to burst out at the seams. Johnny could feel the lump rising in his trousers; he silently thanked the lord he had bought a coat which he had conveniently draped over his lap to hide his bulging erection.

"Mr Carter's on the phone Ken" her voice was sexy and had a slightly southern American drawl to it and Johnny guessed that Kenny had imported her into the country illegally as he had with all his other bits of skirt that occupied his little gold mine, her thick glossy lips puckered as she spoke, sexily pouting in Johnny's direction, the flirtatious flicker in her eyes drawing Johnny in closer. She smelt delicious, clean, her thick luxurious locks bounced as she ran her hands through them playfully. Kenny's eyes grazed the girls voluptuous figure and he licked his lips manically the movement making the ugly old bastard look somewhat feral he smiled then, a vicious sneaky smile that slithered onto his thin lips;

"Tell Mr Carter to go and fuck his mother" Kenny smiled as he spoke, tossing his head back in mock amusement. The girl nodded subtly and turned on her heel, smoothing down her skirt and plumping her hair up with her fingers she gave Johnny a quick wink as she went to walk away. Kenny followed her to the door, giving her a sly pinch on the arse right in front of Johnny, it was a territorial thing and Johnny knew it, it was a simple gesture but Johnny could see the sheer embarrassment on the girls face depicting that she too was absolutely mortified at Kenny's sudden displays of affection. The seldom grin that crept on Kenny's face as he ushered his little dolly bird from the room was one of pure degradation. Silly little tart coming in here and acting all coy in front of his business associates as though Johnny was one of her bloody punters, well he'd fucking have her later. He sat back down at his desk and pulled out two tumblers and a bottle of liquor from the top drawer, he poured two large measures into the glasses and slid one across the table at Johnny. Slowly he sipped at his own glass the liquor burning as it hit his throat, eyeing Johnny as he mulled his little scheme over in his head.

"So Mr Fenton, Do we have a deal?" his voice low and hushed, the darkness of the room putting Johnny on edge, he had stepped into the lion's den and he knew now that it was indeed shit or bust. This was where he either propelled himself into the criminal underworld or he crawled back under his rock and carried on being Kenny Kreegan's skivvy doing drug runs for petty cash and hitting about a few mugs for money.

Kenny extended his hand across the table to the boy, his wrinkly knuckles white with tension his long pianist fingers eerily thin, like matchsticks. Johnny took the man's hand and gave it a quick shake before snatching his hand away, he didn't like this guy one fucking bit he gave him the creeps something rotten. Kenny smiled, dismissing him almost instantly and proclaiming that he would be in touch in the near future when he had the plan drew up and put in place. He showed Johnny out of his office, straight to the front door briskly shooing him past the big titted blonde who ran the house, saying a swift goodbye he turned away slamming the door shut behind him. Johnny grabbed his phone from his pocket and tapped away at the keypad, holding the phone to his ear he listened to the shrill ringing, before it was answered by the man with the husky voice on the end; Johnny smirked as he spoke.

"Man have I got some fucking news for you!"

Chapter Forty Three

Craig stared at the skinny naked red head in front of him, the smirk on his face wild as she took his penis into her mouth for the third time that evening her tiny breasts pert and high on her chest, her skin milky and soft, the small rectangle shaped glasses that sat on her pointy nose making her look almost well educated. Craig's phone had been ringing nonstop for the last hour and he was starting to get sick to the back teeth with Jenna's constant texting. She had really fucked him off at the hospital and he had barely spoken to her since. Fuck her he thought as he turned the stereo up slightly and the sound of chase and status filled the enclosed space, he snorted another fat line off the plate in front of him, the buzz hitting him instantly. He cocked his head backwards and felt the coke trickling down his throat, it's pure deliciousness enveloping him and his drug fuelled stupor deepened even further, his heart was beating ten to the dozen and his jaw was going for gold. He could feel his eyes bouncing around in his head, the rush invigorating him, sending deep shivers down his spine; he sucked in a deep breath, euphoric now, every single nerve jangled in his system, he lit his joint from the ashtray, the silky smoke caressing his lungs as he took a deep toke. The hazy smoke dancing around his face as he exhaled, his head was completely loose, no worries or stresses, after Johnny Fenton's phone conversation earlier Craig had started plotting his own little scheme to pay back Kenny Fucking Kreegan. It would take time, it would take guts and it would take a good right hand man.. He pulled the girls head down further onto his throbbing cock, drugs making him delirious, passionate, he wanted this little tart more and more with each seductive stroke her tongue took against the soft shaft of his penis. He ran his fingers through her long dip dyed red hair yanking at it slightly as she took him even further into her throat, heaving slightly as his shaft tickled her tonsils. Craig pulled her back away from him and ordered her to go and stand by the window,

"I want you to dance for me" he said playfully as he lay himself back onto the bed sheets that he had only shagged Jenna in a few hours ago. His eyes clouded over in a druggy haze, lust seeping out of every pore of his sweaty body as he scanned every single move the girl made carefully, he carried on puffing away at his joint, the pure stench of the cannabis making the girl feel physically ill, but she wouldn't show it, she had waited months for Craig to even notice her, and now she was going to give him the ride of his fucking life. She strutted over to the window and closed the thin voile curtains, her tiny body winding as she seductively grinded to the sound of Ke$ha's "crazy kids" Craig had to laugh at the irony of this little piece shaking herself to Jenna's favourite song, he turned the stereo up louder, hoping that the little slapper in the flats downstairs could hear him. Fuck Jenna Shearan and her bastard child Craig thought as he gripped the plate and his rolled up twenty and took another big fat line from the china surface before resting back and taking in the floor show.

Jenna sat in bed with a cup of tea staring lovingly at the scan picture in her hand, rubbing her swollen stomach beneath her fluffy cotton dressing gown. She smiled sadly, there was no way that she could tell Craig that he was the baby's father now. She wasn't even sure that she wanted to; he was so unpredictable and unreliable lately, constantly out and about the estate sniffing coke with the rest of the bastard druggies. He was starting to lose his muscular shape, he was drawn in and sunken his whole appearance screamed druggy. Jenna lay down against the plumped up pillows smelling Craig all over them instantly as her nose dived into the rich cotton on the pillow cases, it was as though he was here in bed with her so strong was his scent, it was everywhere, kissing her senses driving her wild with its sheer intensity. She loved him so much it hurt every single part of her but she couldn't stop herself from loving him not now, not ever. She had to protect him from the truth though; it would kill him to know that she had lied about the father of the baby; he would probably kill her with his bare hands. Craig had vowed after seeing Sammy become such a shit mother to her two kids that he would never ever follow in her footsteps and Jenna knew deep down that he wouldn't. But as it stood, he couldn't know the truth, not until he got himself clean. She took another deep breath inwards and basked in his delirious scent, it smelt like home to her, so clean and manly beneath the musky smell of his aftershave. She slowly closed her eyes and drank him in, drowning in each precious memory they held together and hoping against hope that despite their recent drama's that they would be able to create so many more.

She shot up as she heard Ke$ha blaring from the flat upstairs, she had to do a double take just to make sure she wasn't hearing things, it was definitely her CD and she knew exactly where it was coming from. She smiled as she thought maybe Craig was trying to get her attention by blaring out her favourite song in the middle of the night. She slid out of bed, wrapping the dressing gown loosely around her tiny bump, scraping her hair out of her eyes she tied it back into a tight ponytail. Padding downstairs to the front door she slid on her slippers, she turned the key in the lock and opened the door to a massive gust of wind that howled outside, it was a freezing cold December night and all around Jenna could see the pretty Christmas lights twinkling from the windows of some of the flats around her, although most were plunged into darkness. Jenna went across to the stair well that led to the upstairs flats , climbing each step carefully as the ice beneath her feet threatened to send her flying, she clutched the hand rail tightly. The music was blaring now. Getting louder and louder with every footstep Jenna took. She reached the top of the veranda, shuffling along not to disturb any of the other flats around her she walked across to Claire's flat, bending down she scrabbled for something to throw at Craig's window to grab his attention. Finding a few pebbles scattered on the veranda she grabbed them up in her hands. Turning ready to throw them, she looked up playfully at Craig's window, the music blaring out now, it was starting to give her a headache with the high volume and the bass combined. The stones instantly fell from her hand as she caught sight of the two silhouettes in the small window space and for a moment she was utterly speechless. She held her hand to her mouth in shock trying to stifle the scream that threatened to escape her lips, she couldn't take her eyes away from the scene unfolding before her. The blood rushed to her head making her feel overwhelmingly dizzy and the shakes that enveloped her seemed to rack her tiny frame, the tears rolled down her eyes but she couldn't look away, the shock was setting in and she was finding that everything was happening in slow motion, the whistling in the music was all she could hear, that cheeky little whistle, she couldn't get it out of her head. Her hand still clamped to her mouth tightly, she was scared if she let it drop then she wouldn't be able to stop herself from screaming. Her eyes wouldn't come away from the window no matter how hard she begged for them to. There he was stark fucking naked pumping away at some ginger bird, her face was distorted with ecstasy and Jenna could hear her distinct over the top moans from where she was stood, Craig's eyes were closed shut tight, lost in the moment, pulling all the same face that she had once found such a turn on now they sickened her, her hand instinctively reached for her stomach, she clutched at it desperately, trying to swallow down the sobs that were coming from her now. There was a horrid high pitched gut wrenching screech that pierced her ear drums and it took her a while to register that it was coming from her. She glared at the window, ginger kid was clutching a t shirt to her naked flesh shouting and pointing at her, Craig's face was picture perfect, his mouth shaped into the perfect O as he realised he had been caught out. Jenna turned on her heel and scuttled across the veranda tears flowing down her face, her cheeks flushed red with embarrassment. She took to the stairs, in fear forgetting the icy structure, she lunged forward, her grip on the handrail lost as she was sent sprawling down the metal steps in a heap. She smacked her head on the bar as she hit the bottom. She looked up, blood spewing down her face as the song played the final notes, the sound of Ke$ha's faint whisper saying "we are the crazy people" she saw Craig at the top of the staircase completely stark naked apart from a pair of Santa boxers she had bought him last Christmas, brow creased, face screwed up in anger and it took a moment for Jenna to try establish whether she had fallen or whether Craig had inevitably `pushed her. She could see the sadness in his eyes as he bounded towards her, eyes wild, pupils dilated heavy and hooded by those thick lashes. He was close. She could feel his hand touch the back of her head, hear his voice calling her name but it sounded so far away, the song had changed now but she couldn't place it. Her body felt heavy, tired and achy, her eyes were rolling and she could feel a throbbing in her back. He hand clutched at her bump hoping to fucking God her little baby would be ok, she closed her eyes praying that the baby would survive, she heard Claire, she was shouting, high pitched and loud, then as she felt the change in hands on her head there was her soft baby pitched voice melodically shushing and tell her everything would be alright. Her eyes wouldn't open, she was too tired, she lay back in Claire's arms, the sound of the ambulance sirens in the distance threatening to block out the sound of the music, Jenna slumped back unaware of the pure horror that was unfolding beyond her, she was in her safe place, a melancholic slumber where no one could hurt her, she hadn't seen what she thought she had seen she couldn't have. Craig loved her, he had told her so that morning. She felt a hot flush between her legs and distinctively she knew that something was dreadfully wrong, she could hear the voices around her head, blood, so much blood, where was it coming from she wondered? Was it her head maybe? She had hit that quite hard, yes it must have been her head she bargained. She drifted off to her little place in her head blocking out all of the noise around her, then she was plunged into darkness, her whole body stifled and she started to wonder whether she was indeed dead.

Chapter Forty Four

"Mum call the fucking ambulance quick!" Craig screamed, looking over his muscular shoulder towards his mother's front door. He bundled down the steps, every step bringing him closer to Jenna's beautiful crumpled body lying at the foot of the stairs, her legs twisted in a disgusting mutated form, her head spitting blood all over the icy concrete. Her bump poking out from under the slightly small t shirt that she was wearing and Craig instinctively ran his hand over it as he held her close to his naked chest she was so limp, her tiny body feeling so lifeless in his strong arms, his bare knees collided with the ice but all he could feel was red hot rage, rage for being so fucking childish as to set Jenna up like he had he had been so stupid and he could actually fucking shoot himself for treating her so horribly. He set his gaze on the blood that was pouring from the gaping wound on her head, he placed his hand there, instantly saturating it with sticky hot blood, the bile rising in his throat, swallowing hard he whispered endless apologies to her, kissing her sticky hair, the blood instantly tinting his lips. He could taste its metallic oiliness as his tongue snaked out of his mouth his lips so incredibly dry he felt as though he hadn't drank a drop in weeks. He could hear his mothers pounding footsteps behind him and he turned to glance up at her the slap that connected with his cheek sending his head bobbing sideward, she nudged him away from Jenna forcefully, taking the girls lifeless body into her own arms and glaring at Craig through bitter eyes, the tears stinging her eyes as she sent him away, screaming for him to go and fucking deal with the mess he'd made. He battled Claire's authority, trying to grab his mother's hands away from Jenna being met with another slap to his already stinging cheek, the ice cold air ripping the tension between them, he turned away, but the sickening pop that came from Jenna made him instantly snap back around, her waters had gone in a torrent all over the ice covered concrete, the hot gush filling the cold December air with condensation. His eyes widened as he searched his mothers face for answers, she did nothing but turn away, huddling the beautiful girl closer, stemming the bleeding on Jenna's head with her dressing gown. Cradling the girl ever so carefully she held her tightly to her chest, all the while telling her that everything was going to be alright. The distinct ambulance sirens in the background fetching her back to reality, she gripped Craig's arm;

"Get dressed and get ready to take her to hospital you little fucking prick!" she sneered, nostrils flaring in anger, her usually sleek bob mangled in all manner of directions the nightdress she was wearing now dripping with blood, his best friends blood. The thought sent Craig into a frenzy of drug fuelled paranoia, he had done this to his best friend. He turned and ran up the stairs, tripping uncontrollably as he went. She was convulsing now, hard forceful convulsions that sent her eyes rolling in her beautiful head, her lip hung awkwardly and for an instant Craig was wondering whether she was indeed having a stroke. He rushed back into the flat, scurrying around scrabbling as he began grabbing at clothes from the washing basket. Pulling on yesterday's jeans and one of his tracksuit tops, his nose wrinkling at the unwashed smell that emitted from them, he instantly felt disgusting. He threw on his trainers, stuffing the laces angrily into the sides of them, huffing madly as he made his way back through the passage, he looked up the stairs and saw the red head he had been fucking earlier sitting on the top of the stairs, sat there in his favourite baby blue t shirt that Jen had bought him, the anger bubbling in the pit of his stomach threatening to explode at any given moment, he hurtled up the stairs, gripping the girl by her bony wrists and half dragged half hurtled her down the thick striped carpet, he lunged at her punching her square in the jaw before sending her tumbling out of the front door.

"This is your fucking fault" he screamed at the top of his lungs; his patience had finally ran out and he could feel himself burning with an inconsolable rage she was crying now, her pathetic sobs filling his eardrums as he dragged her away from his mothers door, down the veranda to the stairwell. He gripped the girl's face, his fingers boring into her thin flesh, leaving dark red marks on her cheeks he pointed to the heap that was Jenna Shearan at the bottom of the staircase and continued loudly

"See that you muggy little cunt, you did this, you fucking pushed her, got it?!" he said vindictively, knowing that the girl would happily take the blame if she thought for a second that it would make Craig happy. He smiled as she nodded her head weakly, her eyes rolling viciously, voice slurring from a little too much booze and more than enough drugs. Craig, satisfied that she would go along with his little story slammed her head against the concrete before making his way back to Jenna. He could feel the tears crowning in his eyes as he held her soft hand in his, stroking the small fingers, feeling how perfectly they fit in his; he had never felt so fucking worthless in all his life and he knew; that without this beautiful, amazing girl he was nothing. Life was completely pointless without her and he promised himself in that stunning moment of clarity that he would never ever hurt her again. He held her dainty lifeless hand to his face, she was so cold. He kissed the tips of her fingers, the tears came then thick and fast in a torrent that splashed off the skin of Jenna's pale arms as they fell like willows from his sad eyes. He whispered sweet nothings to her, willing for her to wake up, willing for this to all be a dream, he closed his eyes and held her close all the while praying for a miracle. The ambulance pulled up a few minutes later, the rest of the night was a hazy blur..... But it was the night that changed Craig Carters life forever.

Chapter Forty Five

Eight Weeks later

Craig cuddled the tiny bundle to his chest and took in her beautiful tiny little features. She was perfect in every single way from her soft downy hair, to her big bulging baby eyes that seemed to simply intoxicate him every time he looked at her, he kissed her soft baby skin and let her curl her tiny fingers around his. It was the first time she had been able to hold her properly since she had been born at a critical twenty seven weeks gestation. She had been too tiny, her little body like a skinned rabbit as she had been tugged from Jenna's stomach. The special care baby unit had become a second home to him ever since, every single day he came to see her and Jenna. Little Kiki Marie Shearan had become a little piece of his heart and he could never ever imagine his life without her, here it was the moment he had been dreaming about for weeks, holding her for the very first time. It had been touch and go for a long time and she had fought off numerous infections but here she was, like a porcelain doll. Soft pink skin, gorgeous little button nose and the presence of an angel about her. Craig kissed her little forehead, a beaming smile appearing on his handsome face as she creased her brow into a scowling little frown, her little nose wrinkling slightly. He knew in that moment that he would do anything on this earth to protect this little girl.

"Oi Mr Carter, you gunna give me a hold of my own daughter then?" Jenna giggled from the chair beside the incubator, voice bursting with pride as she witnessed the glorious scene before her. She smiled, a genuinely stunning smile, despite the odds here they were, she was still a bit battered, still a bit sore, but she was over the worst. She had her best friend back on her arm, despite how furious she had been with him when she had first come around from the fall. He had proved himself more than worthy by staying at her bedside despite telling him countless times to go and fucking die, Keeping an eye on Kiki morning noon and night in the special care baby unit spending his days just talking to her, making a fuss of her and truly just loving her above everything else. Jenna knew he would do absolutely anything for their little girl. Not that he knew yet that she was his. That would come in time. She laughed again as Craig protested sadly that he wasn't quite ready to hand little Kiki over yet, his beautiful lips pouting sexily at her and they both smiled at the irony of the situation. Despite his reservations Craig had fallen head over heels in love with the little bundle that lay in his arms and he would happily take a bullet for the little missy. He walked tentatively over to Jenna and placed the baby into her mother's arms. He gazed at them both for a long moment, drowning in their happiness, Jenna was a fantastic mother, it was so natural to her and he knew that Kiki would have an amazing childhood with her. He leant over and kissed Jenna softly on the lips;

"You did so good babe" he whispered gently against her lips, feeling the small smile that that came from her pressed against his cheek. His stomach somersaulting inside, his heart leaping in his chest, he felt so delirious with happiness. They could have been the most perfect little family, but Craig wouldn't get into the routine of raising another man's child, he would feel disrespectful to not only the baby but to Jenna too. He shook the thought away immediately he had already got too involved with Jenna, despite always knowing that he loved her undeniably with a passion he couldn't control, he would hate to ruin their perfect relationship. He had seen in her eyes how hurt she had been the night he had caught her shagging Nikki the cokehead from the estate, how stupid he had been and it had taken almost losing her to make him realise that he would never jeopardise their friendship again in the name of jealousy. He knew that she loved him equally as much as he did her, but what was to say, if they tried to make something out of it, that two or three years down the line they'd split and never speak to each other again. There was no way he could be without her, he knew that without a doubt she would always have to be a constant. He looked so uncertainly into her eyes and saw his own fears mirrored there, her big green eyes sparkling of the mystery that was their future together the complete fear of constantly having to fight her feelings, he looked away, dropped his guard for a second and he really realised how innocent and vulnerable he felt in her presence. She was simply stunning despite being sat in a pair of joggers and a tracksuit jumper, hair scraped onto her head in a neat topknot, whispers of her long dark hair slithering down the side of her cheeks, her face devoid of any make up and still she was fucking gorgeous. Not a single blemish on her milky skin, back in her pre pregnancy clothes and still feeling the same body woes of every single first time mum. She looked fuller, every perfect curve enhanced beautifully from the pregnancy. She was glowing, healthy looking and full of content at the presence of her gorgeous little girl. Craig had never wanted her, craved her so badly in all his life. But as usual his head ruled his heart and he wouldn't allow himself to take that death defying leap of fate.

Chapter Forty Six

Johnny Fenton squirmed beneath the buxom prostitute currently riding him like a fucking cowgirl for all he was worth, his body pinned to the used cheap feeling cotton of the Argos value bedspread, the room lit sensuously with scented purple tea lights creating an eerie glow in the darkness, the young girl's skin tight snakeskin leather corset sucking in every single inch of her ample body, her dimpled thighs slapping hard against Johnny's stomach as he watched her arse humping him in slow delectable strides that consumed him entirely. His balls felt ready to burst as she started moaning breathlessly, sexily winding her hips as he plunged his cock deeper inside her with a simple slip of his hips. The feeling of her skin against his pure deliciousness, he arched his back slightly as she pushed down on him harder, he gasped if only for a second, the pleasure consuming him entirely as he came inside her, spurting deep into her wet crevice, hot and dripping as he held himself inside her, her moans gradually subsiding, resting back, her weight laid on her hands as they gripped at the bed sheets. Gradually coming down from her euphoric high she rested slightly, her hips dropping as his floppy lifeless member slipped out of her like some sort of foreign object. She glanced back, her eyes met with a flash of Johnny's beautiful smile. His gleaming white teeth glistening in the subtle candlelight, his naked body tight and muscular, His taught six pack oiled lightly by his light perspiration his adorable face, not yet rid of its teenage innocence, he was young, extremely handsome and successful everything any woman would find attractive in a man. His floppy blonde hair ash coloured and hazy in the dim lighting, his piercing eyes dark and smoky, he was god like in appearance, the mouth of the gutter, the face of an angel that summed up Johnny Fenton quite perfectly.

He glanced up, locking his steely eyes on her body, he looked at her as if she was the only woman in the world, which of course to Johnny she was. He kissed Cath's lips and drew her close to his naked chest. Her vivid tired eyes hooded as she snuggled against him, she hated all this sneaking around, but Kenny would blow a fuse if he found out they were sleeping together. They had been sneaking around in hotel rooms for weeks, and now he had invited her round to his place. His small, protection paid flat on the Belmonte, Cath loved it here, despite knowing that it was indeed her boss that kept Johnny in his plush lifestyle in the flat. She cuddled into him, feeling each groove of his taught muscular flesh against her naked skin. He was gorgeous, simply stunning despite his teenage years and Cath could feel herself falling for him with each passing moment that they spent together. She had slept with only a slight few of Kenny's business associates, not that it was strictly "allowed" but she had ever fallen for someone as hard as she had for Johnny. She turned and picked up the glass of red that sat on the bedside cabinet, she took a mouthful, all the while glancing through the corner of her eyes at Johnny who had taken to making himself a joint from the spliff box beside the bed, Cath had never been so happy and she knew that she never would be again, not under Kenny's control anyway. The sound of Westlife filled the small room, as Johnny poured them both another large measure of wine from the bottle in his hand, he sure was a charmer. Cath grinned at him as he filled her glass, urging her to sip, holding it to her lips, it was a simple motion and she took it undoubtedly as nothing more than a romantic gesture. He was simply stunning, even with his hair on end from their passionate encounter, he was still breathtaking. He began to croon the melodic words of "unbreakable" to her, he was a little drunk, she could see from the way his eyes lazily locked onto hers, glazed over and slightly hooded, his mouth slightly dipped. Yet he was still a picture to look at. She giggled childishly as he started belting out the song at the top of his voice, shushing him slightly as he hit the top notes, his small muscles flexing as he continued to punch the air dramatically in song. He was in the moment and she couldn't help but love him all the more. They sat back against the sheets, simply enjoying one another's company. For a moment Cath closed her eyes and imagined what it would be like to have Johnny as her own, far away from London, far away from the Belmonte, far away from the drugs and prostitution, far away from life itself. She knew he was destined to be hers. But life had dealt her the joker card and as usual she felt as though she had been handed the bum prize in the deal of love. She would never escape Kenny's clutches and she knew herself she would always be in debt to Kenny and his life. Kenny had saved her from the grips of a crippling crack addiction, made her go cold turkey, pulled her back to reality before it had indeed been too late. Yes she had become one of his working girls, but she had moved throughout the ranks of prostitution, from the streets to the Belmonte whorehouse and now she was madam of the brothel, all of the girls worked under her, all the men around the Belmonte answered to her, succumbed to her charms. Yet it wasn't enough, all Cath craved was normality. A family, maybe a few kids, council house in the suburbs, school runs at nine and four, She knew herself though it would never happen. She owed Kenny way too much for him to let her go quietly.

She kissed Johnny hard on the lips, savouring every single moment of his tongue entwined with hers, his breath harsh, brushing against her cheek as he pulled her close in the eerie darkness, running her thin fingers through the vigorous chest hair that flurried his pecks, entwining the hair between her fingers, playfully looking direct into his beautiful eyes, steely and seductive, she leant into him, drinking in his scent, the overtone of expensive aftershave mixed with his soft sweat, simply addictive and she wouldn't for a second let him go, pulling him closer against her naked breasts, the skin beneath puckering with excitement with his fragile touch. Her nipples jutting forward as his mouth skimmed them, his eyes wild and seductive as he lapped at them his tongue tantalising her, he could feel her skin shiver at his touch, the tiny goose bumps that slivered across her pale skin driving him slightly demented. He kissed her hard on her small rosebud mouth, running his tongue around her mouth each stroke deeper than the last. He knew he was playing with fire but he couldn't help it. He had never ever in his wildest dreams imagined that he would fall for a brass, but he loved Cath. There was nothing he could do to change that.

Chapter Forty Seven

Kenny Kreegan sat behind his desk counting a thick wad of money from the open gym bag before him. His eyes mad with envy as the notes slid between his long tentacle like fingers, each one feeling like pure gold to his skin, his profits for selling these girls like the whores that they were. He had to laugh at the irony, the dirty game, the oldest profession there was but it was the wives of the men who frequented these dives who would never realise the money that was to be made from sex. The sheer vanity of those stuck up bitches made Kenny's skin crawl, there was nothing better than to watch a snobby cunts husband fucking a brass, there was something about it that made Kenny's cock squirm around in his pants. He loved his business empire and the he loved the girls who made it so successful, even mad Sheila had a place in his heart after all these years. Despite the fact that she was a batty old hag with a greying curly perm and saggy skin that looked as though a dog had mistaken it for a chew toy, he still cared for her dearly. She knew exactly how to create him a buck, all his girls did, and that was why he commanded so much respect be shown towards them. He turned to the safe and slung the bag none too casually back inside, peanuts to him, petty cash for when the girls needed some new shoes or knickers. Unbuttoning the top button of his shirt and loosening his tie from around his weasel like neck, he lit himself a cigarette and recoiled into the high backed leather chair that frequented his desk, taking in the thick dense tobacco smoke, hugging his lungs so lovingly with its smoggy caress, he smiled deeply, puffing the remnants in little hoops that filled the blank space in front of him. He was a content old sod despite his wife Rosa being in a nursing home on the other side of the country, the dementia eating away at her, taking away every last drop of sanity that she had so desperately clung to. These days she didn't even recognise him or the fruitful life they had once shared. Thirty years they had lived a happy marriage, facing each day without any fears, she sat at the front of house greeting the punters, always so full of character, lust and passion for life. She was an exuberant character and everyone she met instantly took a like to her. Kenny had fought long and hard to keep her with him, but in the end she was becoming a danger to herself and his business, the straw that broke the camel's back was when people started taking advantage of her good nature by pretending to be Kenny's friends just to get in on his business deals. He had put her up in a five star nursing home with the best medical professional help that money could buy. A little house girl keeping her company as she spent her days trying to filter and make sense of her memories. Some days Kenny would phone and she would be sociable, a slight shade of the woman she had once been. On other days she sat in her room for hours acting violently towards the staff and sinking into evil states of depression where she would self harm by biting herself and screeching at the tops of her lungs. Even now at the age of seventy and well into the clutches of her illness, Kenny knew she would live many more sad years in the horrid confusion of her own mind. He still loved her dearly; she had been his one true love in life and he held on to his precious memories of her when she was alive and well, unlike the dark secrets he harboured of her illness. The girls never spoke of her; they all remembered Rosa

Kreegan, but none of them dared upset the applecart with Kenny, so they all acted as though Rosa had never existed. Kenny smiled sadly as he thought of his wife, no matter how much he surrounded himself with all these pretty girls his heart still ached for his true love. She had been his whole world, he remembered taking her out dancing at the old Soho clubs in the sixties, and she had been so stunning. All puff skirts blood red lips and hairspray, infectious laugh that would knock any man dead and a personality that was feisty and sexy. She had always been hard faced, typical cockney girl, mouth full of slang and swears but she had been a lady, a truly special lady. Even now that the dementia had taken hold, she still painted that blood red lipstick onto her lips every morning and coiffured her bouffant hair to perfection. Still she wore the powder pastel coloured two pieces and pearly white stiletto shoes she had always worn, yet now she didn't manage to carry them with as much class and grandeur that she once had. Kenny lit himself another cigarette and poured himself a small shot of liquor from the drawer, he held up his glass and held a quiet toast to his lovely East ender Rosa, all that she was, and all that she never would be. He drank in silence, his mind fishing over the past, the smile not quite reaching his eyes.

Chapter Forty Eight

Ub40 sang out loudly across the Belmonte, it was early morning and Craig was pacing back and forth his mothers living room nursing little Kiki in his dead weight arms, he had been singing softly to the little angel for over an hour now and she was loving every single second. Clad in his mothers fluffy slippers and a pair of boxers Craig felt every bit the prick as he did his best Ali Campbell impression for the little girl.

"Listen now Kiki Marie your gunna love this guy as much as I do despite what that mother of yours says" he soothed, kissing the babies tiny little forehead softly taking in her sweet little baby smell as he held her tightly. The little snuffles and the big toothless grin that followed making him grin like a Cheshire cat as he continued to rock her tiny body in his strong arms, she truly was a little treasure and Craig's love for her was simply beyond words. She had taken his whole heart and made it her own and Craig would never ever be able to describe the lengths he would go for this gorgeous little bundle, her soft baby skin so delicate and fragile against his, the silly little sounds that emitted from her simply took his breath away. He turned to the stereo and turned it up a little more as "I'll be your baby tonight" filled the small space. Craig smiled uncannily at the precious little doll as he sang the words so lovingly at her, not realising that he was being watched by Jenna and Claire who had been stood in the doorway watching him for what seemed like hours. Taken aback by Craig's soft, loving attitude towards the little girl they both hid away from his glances, knowing that he would be all embarrassed if they saw him in his true light. Cradling the little bundle in his arms so carefree so self absorbed by the beautiful little doll. The smile on his handsome face was literally breathtaking as he grinned at the gorgeous little girl the soft tinkling of Claire's fragranced tea lights bouncing off his slightly tanned skin lighting up the shadows in the small living space, highlighting the boys rippled muscles perfectly as he held the little girl tightly to his bare chest. He was sober for the first time in months and Claire had never been more proud of her son. Even now in all his simple splendour Craig shone, he was so engrossed in the little girl. He had stepped up to the plate somewhat since Kiki had been born, constantly wanting to babysit for Jenna or offering Jenna to stay at Claire's with the baby, she had somewhat become his new addiction. Jenna smiled wholeheartedly as she observed Craig with their perfect daughter, the little secret of Kiki's paternity was something that she was holding tight to her chest and that was the way it would stay for now at least. As Craig had always told her since they had been kids "if it aint broke don't fix it Jen!" Never a truer word spoken she thought as she smiled secretively behind her fingers that were subtly placed at her mouth. Her eyes caught Claire's luminous with pure love for her only son, she was mesmerised by him, completely in awe of him and Jenna was soothed by the thought. They had all taken Kiki in as their own, even Sammy had loved the little girls company. She had brought some much needed light into their lives and for the first time in years Claire looked and felt complete. Jenna held her friends her hand and led her into the living room, Craig instantly startled as they disturbed his little singsong. His gaze turned to his mother and Jenna, the grin on his face spreading as he started to chuckle, he knew they had been there a while, their faces had that warm glow to them that they always had when they saw him with Kiki. It was as though they had expected him to reject the child. But no he had taken her under his wings and made her in a way his own. Even he surprised himself with the love he felt for her. Unconditional, unending pure devotion. Craig knew that that would never change in a million years, he loved Kiki and she adored him equally, for that he would be eternally proud.

Chapter Forty Nine

Kenny sat back in the shitty fabric lawn chair and took a sip from his tumbler of sour lemonade, despite it being early February being minus Moscow outside and his arse was damp from the freezing cold padding of the chair, he sat in the gardens of the Calmer Seas nursing home with his beloved wife Rosa. He couldn't bear the thought of sitting indoors, the stuffy overheated rooms, the patronising eyes of the nurses watching every move they made, the other nursing home patients all hovering around in a world of their own dosed up on sedatives no he couldn't handle that one bit. He eyed Rosa with pin point precision, watched how she nervously smoothed her skirt, played about with her bouffant hair, then smoothed the powder blue skirt again, eyes manic from medication and sheer confusion. Her beautiful seductive rosebud lips painted scarlet set in a deep thin grimace as she stared out into the nothingness before her. The stiletto shoes she wore so daintily sunk into the soft grass, her legs mottled blue from the cold, yet here they were as though it was summertime, no raincoat, not even a shawl, sitting so separately mulling over their plans for the year ahead, picking for conversation to fill the awkward silence that hung between them. The sound of the local radio hummed gently from the small portable stereo that sat on the little lawn table between them. Kenny handed Rosa her last Christmas present from the silver holograph gift bag that lay clumsily at his feet   The gorgeous red wrapping paper neatly packed and tied with a bright green bow, Only the best for my girl, he thought as he handed to her, her fragile hand took the gift, he could see the confusion on her face as she said "oh is it Christmas Ken yeah? Must have forgot" she said taking the parcel from him and placing it on her lap Kenny didn't have the heart to tell her that Christmas had been just over two months ago and that he hadn't bothered coming up here because he was too busy screwing his new bird and having Christmas dinner at hers to even think about his fucking loony wife. It was a fairly large box and Kenny couldn't help but burst into laughter as she said "it's not earrings again is it?" her face dead serious, the grimace on her face deepened as she wondered why the fuck he was laughing.

"You girl make my fucking day best thing that ever happened to you, losing your marbles!" he chuckled taking another sip of his drink. He urged her hurriedly to open her present as she glared at him for his rude remark about her mental health, waving his hand in consternation, trying to shake off the comment that had obviously offended her.

"Fuck me your an ugly old bastard Kenny Kreegan" she smirked, never one to mince her words, Rosa stared straight through him, her glassy hooded eyes unsure of him, clinging on to her barely there memories, trying not to confuse herself as she again had to try and place his younger face, the more tolerable one in place of his haggard ugly new one. He had never been a looker, not even in his teens, he was all buck teeth and weird bulgy eyes, but he had been so charming, so lovely, yet so dangerous in business and power. She had loved their little empire on the Belmonte, the nights she spent with her girls, preening them to perfection, taking them shopping up west for their tarty little outfits, squeezing them into the most expensive leather corsets and fine cotton fishnets. Every girl gave her the utmost respect, as though she was the mother they had never had, each one trying to be her favourite and each working so hard to earn the top cash. Rosa remembered her grandeur, her sheer dominance in the gang world, no one ever messed with Rosa K and her entourage of sluts. Now look at me; she thought ironically smoothing the hem of her tight powder blue skirt, her soft fingertips tracing the lumps of the stitching, comforting her manic thoughts if only momentarily. Today was one of her better days, she could still picture faces, names, places. These were the days she felt were worth living. It was the torturous days where she had no recognition of who she even was that nearly tipped her over the edge. The days where even she questioned her own sanity, it was an all consuming disease, eating away at your mind first, then your body, until you were left nothing but a shell, abandoned by your own memories. Rosa sat back, taking in the scene of abandonment before her, when her and Kenny had got married he promised her the world and more, promised to stick with her in sickness and in health and here she was in a fucking nursing home surrounded by pissy smelling delinquents who's only goal in life was to win the weekly game of monopoly, unless they threw a paddy fit half way through because they forgot what bastard piece they were meant to be playing as. How ironic, Rosa thought, nothing had changed for Kenny, he was still the wheeler dealer that he had always been, still selling sex, still trying to earn a fast buck, still living their life, and here she was struggling to remember what day it was. It didn't seem fair somehow. She glanced over at the old toad playing with his tie, knee shaking ten to the dozen counting down the seconds until he could run away from her for another six bastard months, an hour twice a year was all she was worth now, and he struggled through that! Rosa felt defeated, she stood to her feet, sinking her heels further into the weather beaten grass, threw the still wrapped box onto Kenny's lap and walked away, not even glancing back when he started calling after her.

"Christmas was two months ago you prick" she laughed sarcastically as she walked away. Fuck Kenny Kreegan and his visits she thought as she strode towards the out building of the care home, and then he was forgotten again, literally.

Chapter Fifty

Craig sat along in the Belmonte estate gardens, swigging from a can of Stella, his head working overtime as he digested the information he had been given, The sounds of the Belmonte enveloping him, comforting him somewhat in his loneliness, the noisy screams of mothers calling their errant children, the druggies scuttling around like beetles looking for their next fix, some random drunk stumbling home after one too many down The Crown, various music blaring out from the flats surrounding him each sound individual yet each one so familiar to life here. It was the same thing day in day out, yet it was so normal. It wouldn't be the Belmonte without the waifs and strays of the world. People who didn't belong in the real world came here, it was crawling with druggies, prostitutes and the like. Wannabe gangsters who shunted cocaine around like it was part of the parcel, barely dressed teens strutting around with their fresh pussy for sale to the highest bidder, it was a fucked up warped little world but it was theirs. Everyone who lived here appreciated its safety, despite it not being very safe at all. Craig smirked at the irony of it all, the sounds of some idiot blaring French Montana somewhere close by, probably some teenage coke head in their Lonsdale tracksuit walking with their fake gangster limp. Oh the irony of it all Craig thought as he tossed his empty can into the metal bin beside him, he stood dusting off his hands off on his jeans. Walking away he knew he had signed his own death warrant and now he would have to put his own devious plan into motion before the enemy attacked. He looked out across the estate, the place he had called home for so many years, his heart heavy as he realised that he wouldn't be here much longer to see it grow, wouldn't see what was to become of the old place, this saddened Craig equally as much as it excited him, his new life was waiting just around the corner and he couldn't wait to start living it.

Claire was plating up hearty portions of her famous cottage pie when Craig returned home, the smell hitting him instantly, intoxicating as he drew a deep suck of breath through his nose. He wandered into the dimly lit kitchen, smiling sweetly at Claire as he plonked himself lazily onto a chair, she glanced at him momentarily, busying herself by pottering around him scrubbing the units and stirring the gravy that bubbled away on the stove. Her eyes caught Craig's momentarily, the echo of a faint smile kissed her lips, she seemed troubled somewhat, her usual upbeat persona opaque suddenly. Craig stood, confusion etched on his face as he went to his mothers aid. Holding her close as a single tear rolled down her cheek.

"What is it mum?" he asked, his breath catching in his throat as he cuddled her into him, he was worried, she never ever acted like this and this scared Craig slightly. He held her chin in his loose grasp, his fingers trailing the thick pale skin of her lower jaw, pressing against pure flesh, turning the thumb prints left on her face an off white colour, momentarily she looked almost ghost like But she shook it off, her fingers easing Craig's away from her face. Her smile half hearted as she turned away from him and continued to potter away. Craig returned to his seat, he glanced back at his mother for long moments the silence between them excruciating.

"Mum what's going on?" He whispered, his voice almost mute in the dense atmosphere. Claire turned arrogantly on her heel, her slipper grinding into the lino floor, squeaking slightly as she came full circle, she glared at her son now a full evil glare.

"Word has it your back with Kenny's mob" she shrugged pitifully, taking in a harsh quickened breath her eyes set firmly on her son they bounced wildly in her head, her pupils dilated and Craig took a wild guess that she had been drinking such was the bitterness that was so vividly etched on her face. Her words filled with sickening malice, she was angry there was no denying that. She strutted over to where Craig was sat and slapped him hard across his naked cheek, her eyes ablaze as she stared at him ruthlessly; she was disgusted, furious even as she shot a wild glance at her favoured son. Her hands trembling nervously from the ricochet of the hard hitting slap, her face crumpled, her eyes still locked onto Craig. Her handsome boy, her two eyes and more. He was perfect in every single way, gorgeous thick lashed eyes staring at him innocently, she shook her head trying to get away from his devious gaze, he was truly beautiful in each and every single way, yet Claire couldn't help but drown in the worry that her son was canoodling with the likes of Kenny Kreegan and the like. Her lips pursed tightly as she pushed a steaming plate of pie in front of Craig, he turned slightly and grinned at her his smile simply mesmerising, yet she didn't have it in heart to grin back. He picked up his knife and fork and slid his meal around the plate, all the while taking in every single perfect feature of her face. He knew she was hurting, but business was business and he had to keep Kenny off his back or they were all in danger. Claire slid onto the chair opposite him, snatching the bottle of wine off the table she poured herself a generous measure into a china tea mug, her gaze didn't leave Craig not even for an instant. Her glare making him feel weak, she had a way of making him feel like a little kid every time she was angry. He pushed his plate towards her, stood to rise and turned on his heel and headed for the door, it was then the plate came hurtling towards him and smashed into three clean pieces as it hit the wall beside him. The thick globules of meat and potato slid down the wall leaving a thick trail of gravy in their wake, Craig didn't even look back, his eyes remained fixed on the sodden mess as it hit the tiled floor with a sickening splat.

"I'm off down Jenna's, sober up by the time I get back aye mum?" he spat angrily pulling up the hood of his jacket as he went, slamming the door behind him. He could feel Claire's eyes stabbing his back as he left, her evil drunken glare burning him with each step he took. She was a fucking nightmare in drink was his mother. Craig wondered though who had told her about him working for Kenny again, he had only been on a few jobs for him and he'd kill Jenna if she had been the one to let slip, best friend or not. He trudged down the metal steps, stopping at the bottom to light himself a cigarette, He smiled casually at Lisa as she stood on her doorstep shaking a bright red shag pile rug, cursing under her breath;

"Orite Lis, Want a hand?" He smirked as he spoke, cigarette clamped neatly between his teeth. Lisa dropped the rug onto the doorstep and strutted up to Craig, much shorter than Craig she stood close and poked him hard in his muscular chest;

"You Craig Carter" she snarled poking him again "Can take that lousy prick in there out with you tonight or so fucking help me. I need a bottle of wine and a whinge with my girl!" she laughed at the latter end of the statement. Craig laughed then a hearty laugh as he replied;

"What the fucks he done now?"

Lisa stepped back, her hand clamped firmly on her hip as she saw her fiancée Lee come bundling out of the front door, an angry purple hand mark on his cheek, he was obviously pissed out of his head he stood laughing his head off hysterically, pointing at his raging girlfriend. The can of super strength lager in his hand spilling out of the can as he stumbled around on the front doorstep attempting to light a fag.

"That" Lisa continued pointing angrily at Lee "has only gone and tipped a three and half on my fucking shagpile the coke head cunt!" she screeched. Her voice high pitched and filled with maliciousness, the posture making her look much younger than her years. She pouted sulkily like an upset child. Unlike Lee, Lisa had grown up with the finer things and appreciated the money she spent on her home; each and every item of furniture was picked accordingly to a specific colour scheme and was placed in a specific part of the flat. Their house was beautiful and Craig knew that she would be fucking furious at Lee tipping his bag of coke all over her rug! Craig shrugged taking a deep drawl on his cigarette, glancing back at Lee and then fixing his gaze back onto Lisa.

"I'm not taking him fucking anywhere, look at the bastard state of him!" Craig chortled, swerving past Lisa and heading towards Jenna's door. He ran quickly to Lee as he passed out, Catching his friend from almost plummeting face first into the concrete. He placed his arms around Lee's wide shoulders and carried him back into the flat, which coincidentally stank of weed and booze and Craig had to hold his breath as he plonked Lee down onto the leather corner style sofa. He was fucking smashed, his whole body shook through too much drink and drugs. His eyes glazed over and Craig had to stop him from tumbling to the floor twice before he finally settled down and succumb to sleep. Craig looked around the usually immaculate flat and sadly took in the scene before him. There were crack pipes strewn on the polished oak coffee table, a broken ashtray lay scattered over the dark carpet, highlighting the silver ash that littered the fluffy surface. The amount of empty cans that were overflowing from the wastepaper basket shocked Craig as much as it worried him, he saw Lisa stood trembling by the door frame, her face pale and slightly awkward as she whispered.

"See what I've got to put up with?" her face sad as she spoke, her forehead creased into an anxious frown she was usually a stunning girl, but she looked so down and upset and it showed on her usually gorgeous face. Her eyes trailed around the filthy room and Craig knew she was embarrassed that he had seen this.

"How longs he been on this shit?" Craig glanced at her, nodding toward the pipe and the rocks of crack that sat amongst dirty foil and empty cans on the table.

"Few weeks" she muttered under her breath, sinking deeper against the doorframe, her head resting against the wood for support.

"Who's he getting it from?" Craig added. His eyes burning into her now, he knew Lee loved his coke, always had done but this was something completely different. White heroin was a whole different league.

"I can't say Craig" she stuttered through gritted teeth, as quick as a shot he was on her hands clutching her thin throat, his breath whispering on her cheek in heavy bursts, his mouth was on her ear as he asked again viciously who was supplying Lee with the drugs. His fingers digging deeper into her pale skin his eyes wild with fury and for a second Lisa thought her would kill her there and then. She coughed and spluttered painfully as he clenched even harder.

"It was Sammy!" she shrieked in agony as he applied another forceful squeeze, blocking her windpipe. He snapped back suddenly, the pure shock written on his face was simply picture perfect. Lisa watched as his hands dropped to his sides, then to his mouth, his gorgeous lips the most perfect "O" as he turned away from her. There was an agonising roar and a shower of glass and Craig put his fist through the glass picture frame above Lisa's head, she shielded her face with her hands as glistening shards poured down over her. She gazed around in a state of confusion, the door slammed shut behind her and he was gone.

Chapter Fifty One

Sammy Carter lay naked out stretched on the plush cotton sheets, sucking away noisily on a half smoked cigarette, her free hand stroking her naked clitoris delight the only emotion on her usually haggard face, her smiling eyes alight with drugs and lust as she watched her new squeeze Leam Reynolds touching himself over her. She was completely drunk on Leam; he was a drug all on his own. Handsome beyond belief thick glossy hair with a rebellious pinstripe of bleach blonde through the middle, slight beard that was trimmed stylishly, slight gap in his front teeth which was completely adorable, he was slim and muscular with dark chocolate coloured eyes that literally drowned her. She was mad for him. He had money, plenty of it, which of course was the main perk of dealing drugs. He hated skag it wasn't something he familiarised himself with, despite selling it on a regular basis. He knew Sammy dabbled in it and he of course was disgusted by it but he found her quite attractive, she wasn't that bad when you got past the skinny body and the drugged up eyes. She was quite a nice girl too, they talked for hours and hours about nothing at all and yet he still found her company quite necessary. They had been dating a while now but of course word couldn't get out about it or Leam would be considered a joke. Sammy Carter was a wild one of epic standards and even he wondered sometimes what the fuck he was thinking. But he had never been one to listen to gossip and had found her quite funny when she wasn't smacked off her head. She was kind, loving and above all she was a genuinely nice girl despite her rugged exterior. He liked that she was young and reckless and what he liked more was the fact that she got jealous of other girls. It turned him on to know that she wanted him so badly.

 She smiled now a truly happy smile as she doubted her fag out in the ashtray and slid beside him, taking his semi hard penis in her hand she continued to tug at it manically, all the while staring deep into his dark eyes, his face rigid with ecstasy as he shot all over her pin marked hand. He planted a soft kiss onto her greasy damp hair and laid back against the pillow, she hugged the thin cotton blanket around herself fighting nervously to cover herself up. She was so self conscious it hurt Leam to see her so desperately trying to cover herself up despite the number of times they had seen each other naked. And every single time it ended like this. He was shattered, it was early afternoon they had been shagging all morning and he was ready to grab a few hours before he was due to go on a number of drug runs that evening. He winked at Sammy lovingly and closed his eyes, hugging her close as he slowly dosed off.....

The banging that commenced not long after both startled and unnerved a naked Sammy as the bedroom door swung open and there in the doorway stood her brother, face purple with anger, eyes dense with malice, breathing heavy and off rhythm, he was sweating profusely and Sammy could see in his eyes that for whatever reason he was fucking furious. He didn't even look at Leam, who had suddenly come to, he instantly lunged at his sister, grappling with handfuls of her disgusting grease laden hair and yanking her clean off the bed. Her naked body on show for all to see and her face flashed scarlet with humiliation as Craig eyed her with disgust. He threw her across the room, all the while grunting and groaning in sheer anger, scooping up and armful of her clothes from the floor her threw them blind sighted at her, trying not to look at his sisters sick needle pricked skin. She truly was fucking awful. Her bleach dyed hair tangled around her sullen face, tears streaming as she hurriedly pulled on a pair of skin tight jeans that still hung off Sammy's skinny frame no underwear or no bra beneath her attire. Craig looked at Leam who was sat rigid in the bed, shock plastered on his handsome face, he didn't move, he had been rendered literally speechless. Craig smirked at the boy, for all Craig's bravado there was nothing more amusing than catching his prey off guard. He waited for Sammy to feebly finish getting dressed before dragging her out of the room by her skinny lifeless arm. There was no fight in her; she just followed her brother without a word. Craig nodded politely at Leam as he closed the bedroom door behind him, all the while none too kindly ragging his sister from the small flat. He reached the unhinged front door and smiled at his handy work, pulling a barefooted Sammy out onto the veranda he slapped her hard across the mouth a reverberating slap that echoed violently out into the air. She slumped against the wall, begging for Craig to leave her go, the sickening metallic taste of her own blood in her mouth making her feel dizzy and unsteady. She stumbled as another vicious blow caught her on the side of the jaw; she sucked in a harsh breath, tumbling against the pebble dashed surface, scraping her naked arms, leaving thick angry gashes on her flesh in their wake. She yelped as another painful blow engulfed her this time to her stomach, she fell back hitting the wall hard, her head bouncing off the concrete surface. Her pale hazy eyes glared at her brother, this monster before her, He grappled with her scraggy locks plucking some of the stray hair straight from the roots and she winced painfully, trying her hardest not to show her fear of him. He yanked her upright, his face barely an inch away from hers, his breath receding in harsh warm torrents across her bony cheeks; she flushed red, her upset apparent as he snarled viciously through gritted teeth "Where you getting the skag you muggy cunt?" straight into her face, tiny specks of spittle spraying her as he spoke. Her eyes widened, a look of pure horror in her drugged up eyes. Sammy knew Craig would batter her for this, absolutely annihilate her for beseeching their family name. Taking drugs was one thing but in Craig's books, to sell drugs, especially crack or heroin, then you were classed in his books as the fucking devil himself. She cried then, thick rancid salty tears that streamed down her barely there cheeks, the snot running from her nose splashing onto the concrete below her, she knew that she had to lay it on thick now, make him think that she had made a terrible mistake.

"Craig I'm sorry!" she shrieked her eyes catching his milky gaze, his body spent from giving her a slap she could see the fury etched on his handsome face. He just stared at her like she was a piece of fucking shit on his shoes, the sweat bouncing off him as he caught his breath in harsh drawls. He slung Sammy then, straight into the wall and he walked away, not even looking back once.

Chapter Fifty Two

Cath wretched over the pristine china toilet bowl, her stomach was as dry as bone the thick congealed bile that rose from her empty gut making her splutter in disgust. The cold sweat that broke out all over her body making her shiver as she coughed the last of her lunch back up, choking as she bought up what she believed to be the last, she wiped her sticky fingers in a few sheets of the cheap toilet paper from the windowsill and flushed away the evidence. A few stray tears trickled down her face as she leant against the toilet door, sucking in the stale air as she tried to compose herself. She had always been a curvy girl, not fat as such but bigger than the other girls she worked with. All Kenny's girls were stick thin, beautiful, tiny waisted and big breasted and Cath felt somewhat over shadowed by each and every one of them. They all seemed so glamorous in comparison. She sold sex for a living, keeping each girl in casual fucks and compliments but the trauma and everyday battles she had over her own body was getting completely ridiculous. She hated the way she looked, each time she forced herself to look in the mirror she saw nothing but sick rolls of fat, her own body so grotesque, so unfeminine so vulgar, in her own eyes she was disgusting. This had been her last resort, she had yoyo'd from a size twelve to fourteen for years now and she had promised herself on so many occasions now that the bulimia would stop, indefinitely, but yet here she was still bringing up every single morsel that passed her lips in a desperate attempt to be thin. She knew that It was wrong to abuse her body so brutally but it was a force of habit now, she ate, she was sick, she was better. It was a simple sickening cycle but in her own deluded thoughts she immediately comforted by the fact that she had control. It didn't help that Johnny was taking her out on all these expensive fucking meals! For a seventeen year old kid he could sure put his grub away, yet he was still so fucking handsome, so gorgeous and kind and Cath didn't honestly know what the fuck he saw in her. Cath sighed, exiting the restaurants toilet cubicle and running her hands under the hot water in the sink, washing away the smell of vomit and sadness. She smiled a half hearted smile at her reflection as she tidied up her slightly smudged makeup, tracing her smile with the vivid scarlet lipstick, her perfect cupids bow lips the only part of her face that she truly loved, they still reeled from the feel of Johnny's tender mouth on hers, still despaired for his touch. He was so young, yet so ruggedly adult in the way he carried himself in business and in pleasure. He was by no means a child in neither the office nor the bedroom and Cath loved his sense of reality. Johnny knew what people thought of him, wannabe gangster, a kid trying to be a big man, but he didn't care. He knew what true loyalty was whether he pleased or offended. And Cath knew that despite trying her fucking hardest not to, she was falling for Johnny hook line and bloody sinker. Despite being a brothel Madame he still loved every inch of her still doted on her as though she was the fucking queen Ma'am herself and the sex was completely mind blowing, he was an exceptional lover, both gentle but rough and he wasn't selfish he tended to her needs above his own and kept her begging for more. He was such a beautiful person, constantly complimenting her on how gorgeous she was and Cath knew that she wanted to spend out the rest of her days with him. He completed her.

She checked her reflection over one more, tousling her soft hair into place before she went back out to the dining room of the restaurant. Sucking her stomach in as tight as she could as she strutted confidently back to the table her curves hugged tightly by the gorgeous black cocktail dress that she wore so effortlessly, the neck line plunging just enough to show a small amount of cleavage, subtle not slutty but enough to turn heads. Johnny was gazing at her from over his menu, a look of pure lust on his youthful face, his playful smile edging on his perfect thin lips he seemed so mesmerised by her, standing up almost instantly as she appeared at the table, he pulled up her chair and waited for her to sit gracefully before returning to his own seat. He just stared at her with those piercing eyes of his that drew her in breathlessly each blink stolen with those long shielding lashes of his, his head tilted to the side just staring so intensely as if he was looking deep into her soul.

"You're so lucky we're not alone or you would be bent over this fucking table" he whispered, a slight chuckle in his voice, he winked at her cheekily staring at her cleavage subtly spewing out of the top of her dress, she truly was beautiful, all silky hair and exquisitely polished makeup that enhanced every flawless feature of her stunning face. Johnny was left simply speechless every time his eyes met hers he felt every single ounce of his body quiver with pure lust for her. Every movement was ladylike and mystifying and Johnny was definitely under the spell. He watched her intently as she sipped water from a large glass tumbler, watched her swan like throat as she swallowed, how her lips pursed as she finished, each movement exquisite. She smoothed over the front of her dress with her thin fingers, the finely manicured nails running against the sequined material finally she rested her hands on the tabletop, her fingers playing with the large cocktail ring on her middle finger, delicate black stones set in silver suited her outfit perfectly. She ran a hand through her hair her eyes caught Johnny's and she smiled effortlessly at him. Then they each returned to their meals in silence, finding comfort in the fact that they were just together.

Chapter Fifty Three

Emma's eyes met Freddie's steely gaze, his face a mixture of congealed sweat and blood stains, His eyes glazed over in a drunken stupor, his stale breath reeked of cigarettes and cheap beer. She stood with one hand firmly perched on her tiny hip, a fleece blanket neatly rolled in the other arm, shaking her head as he stumbled in the doorway there was no way she was sleeping in the same room as him tonight!. She had never understood his drinking, why it was so heavy, frequent and above anything troublesome. In truth she felt more like his carer than his wife, the constant beatings, the screaming, the fights were a constant reminder to her of the bastard he had become. And as she stared at him through a half opened eyelid, she sighed a heavy breath knowing that tonight would be exactly the same as any other. She'd have to carry him up to bed, after of course taking another lashing from his vile mouth, each sentence he'd manage to string together in a deep slur was full of the shattering words that cut her deeper than any knife ever could, how hadn't she realised that life was going to be like this? And as he threw up all over her freshly mopped kitchen floor, she felt the tears well up in her eyes. Then came the heavy blows that covered her face his tightened fists raining down on her bruised skin, the sweat from his face colliding with hers in a bitter-sweet symphony of lust and complete and utter hatred. She despised him so much, yet she found herself in the tangled web of love that he kept her constantly trapped in. What she had yet to realise was that she no longer loved him...she just felt sorry for him. He was a stranger to her now.... no longer was he the handsome man she had married. His jet black hair, once glossy and rich hung on his shoulders in a pitiful mass that hid his sweat stained neck. His once beautiful blue eyes were now dead in their sockets, his gaze so vacant and far away that he himself looked distanced from his whole body. The stale smell of smoke and lager that hung on his breath like a lead weight around his sunken shoulders, he was a vile skeletal little creature that had taken the place of her once burly husband. Yes she realised then that this was as good as it got for her. Yet she was addicted to the violence and the thrill it gave him, the control he had over her was her poison, in a way it made her feel like he needed her, wanted her, desired her every affections, this was the only thought that kept her sane on nights like these and as he threw his fist down hard on her face for the last time, she knew that it was only these vague dreams that kept her alive.

She woke to the sound of her head pounding and the music blaring from the flat upstairs, crying children drowned out the mix match of noises that came flooding into her ear drums all at once. The smell of dried blood and piss filled her nose as she took in a deep disgruntled breath, suddenly wishing that she hadn't. She placed her hands out before her and pulled herself up onto her hands and knees, letting the familiarities of her surroundings bring her back to any sense of normality. The kitchen floor was covered in puddles of vomit and blood so she knew that last night's beating had been a good one, although she dreaded having to face looking in a mirror at any point during that day. Her hair was clumped together in dirty knots riddled with whatever was on the floor, broken glass, food, vomit, it was all there, her clothes were damp with urine and stale sweat, the first thing to enter her mind was the bath tub. She needed to get herself together before he came back, otherwise there would be hell to pay. Slowly she heaved herself onto her feet, staggering slightly as the warm rays from the sun outside came pouring in through the window, she slumped back against the fridge, her ankle twisting slightly inwards, the signs of broken bones had never been so apparent, yet she knew that she would have to grit her teeth and bare it, she had done it before, she would have to do it again. She edged her way to the bathroom, dragging her broken leg behind her, each step was daunting and painful, deep throbbing pains that shot straight through her body. Her leg felt heavier than a tonne of bricks, as she winced at the thought of having to climb the stairs in this vicious state. It had taken her until now to realise that she was completely naked, as she stared down at her mutilated body she broke down in floods of tears, the thick black and purple blotches that covered every inch of her skin looked puffy and swollen, her fingers were crooked from where he had trampled on them with his steel work boots. Her whole body was covered in bloody streaks and scratches, even she would have to admit that she was a complete and utter mess. But discreetly as she stumbled up the stairs she smiled, a small sacrificial smile that told her that he had not yet defeated her, she was still in the twisted playground game that was her life.

The sound of evil silence filled the kitchen as she slowly swept up the broken glass and set the kitchen back to its original homely state, brushing the tears from her burning cheeks with the back of a blood stained fingers. She strutted over to the side board of the kitchen unit and took out a glass and a bottle of Bells Whiskey, pouring a generous measure she toasted thin air before gulping down the harsh liquid in one go breathing a sigh of release deeply to ease her burning throat. She scraped her hair back into a neat bun on the top of her head before retiring to the lounge taking the bottle of Bells and the crystal glass with her.... no matter what he wouldn't beat her sober, not tonight anyway.

Freddie sat propping the bar of the 'Fox and Badger' inn gulping down the remains of his pint of lager which had been standing for well over an hour and was now warm and sickly, he smiled at the barmaid gently as she shuffled her buxomly built body across the bar area smiling with her jutting teeth and ill fitting attire that was slightly childish for her years, the small pale blue skirt and ill fitting snake skin shirt were an impossible match even to the East ends standards as her heels clapped against the solid oak flooring she created a melody all of her own, she noticed him staring and remarked in her screechy tone "Oi Jase put your tongue away my boy, your missus would have a fit! And anyway you couldn't afford these babies even if you won the lottery!" she giggled with this pushing up her small breasts and showing her horsey mouth once more, Freddie began to bellow with laughter so much so that the whole pub looked at him in bewilderment

"haa as if Sheila love, your barking way up the wrong tree!" he proclaimed ordering himself another pint before going outside and lighting himself a cigarette the smoking ban had killed pub culture in London, the social scene had squandered, people preferred to stay in with a couple of cans and the comfort of not having to go outside for a smoke, god damn British politics Freddie thought taking a deep draw of smoke into his already wheezing lungs, taking in the warmth it gave him, holding it for a few seconds then breathing out the smoke in a big grey cloud. He stubbed the cigarette on the wall before going back inside for his drink.

Emma was pissed and by God did she know it, she stumbled around the living room singing to her favourite Celine Dion album the music giving her a subtle rush of love that these days she never felt from human contact, her husband had put pay to that! God why did she love him so much? Emma didn't even realise the answer to that question herself, as she nursed her pain in her swollen face with yet another large measure of brandy, she could feel the burning liquid hit her stomach, only then was she satisfied and already pouring herself another glass, it was only when the vomit hit the carpet did she then decide to give up and go to bed.

Freddie stumbled through the door at around eleven thirty carrying a four pack of cider and a greasy kebab in his arms as though he was in possession of the crown jewels. He smiled as he realised that Emma was in bed, fucking lazy bitch he thought to himself, he had been hoping to get his leg over, give her the sob story, promise he'd stop hitting her and then she would be up for anything.... or so he'd hoped. But he was sadly disappointed when he strutted upstairs to find Emma on the bathroom floor sleeping soundly in a pool of her own vomit, only then did Jason feel his own vomit bubbling in his gut, the acid rising high in his throat and it took all his might to swallow it back down.... there was no way he was wasting four quid on his greasy feast just to spew it back up! Instead he kicked Emma in the head, a hard blow and he felt her head slam against the bath tub. He brushed his teeth and sloped into bed sticking a Porn film in the DVD player and forgetting that his wife was lying unconscious on the cold bathroom tiles. Well if she wasn't going to give him his kicks he thought to himself, then he'd get them elsewhere.

Donny Anderson was sprucing himself up for work, his precious suit ironed and starched to a crisp his hair slicked back neatly and his tie shaped in the perfect knot, Donny knew he was slick, probably the slickest face in the smoke, he was known as a hard man famous for being fierce but fair. If he owed you a debt, then he would pay it... if a hiding was to be dished out, then he would dish one out with seconds and a desert. He was loved by all the ladies and feared by all the men. A reputation Donny highly claimed, being only on the fresh side of thirty he was more than a force to be reckoned with. He tidied up his briefcase and went downstairs where he saw his beautiful fiancée Sandra preparing them a hearty breakfast of sausage, egg and toast... she smiled as he hugged her waist tightly turning her into his and kissing her gently on the head, trailing little butterfly kisses down to her perfect rosebud lips.

"Donny you'll get lipstick on your face" she chuckled heartily as he kissed her hard on the mouth, muffling her words.

They sat down at the breakfast bar where Sandra poured them each a steaming mug of fresh coffee and presented Donny with the morning paper, leaving him to glance over the headlines before she vacated to the lounge to watch the morning's television. She was a diamond was Sandra, but she could be a nosey bloody bugger, always gossiping. The week before last she has decided that the woman in the house next door was on the game, just because the girl had three kids and was doing the school run dressed in a mini dress and heels in September, Sandra had forgotten to point out that it was an absolutely gorgeous day and the girl worked in a salon in town. That was his Sandra always willing to make a mountain out of a mole hill. But in Donny's eyes she could do no wrong, she was perfect, with her flowing locks of brown hair, the perfect size 8 figure, ample breasts and gorgeous icy blue eyes... she was as pretty as a picture and Donny had vowed that one day, when he retired, he would make Sandra Hemming his wife. She had been his childhood sweetheart, had been together since they were fifteen, she had been patiently waiting thirteen years for him to set a date, he decided there and then that he would marry her sooner rather than later! She was his soul mate, Donny Anderson was as sure of that little nugget of information as he was his own name.

Emma slithered down the stairs, her hair a mangle of dried blood and vomit, her head was not her own, the hangover she had was simply diabolical, she crawled to the kitchen and popped herself a few tablets and propped herself up on the kitchen table. Her mouth was dry, her head was pounding like a big bass drum, her knees where weak and she wasn't sure if she was still drunk or just a little giddy from her night on the bathroom floor. Emma stood up and set about making herself a cup of tea trying to shake off the feeling of suffocation that was wrapped around her head like a tight thick rope, she felt ill... really ill. She tried her best to stay quiet in fear of waking the mammoth from his cave. She had peeked in on him before she had come downstairs, fortunately the image of her husband sprawled naked on the bed with a porn film on replay in the background was something of a regular occurrence to her. She cupped her head in her hands staring at the creamy rim that had appeared on the top of her teacup, a single tear rolled down her cheek, she was tired, she was in immense pain and her head hurt with the millions of thoughts buzzing around in her small mind. As she heard the creaking of the mattress from upstairs her shoulders tensed and she ran to the sink quickly filling the kettle and putting it to boil, she knew how grumpy he could get in the mornings and she had vowed that she would not provoke him in any manner today, in all honesty she didn't have the energy nor the regard to even flare his temper. As Freddie came strutting into the kitchen stark naked cupping his testicles with his hand and yawning with the pitch of a grizzly bear she scanned him over, looking at his taught body and ample buttocks as he reached into the kitchen cupboard for a mug, she smiled tenderly greeting him with a casual "good Morning" before setting about getting the breakfast things ready, from the smell of stale alcohol that emitted from both their breaths they both knew they needed something to line their stomachs.

Freddie sat watching his wife with a squinted beady eye, he knew she was in pain but to be honest with himself he found he didn't really care, she had become something of an annoyance to him in the last passing weeks, and last night finding her hugging the toilet bowl drowning in her own vomit had really put the cherry on top of a very large, very sour tasting cake.

Donny Anderson was late, his meeting with his old pal Kenny was due to start in fifteen minutes and he was nowhere near the Café Rouge on the high street where he was meeting the wannabe hard man regarding a big warehouse conversion that he had just taken on. He wanted to branch out his business into stock markets and property development, he planned to convert the old warehouse into offices where he could keep his private effects that were just too bulky to be kept at home. That and he knew of a few girls who had been shipped over illegally from Russia who wanted to meet up with Kenny for some work at his little whore house. His Sandra had no concern for his work ethic she just sat back and enjoyed the life of Riley while he was out earning a wedge. Sandra was a trained interior designer so most of her social hours were spend picking themes and colour schemes and forever transforming their small three bed terrace just a few miles out of the Belmonte estate. Donny knew that Sandra was longing for a family, had been for years... but he didn't have any interest in having children, his time was purely dedicated to his work and his businesses, he just didn't have the heart to tell Sandra that she would be picking paint swatches for more than a couple of years just yet.

Chapter Fifty Four

Finley Monroe was angry, it was Monday morning and already everything had seemingly turned out for the worst. His thirteen year old daughter, he had just found out was shagging a vagrant gypsy from Ireland who was in fact seven years her senior and one of the biggest drug users known in east London. He had left the house with a fresh hand mark on his face thanks to his lovely wife Jolene who had more than vocally stood up for the little slut. Thirteen and already on her back, Finley was devastated, he knew he would be a bloody laughing stock when this little gem became public knowledge, something which he wanted to avoid at all costs. He hadn't the guts to admit to himself that this was all his fault, if only he'd been there more, supported his little girl, but no he had been too busy running his precious gentlemen's club exploiting young girls just like his daughter. He felt like a total fucking idiot. He pulled the car into a nearby parking bay and cried his eyes out..... He was glad that he now had a buyer for the old place, some chancer called Jamie Collins from the East end but he would be extremely sad to see it go but business was business and unfortunately despite his efforts family had to come first. He hoped today would fly by god knew he needed to get a stiff drink and a joint to calm down.

Emma Fenton sat on the edge of the bathtub staring at her small wrist watch, three minutes seemingly taking forever to tick away, she knew what was happening she just needed to clarify herself doubt with cold hard evidence. As she glanced at the little white stick in her hand she felt her stomach wretch with absolute disgust, the two pink lines on the test were there as clear as day, she was pregnant. Emma felt her eyes well up with feelings a mixture of excitement and sheer terror, how was she going to explain this one to Freddie? She plotted it over and over in her head trying to string together a valid sentence that would sound appealing to him, as if this whole sorry situation was a good thing, deep down in her heart she knew it wasn't. He would never ever ever think this was a good thing, he'd make her get rid of it or he'd get rid of it himself.... either way she knew that this feeling of elation was to be short lived. She found herself dreaming of her baby, what it would look like, who it would act like, would the twins love him or her then the harsh reality of the fact hit her that even if she were to have this child she could never provide it with a life, and who knows maybe Freddie would get bored of hitting her and turn on their babies? The twins were only a few weeks old and she couldn't believe that she was back in this ever familiar situation despite her young years. She couldn't even breathe with the spine chilling anxiety that had taken over her whole body, she felt terrified, absolutely terrified. As she gently rubbed a hand over her flat tummy she felt a small swelling sense of pride wash over her, she savoured every dragging second knowing that this was the happiest she had ever felt in her small life, to have that snatched away from her now would be the end of her. She stared at her bruised battered body and realised she wasn't carrying a child, she was carrying her one way ticket to a life of endless misery, Freddie would make sure of that, Emma knew that as well as she knew her own name. Pulling her bathrobe a little tighter round her body she left the bathroom quietly stuffing the pregnancy test into the waste paper basket covering it in toilet tissue and a face cloth. Slowly she crept downstairs, the drinks cabinet was whispering her name, she was seeking oblivion and she knew that she had to find it.

Freddie sat nursing a large brandy in his hand as his wife entered the room, his eyes shunted straight at her watching her ample silhouette prance around the open living area, her slippers making a scratching noise on the carpet that began to annoy him slightly. He gestured for her to sit with him, an act of kindness that even Emma felt grateful of, pouring them both another large glass of brandy she joined him on the tatty printed sofa handing him the glass before taking him a sip of her own drink, tasting the venom of the amber liquid burning her throat, gagging slightly as it hit the pit of her wavering stomach. She patted her husband gently on the arm as if trying her hardest to gain his attention;

"Fred" she whispered in a slightly melodic tone,

He grunted vaguely in reply his eyes transfixed on the TV set in the corner of the room, he was watching the repeats of Jeremy Kyle or at least he looked like he was.

"Fred I'm pregnant again" she stammered almost knocking the glass out of her own hand she was shaking so much.

His eyes didn't move off the television as he brought his arm up and smacked her clean in the face, the stinging sensation sprung into her face like a snapping elastic. His face grimacing in fury as he continued to rain blows on her face evil profanities spewing from his mouth like a flowing river. He brought his foot down on her ribs in big stomping motions leaving her winded and gagging for breath begging and pleading with him in ample gasps to stop. It was only when he heard the loud popping of her jaw did he stand back and admire his work, like and intricate oil painting she lay sprawled on the black fluffy rug, her limbs bent and broken in shapes that appeared almost impossible, she looked alien, and like a skilful artist he just stood there with his arms crossed over his chest admiring his work. He panted eagerly as he laid the boot into her jaw one last time before piling into the kitchen to wash his dirty hands.

Chapter Fifty Five

Finley Monroe was gasping for a fag but the inspector of the dock yard would be doing his rounds soon and he had already been caught three times in the last week off duty. He pulled his steel capped boots on and shoved his trainers in his gym bag. His mind was reeling about his daughter, his bloody Stella a tart, God it hadn't seemed that long ago she was running around in nappies singing to the Spice Girls, now look at her, how the fuck she'd gotten acquainted with Paddy McDowell had bugged him all morning, he had rallied all the possible situations around in his mind like a relay race. It was apparently obvious that she had been bothering around the gypsy camp sites just outside the East end. Finley just hoped upon hope that she had had the sense to use protection with that dirty little bastard, it turned Finley's gut just thinking of the diseases that cunt was riddled with. Finley slammed his fist hard against the aluminium barrel in front of him his temper suddenly reaching boiling point. He knew just the person he would go and see to sort this little problem out, reaching into his pocket for his mobile phone he grinned slyly.... Oh Paddy McDowell best start getting his fast daps on and getting the fuck out of London, because when Finley and his boys got hold of him there would be more than just a typical bloodbath. There would be riots over this.... Finley would make sure of it.

Donny Anderson was pleased with himself, the phone call from Finley Monroe had sent some well over due business his way, he was looking forward to taking McDowell down to his maker the bloody dirty little bastard going round shagging kids! Her bloody chest was flatter than his and he had her on her back already! It made Donny sick to his stomach and he had to suddenly force the bile to remain in his throat. He hated the Irish lot anyway, nothing but thieving, murdering, lying little trolls, in Donny's book the gypsies were the scum of the earth. He would put a price on Paddy McDowell's head and then get back to Finley Monroe; nothing was set in a solid cast iron guarantee until the wedge had changed hands. Only then would Finley Monroe get his revenge, until then his words were about as much use as a piss in the wind. Donny was excited and it showed in the devilish grin that had suddenly spread across his handsome face. He pulled his mobile from his pocket and made a call to his old mate Kenny and asked him to send over two of his best boys for a meet, he had to call together a bunch of meat heads to solve this little problem and Kenny had just the muscle to back him up.

Chapter Fifty Six

Dr Liam Gold sat behind his desk bewildered, this was the fifth time Emma Fenton had sat in front of him this month and if he was honest with himself he was sick of seeing her face, she always sat slouched over her shoulders hunched and her body he knew was black with thick welts and bruises. Yet time and time again Emma sat in front of him sympathy seeking, seeking pills that would make her forget her husband's violence, she had put herself in that position and had proceeded to stay in that position until it would undoubtedly kill her. Dr Gold pushed his fringe away from his face, his youthful skin showing shining pools of sweat in the harsh daylight that flooded the small consultation area his shirt marked with fresh sweat patches that his strong smelling deodorant had failed to mask.

"Mrs Fenton" he cleared his throat before continuing "Have you thought of placing yourself into a woman's aid refuge? This abuse cannot continue not with your two children and even more so now that your with child don't you see that?" he opposed the question with a tone of arrogance as if he already knew the answer was negative before she even opened her mouth.

"I want a fucking termination and me pills doc that's all I didn't come here for a counselling session I thought you were a GP not a pissing shrink!" she retorted in haste, her voice croaked with the dryness of thirst that lingered in her mouth.

Dr Gold shook his head in consternation at the complete brass cheek of the Muppet sat in front of him, oh Liam Gold had seen them all, drug addicts looking for a sick paper, pensioners trying to gain more benefits off the state, mouthy children who were pregnant at the age of twelve, It was the curse of the Belmonte and all of the filthy vagrants who occupied it but none of them had the utter bravado that Emma Fenton had just slapped on the table. It was as though she thrived on violence, she found some sick pleasure in being beaten! Her husband was well known in London, Yes Freddie was a definite character of sorts. Dr Gold grinned showing his pearly white teeth that were like ivory in his mouth.

"Mrs Fenton I'm taking you off your anti-depressants and your sleeping tablets with immediate effect until you seek professional advice from a drug councillor. As for a termination you may book one through the NHS via the hospital itself, please call the number on this card between the hours of nine and five, now if that is all I do have other people to see today" he announced with a rather jovial tone of voice.

Emma's face was an absolute blank and she wasn't sure she had heard the doctor properly, the bastard couldn't be taking her pills, could he?

"What!" she screeched the dryness of her throat suddenly easing as she began spouting her vile language at the doctor,

"You Cunt! You know those pills are the only things that keep me fucking sane! How could you!?" she wretched, feeling her whole body tighten as the good doctor began to laugh at her hysterically. Within moments she was being carted out of the building between the burly forearms of the two security guards who had heard the commotion.

Dr Gold's day had been made, he crossed off Emma Fenton's prescription card, if she needed the valium and the anti-depressants so badly she could buy them off one of her druggie mates, maybe her brother even. The good doctor was well and truly sick of funding the habits of no-good idiots like Emma Fenton and the like, to him she wasn't with the proverbial wank.

Chapter Fifty Seven

Craig sat at the breakfast Bar of the Deluxe cafe on the outskirts of town, the decor typical of an all American diner all blue and red pinstripe and retro posters of burlesque girls advertising chocolate donuts and the like, the funky modern decor and the large old school jukebox that stuck out like a sore thumb in the small space blasting out sounds of the sixties. It was a little piece of heaven and Craig loved it here, everything was homemade, American and delicious and the girls who ran the place turned a blind eye to the odd drug deal or the odd gangsters meet and it was completely private here. Craig sat nursing a cup of their famous fudge hot chocolate mulling over the thick wads of cash that sat in the envelopes in front of him, he sat in wait, every now and again looking at his wrist watch not in agitation but more in haste for the excitement of getting his plan into motion! It wasn't everyday you faked your own death he thought laughing at the irony his seductive grin catching the attention of two girls on the table opposite him, he smiled his full beam smile in their direction nodding them a subtle good morning, this turning the girls into silent fits of childish giggles. Craig noticed Johnny's mothers car pull up outside the barbers shop opposite and out stood the handsome Johnny Fenton in a black pinstripe suit and fake aviator sunglasses strutting towards the cafe like something out of an American gangster film. Craig's laugh suddenly turned into a full reverberating cackle that bounced off the walls as Johnny came towards him and pulled up a stool beside him.

"You had your fucking mother to drive you?" he couldn't speak through tears of laughter, Johnny Fenton the wannabe gangster being chauffeured by his mummy dearest the irony of it all hit Craig like a lead weight, they were in reality all just kids. All of them trying to make their way in the big world of crime and deception, yet none of them even finished school yet. Oh the irony thought Craig as he pushed the two cash filled envelopes Johnny's way.

"Count it if you want" Craig shrugged taking another sip of his drink, the girls on the opposite tables staring awestruck at the two handsome money makers at the bar, their tongues literally dragging the colour off the lino tiles as their eyes followed the envelopes of cash as though they were completely mesmerised by them. Craig smiled again in their direction before turning his attention back to Johnny who was just finishing ordering himself a large latte and a sticky donut from the buxom young waitress who was flipping fresh pancakes behind the counter, the smell simply intoxicating making the place feel so homely despite being just another east end eatery.

"Nah I trust you" Johnny grinned pulling a small envelope out of his breast pocket and handing it to Craig, the glint of pure joy in the two boys eyes was evident as Craig dropped out the two fake passports, the fake drivers licence, the fake death certificate and all the agreements for the day of the plan. Johnny had even paid two of his mates to nick an ambulance and some paramedics uniforms and they were going to be the firsts on the scene, there were photos of the murder weapon itself already littered in Johnny's prints and he had already congregated a few of the estate boys to be his mob when the job went down. Craig looked inside the passport "Jamie Collins aye" he grinned as he saw his own picture merged with all the forged information. He couldn't wait to just escape now, hide away for a while do his new club up and then when the time was right Boom he was coming for Kenny Kreegan and his fucking firm the bunch of muggy cunts. This was for Johnny as much as it was himself, Johnny's bird was one of Kenny's possessions and they both knew he wouldn't take kindly to knowing his Madame was fucking the clientele. Craig knew Johnny wanted Cath all for himself and the money from this job was going to set him up for life, that and the prospect of working in Craig's night club when it all came full circle. Of course Johnny knew that he would be going away for a while, he knew that he would be getting done for manslaughter. They already had a few bent coppers and a bent judge on their side just for handing them Kenny on a plate and now it was time for the two young boys to get their retribution. They had so much control already that it was lethal but they both knew that this was the only way that they would be free of Kenny and the firm without any repercussions. It was a simple plan, they had been plotting behind Kenny's back for so long, pretending to hate one another, all the while plotting the death of Craig Carter on Kenny the simple cunts terms. Kenny wanted Craig dead and as soon as the job was done Johnny intended to sing like a birdie to the police, he had recordings of Kenny admitting that he wanted Johnny to stab Craig to death. Johnny of course had filled Craig in on all of this and between them they had concocted to fake Craig's death. He would be stabbed, two single lacerations to the stomach and the chest area above his breast bone, he would be given a shot of some drug that was meant to make your heartbeat practically stop, he would be taken to the morgue for his mother to see him, then carted off to the finest private hospital money could buy in south Wales to recover. There would be blood loss there would be a lot of trauma but he would survive and he would come back bigger and better than ever before and then he would kill Kenny and his fucking mob before opening up his very own lap dancing club right here in London. It was fool proof if played right but the boys were prepared, the police interference would be minimal of course there would be a court case, media interference but they had enough paid protection that everything would play out to their advantage in the end. In six months he would even have a grave to visit but Craig knew that if he didn't do this now then Kenny would kill him and all this would have been for nothing, and then he knew Kenny would make a play for Jenna and he couldn't handle the thought of any harm coming to her or little Kiki. He loved them too much for that. The both boys laughed heartily at their success and hugged each other tightly, the next time they were to see each other Johnny would be taking away Craig Carter and putting Jamie Anthony Collins, twenty seven year old club owner in his place. They were brothers in business and in power and now it was time to take the underworld for their own.

Chapter Fifty Eight

Jenna sat in front of the bedroom mirror running the curlers through her dark mass of glossy black hair, tonight was the night she was going to finally admit to Craig that she was completely and utterly in love with him and that friendship was now no longer an option for them. She needed him now for her own, so far two bottles of wine had been consumed and she was all but a little bit pissed. She stared for long moments at her stunning reflection, the neatly curled lashes coated in thick coats of dark mascara accentuating her gorgeous almond shaped eyes perfectly, her beautiful rosebud mouth perfectly puckered and slathered in thick pink lip gloss, bare legs and a pretty red and black corset dress that pushed out her breasts and skimmed her curvaceous thighs perfectly. She tousled her hair over her shoulders, the tumbling locks just concealing her pert breasts from their tight confines of her dress she was alluring, mysterious and simply drop dead gorgeous and she knew that tonight her and Craig would finally get on the same page. She pouted seductively at her own reflection, eyes fluttering innocently, she looked simply breathtaking and she knew Craig would be spending the night here. She poured herself another large glass of wine, taking a sip she took a second glance at her reflection, yes she was perfect. She smoothed down the skirt of her dress as she stood, trying not to tumble over in the towering stiletto heels that encased her feet, she tripped slightly with each drunken step that she took trying her hardest to maintain a sober front, of course failing miserably and her walk had turned into more or less a stumble. The sound of the doorbell downstairs brought her crashing back to her drunken reality.

Present Day

Craig sat in warm glow of the fireplace, his strong muscles standing out in ripples against the amber glow, the beer in his hand warming slightly from his body heat, his focus on the television not really taking interest in the BDSM porno that he had playing but his eyes were set there never the less dancing between the vivid colours yet not really taking in the full picture. Those steely eyes so captivating, so mystifying, so hard his gaze was simply riveting. The scars across his stomach and chest standing out against the flickering amber flames, turning him sick each time he glanced at them, he took a large gulp of the warm liquid, his parched dry mouth savouring the wetness, his taste buds rejoicing at the feel of something thirst quenching. He was tired, his eyes hooded and heavy, he stretched out his tense bones clicking as his body writhed on the small sofa chair, he ran his hands through his hair contemplating calling it a night and wandering off to bed but his head was all over the place and he needed to figure out his next move, he didn't want to return Kiki to her mother, he knew that much. He couldn't bear to be parted from the little girl again it was unthinkable. She was his fucking daughter for God's sake and Jenna had lied told him some bullshit story, he should have known she didn't have the balls to sleep with another man. He glanced back at the television at the big titted blonde bound and gagged being whipped with the plaited whip, her skin burning red with each stroke, Craig revelled his eyes shutting tightly at the joyous thought of doing this to Jenna. Trouncing the mouthy little bitch with a gag, sounded perfect to him, like music to his ears. His eyes burning an intense smouldering blue as he glared at the moving images before him. He had never admitted his obsession before but as the erection in his pants bulged he couldn't help but admit to himself that he was nothing but a kinky bastard and Jenna Shearan would soon know just how hard he was willing to play. He smiled that picture perfect smile, his hands caressing the bulge in his trousers gently his long fingers twitching beneath his own touch, his eyes smoky with lust and need. He sat up, his revere burst by the sound of his little girl whimpering at the top of the stairs, he flinched, grabbing the television remote and shutting off the film,

"Coming Keeks" he said, running his fingers through his short hair, rubbing the slight stubble that occupied his face. He sunk the last of his can and tumbled up the stairs to the perfect little angel who stood at the top clutching her tatty knitted doll.

"What's up sweet pea?" he hushed, hugging his little daughter's body to his, kissing her silky soft hair his strong arms enveloping the tiny little girl in his embrace.

"When can we go back to mummy's house?" she whispered, sleepily rubbing her tired eyes, tears making her beautiful little eyes puffy and sad. Craig winced, scooping her little body up inhaling her sweet baby smell, cuddling her close to him.

"Don't you want to stay with me Keeks?" he asked her honestly, his voice strained in the darkness, the tears formed in the corners of his eyes threatening to spill, he would be devastated if she were to go home, that would mean revealing himself to Jenna and his mother, something he wasn't yet ready for, but for Kiki he would give the world. He had grown to love her in ways he couldn't even begin to describe, she was his little girl, such a mesmerising, bewitching little thing and even now he only had to look at her and he was drunk on pure love for this little madam. She was strong minded, mouthy like her mother, with a beautiful personality, she had his looks though. He could see it now, straight nose and glossy dark hair. She was a Carter there was no doubting that.

"Daddy's going to take you to mummy soon Princess I promise." He stared into those perfect turquoise eyes, so innocent, so beautiful, his stunning daughter and he promised himself there and then that he would have to take her back to Jenna. It was time.

Previously

Craig stood on the doorstep of Jenna's flat looking simply taken aback with her, stood there on the doorstep all playfully dressed up for his benefit, he smiled a rugged, barely there smile his lips pressed firmly into a grim line, he looked seductively at the little temptress before him, here she was serving it up to him on a plate and he was shell shocked, her beauty something textbook, she truly was stunning there was no other word, her glossy dark hair tumbled in delicious curls down her slightly arched back, her face made up like a china doll her dress hugging every curve exquisitely he stepped into the flat, his eyes locked on Jenna's, cool, fleeting and he knew she was hot for him, he took of his jacket and tossed it none too kindly onto the stairs, his eyes fiery, burning with carnal lust for this pretty young woman who owned him, owned his heart, owned his soul, owned him entirely. Best friends, always, he had said from the beginning that he never wanted anymore than friendship yet now here he was literally frothing at the mouth with need for her, she was his drug of choice stronger than any opiate she was striking, deep down inside him his muscles tensed, his stomach flipping at the thought of having her, there as his own, her eyes flickering at him, her thick glossy lashes that hid those impulsive sexy green eyes|, a beautiful striking green that made him shiver every time his glance stole them. She was completely submissive to him and he loved that, she wanted him, needed him.

"Miss Shearan your looking delectable as ever" he smiled, that perfect smile of his, his teeth straight, whiter than white, he pulled her close, smelling her heady cocktail of shampoo and jasmine bubble bath, she was quite the intoxicating elixir. He pulled her against his strong chest, his nose sinking into her hair, beautiful, precious Jenna whom he loved with every single inch of his being but he couldn't admit it to himself. He raised her chin with his long pianist fingers the tips resting lightly on her fleshy cheeks and kissed her, hard, impressionable, his hands tugging at her glossy mane, his eyes still locked tightly on hers. She reciprocated, her tongue exploring his mouth expertly, He had never ever been so captivated in his young life. She was such a turn on despite being overly dressed, slightly slutty if he was honest but he didn't care. For that singular moment she was his and his alone. His hands trailed from her face down to her breasts, pert despite their tiny confinements of the dress, his nose direct on her neck, the small hushed breaths coming from him making her arch against him, as he trailed simple butterfly kissed down her throat the small of her back against his palms as he skimmed against her buttocks, holding her tightly toward him, tantalising him with her poisonous kiss, Craig pushed his hips against her, smiling as he kissed her deeper.

"Your eager Mr Carter" she whispered against his lips, her tiny body entwined with his. Craig held her there, kissing her deeply, his fingers all over her tiny body, Jenna inhaled deeply, taking in this beautiful man and all his crazy demands, she pulled him in closer, her teeth dragging against his bottom lip, slowly seductively she took his hand and led him into the living room, kicking the door loudly behind her. She sat him down on the couch, knowing he wanted more, his eyes distressed, her hands clinging to his in a desperate assault. He smiled an uneasy smile, clearly confused, he gazed into the empty space between them, his gaze wanting, wondering, the sultry sound of Ellie Goulding's "Explosions" flittering between their hooded glances, Jenna stared at him, hard, her eyes sad, depressed even, she locked her eyes onto his, brushing down her skirt, She held her hand out, he took it effortlessly.

"Craig I need to talk to you" her voice hushed, barely audible against the music, her face devoid of expression, what could he take from this? Nothing of course! She was closed off now, her hands trembling he noticed from the corners of his eyes the vibrations ushering against his own fingers, the awkward glance on his face catching Jenna's equally mirroring each other's distain, he shuffled closer to her, her hand still firm against his, clammy though, the sweat warm against his fingers, he held her hands tighter.

"What?" he croaked, his eyes fleeting between her face and her naked legs, those legs, so pin up perfect, so shapely yet her face so guarded so unsure he leant in, catching the ghost of a breath against his cheek, he wondered what was troubling her, she was different, extremely different, he nuzzled against her naked neck, her breath altered slightly, nervous beneath his touch. She cleared her throat, the sound melancholy, sad and contrite with emotion.

"Craig, I love you" she whispered, her eyes closed against his warm touch, her fingers tensed at her words, his flexed slightly, his fingers on his free hand skimmed her cheek, her skin so polished, coated in makeup yet so soft and needing. His eyes locked again onto hers, steely, hard, piercing blue, tranquil yet as rugged as the sea, he lunged forward planting a soft chastised kiss on her cheek

"I love you too" the words escape his mouth before he's even had a chance to revise them. The breath in his throat hitched as he said the words, unsure whether he really meant them. His finger grazed against her bare cheek. She looked distressed, unsure if his words, she forced her head away from his, her movements fragile, small, he looked direct into her eyes, she trembled beneath his hard stare, trying her hardest to captivate her glare away from him.

"Your Kiki's dad Craig" She swallowed hard as she spoke, Craig's head instantly snapped back, his hand snatched away from hers as thought the words had burnt him a look of sheer sweet confusion etched onto his handsome face. "I beg you're fucking pardon" he scoffed, his eyes full of malice, their usual blue intensified deeply, his hands shaking tremendously, every inch of his skin sensitized, he glared none too kindly at Jenna, his head shook in complete disbelief.

"It's true Craig" the faint whisper left her lips, she held her hand back out to him, he snatched his away instantly, his hands placed on his lap, his scattered brain trying to even comprehend what Jenna was saying to him. A Daughter, what the actual fuck, he thought. His head suddenly flooded with images of the precious little girl whom he loved so much, his? No it couldn't be.

"You're a fucking liar Jen!" he found his voice loud, vibrating off the walls, he looked at her with disgust, his eyes burning into her pale white skin, he had never been so fucking angry in all his life. Who the fuck did Jenna think she was? After all this time; after she had sworn blind to him that Kiki was some random's that she had met, he felt such a fool for believing her. Craig's eyes burned with hate, pure unadulterated hate, he had never been so fucking angry in his life, his stomach was dancing, completely tied in disgusted knots. He exhaled a sharp, almost glass like breath. He looked briefly at Jenna before standing, his lips curved deliciously into a line of disapproval. He was so sexy yet he was destructive and capable of anything if the mood took him. He turned to walk away, Jenna stood and pulled him back toward her, she was pleading now her voice small and pointless barely audible in the small enclosed space, Not that Craig was listening of course; The tiny dress that she wore now bunched up around her milky thighs, his lips puckered, the grim line set even further as he glanced at this foreign object before him. She again smoothed it down with her fingers the silky sheen of the skirt glowing slightly; Craig didn't even look back as her hand grasped his;

"What the fuck is this Jen?" he spat, his voice so distinguished, so bitter as he spoke, his body rejecting her, pulling his hands away from her as though she was dangerous to touch. He stepped away; the electricity between them charged, she stepped closer to him, her eyes begging him to understand, begging him to believe. She glared at this man she loved so much;

"Craig I swear, She is yours" her voice barely a whisper, as she pulled back from him, she knew she had crossed the boundaries tonight but she didn't care. Craig needed to know their little predicament.

"Why now?" he added, his voice filled with emptiness and sadness all at the same time, his neediness simply alien to Jenna, he was usually so strong minded, so hard faced, and here he was tears pooling in the corners of his melancholy eyes, his face crumpled, distraught. His handsome face somewhat sallow, pale, he ran his hands through his hair his fists clenching tightly beneath his touch. Jenna stepped back away from him, her eyes sombre, saddened that it had come to this, her breath hitched in her throat, the sound slicing through the silence.

"I couldn't tell you" she whispered, her voice low and husky "I didn't want it to come between us, you don't WANT me Craig you never have" her voice trailed off as she glanced at a spot on the wall instead of looking directly at him. He tensed, his muscles rippling almost busting out of his shirt;

"It's not that I don't Want you Jen, it's that I don't see the need to complicate things" his voice soft, sad even as he glared at her his eyes dancing in his head, his stare burning into her, angry smouldering making her seemingly defenceless. He leant against the door frame, his gaze hooded, dreamy, his lip hanging sexily, pouting slightly but keeping his feelings concealed and Jenna had never found him more alluring in all the years of knowing him.

"Well Craig that's what I want" her hands spread out in front of her, a gesture of pure need "I need the hearts and flowers, I need you to want me, love me, own me" her voice sickly sweet to his ears, but he couldn't react to her now, it wouldn't be fair knowing that in a few hours from now, to them all, he would be dead. His scorching eyes left hers, she would never understand how much it would hurt him to walk away but he had to play the safe card of this. He made his way to the door, smiling sadly at her and the horrible sad tears in his eyes evident, aching to strain from their confinements.

"I'm sorry Jen but I don't believe you" he whispered, kissing her forehead before leaving, the door slamming none too gently behind him, she was routed to the spit, literally rendered speechless. Her mouth dipped to the perfect "O" the lingering of his kiss trailing her, coursing the blood through her veins to boil. She had never ever been so angry in all her days but she couldn't move, shock had set in and she could feel the sweat pouring off her, each and every inch of her skin over sensitive every single follicle of her hair literally stood on ends saluting her anger. She was breathless, simply taken more than aback at his words "I don't believe you" what did her think she was? Some kind of fucking slut! She was furious, livid even, she wandered into the living room her head all over the place as the tears finally came, racking sobs that completely crippled her, enveloped her in her sadness. She glanced around, the image of his face everywhere, that smiling smug bastard his hands all over her in every picture, she took one of the frames from the mantle and slammed it against the hard wood flooring, seeing it shatter into a thousand pieces she felt her release, a little of the tension erased, her whole body sick with desire and pure unadulterated hate such a heady concoction, so mind numbing in its intensity, her arms swept the set of photo frames from the mantle watching them shatter against the wood, erupting glass around the small space her breath fast paced, angry, her carnal screams reverberating around the blank space. How fucking dare he! Jenna glanced around at the carnage before her, a demented giggle escaping her lips, uncalled for but necessary. She glared around her, her whole body on fire each movement preconceived, she dropped to her knees, her hands tugged at her long glossy mane, her sobs loud, echoing around the confines of her living room, her palms trying to brush away the tears cascading down her face of course getting nowhere. The pang of pure grief struck her stomach, why wouldn't he believe her? She had never given him cause to believe otherwise, he had taken her in every way possible, her virginity was his, her who entire sex life consisted of one name and one name only Craig fucking Carter, Mr Oh my drop your fucking knickers. She felt a fool, a complete fucking idiot and now here she was crying, more than crying, despairing over him, over Craig. Her "so called" Best friend. The man who promised to protect her from the world yet here he was now abandoning her.

And yet here she was.... Never had she wanted him, more than she did now..... Did that make her as fucked up as he was? She didn't quite know.

Chapter Sixty

Claire Horran clutched her glass of wine tightly in her sweaty hands, her whole body quivering with an aching need for her son's precious memory her tears rolling slowly down her face as she listened so intently to Jenna's story her ears pricked with every word. Lee sat beside her, his mouth pressed into a hard grim line. His body rigid, tense, his face giving nothing away, void of expression as he listened to Jenna, her voice sad, somewhat depressing. Craig had been one of his best friends; he had been devastated when he had died. Yet Lee couldn't get his head around Craig's apparent reaction to Kiki being his, he had revelled in that little girls presence since the day she had been born. He couldn't quite put the pieces together, Craig had loved Kiki, loved her with a passion so carnal, he would never have abandoned her... Surely not? He would have killed for that little girl Lee sat silent, sinking further into the background as he pondered over what Jenna was saying, it didn't strike him as the truth. Not for a single second. But he listened; his ears burning as though someone had set them alight with a hot match. He took a large glass of wine and glugged at it maliciously, it had warmed from the atmosphere, sickly on the palate, cheap to taste, but it was wet, just what his mouth needed to recover from the revelry. He said nothing, he glanced at Claire, she had aged a lifetime in the last few hours and she looked so stricken. Her usually plump pink cheeks were slightly sunken, her usually jovial face devoid of any happiness, she look so different, so sad, and Lee automatically felt pity for her. He grasped her hand, in a friendly manner of course, a desperate smile playing on his lips. The atmosphere shifted, slightly awkward in the uncomfortable silence.

"But Jen He loved Kiki, I can't see him abandoning her when he knew she was his" Lee's words silent, barely audible and he regretted them as soon as they had escaped the confines of his big mouth. Claire was still shaking her head, still unsure, still so desperate to claw the information out of Jenna, her precious boy, as if it wasn't enough that he was dead, here they all were like vultures slandering his good name. It was true, he had worshipped Kiki, he would have happily given her the world and that's what Claire couldn't grasp, a few hours after Jenna had spilt her guts to Craig he had been stabbed, for a single split second the horrific thought that Jenna could have been involved crossed her mind. Her stomach tied in knots instantly, she released the thought immediately, no Jenna loved Craig, and Claire knew how much the girl was hurting. Or was it her own guilt she was masking with her grief. Claire suddenly felt light headed, sick even; she gulped the rest of her wine down in one and urged the girl to continue. Her eyes bright with fear, her heart hammering a tattoo in her chest, the blood literally rushing through her veins her anxiousness enveloping her as she filled her glass once more.

Chapter Sixty One

Previously

Johnny Fenton ran his fingers through his hair, his breathing laboured and his face flushed an angry bitter red as he walked into the bathroom to find Cath with a toothbrush rammed down her neck, her eyes wide in sheer terror. She was instantly on the defensive screaming at him to get the fuck out, but Johnny just stared, his whole body froze to the spot, his mouth dry suddenly from simply gaping, he had so many words on the tip of his tongue yet his brain wouldn't let them leave his mouth, his eyeballs flitting from the dirty toothbrush handle, to the vomit that was splashed into the toilet bowl, his hand instantly raised to his mouth but it was a passive movement, his eyes glazed over as he took in the tragic scene before him. Cath's pretty cocktail dress bunched up, her usually straight bob messy from the sweat, her mascara running slightly from crying, her fingers still clasped around the toothbrush handle.

"What the fuck is this Cath" He finally gasped after what seemed like an age. He slid down the doorframe so he was sat opposite her. His head leant against the solid wood, taking in each little movement his beautiful girlfriend made he had never felt so stricken in his life. He had always known Cath hated her body, every time they had attempted sex it was always the same old drama of turning the light off. Despite constantly reassuring her that he thought she was fucking beautiful, and she was of course. Johnny gazed at her with wide eyes, his expression saddened now as he saw the tears trickling down Cath's sallow cheeks. She dropped the toothbrush onto the floor and turned to flush the evidence of her foul illness away. Johnny scooted over to her and reluctantly rested her head against his chest, her sobs came then, fast and heavy racking her body. Finally someone had caught her, maybe now she could find it in herself to stop. Johnny kissed the top of her head running his fingers against the small of her back whispering her worries away with his delicate voice. He had genuinely had no idea about her being this fragile about her looks. To him, she was absolutely perfect, flawless and here she was feeling so low and upset with herself that she was making herself ill to try and be thin! The thought depressed Johnny and he kissed her once more, holding her tighter to his beating chest, holding back his tears as he choked on the words that barely came from his mouth, he had been rendered literally speechless for the first time in his life.

"How long" he whispered against her soft, slightly damp hair.

"Years" was all she could muster as a reply. Johnny sagged against the bathtub, his long fingers skimming her soft flesh, pricking her skin; he had never felt so vulnerable to someone in his life. But this woman had him completely mesmerized. He had always been so hard faced, so empty before he met Cath, and now he felt serene, happy there was nothing he wouldn't do for her. She made his life worth every single waking moment and he would do anything in his power to make her better, to make her see how beautiful she truly was. He pulled her tighter to him, his muscular arms hugging her hard with a carnal need to feel her body on his.

"Why didn't you tell me?" his voice soft against her skin, melodic even and he felt a tiny shiver creep over Cath's body, she relaxed into his embrace and he huddled her closer, smelling her musky perfume drinking in her beautiful Cath smell. He was terrified; he had never felt so child like in all his days, he swallowed down the painful lump that appeared in his throat, holding back the salty tears that threatened to spill from his eyes. She simply shrugged her shoulders rigid against his chest, her breathing low despite her whole body shivering.

"Jon" she whispered silently, her fingers knotting in his own, her usually finely manicured nails bitten to the quick "I've got to tell you something" she continued, her whole body trembling now as she turned her gaze toward him. Johnny's eyes flitted back and forth from her eyes to her mouth, confusion etched on his beautiful young face. He shook his head glumly; he didn't feel like his head could take anymore but he sucked back a harsh breath before nodding his head for her to continue.

The words were out of her mouth before Johnny could even think of processing them, Pregnant, she couldn't be? Not after doing this to herself, Johnny pushed her away from him, his face etched with anger, his lip curled into a devious snarl as he snorted violently in her direction, his look almost feral as he rose to his feet, his eyes never leaving Cath, even as he put his fist through the bathroom mirror and a million shards of glass showered her body falling like razor sharp confetti around her, the vindictive flicker of a smile playing on his beautiful lips, but it wasn't a happy grin, it was malicious, unbelieving, He wasn't her Johnny anymore, she could see that plain from his face, the blood pumping from his clenched fists drenching the sterile white bathroom tiles, splattering the hem of her skimpy cocktail dress. He turned on his heel, his shoes sticky with his own blood leaving imprints on the carpeted hall as he walked away, laughing hysterically.

Chapter Sixty Two

As the fresh air hit Johnny he gasped breathlessly, fear choking every single inch of his lean body, he slid down the thick concrete wall and the tears that he had been holding back finally came rushing down his cheeks, his whole body was shaking nervously, his long fingers running through his hair as sheer desperation gripped him, his shoulders slumped forward as he vomited violently all over the cold concrete veranda, his expression ashen as the anxiety that had built inside him came exploding out. He waited as his breathing slowed back to a reasonable level, the harsh breaths constricting in his throat, he gasped as he wiped his eyes on the back of his jacket. He slipped his mobile from his pocket and punched a number on the keypad, wiping his mouth with the back of his cuff as he held the phone to his ear.

"We need to meet, now! Fifteen minutes, your place" his voice was unrecognisable as the words tumbled from his dry lips. Hanging up he slipped his phone back in his pocket, checking his face in one of the neighbour's windows he noticed his hair was tangled, unruly, and messy on the top of his head, his skin milky pale, he looked as though he had aged a decade in the last fifteen minutes. He made his way down the steps and across the Belmonte, He had to see Craig, and he had to see him fucking now

∎∎

Johnny sat on the edge of Craig's bed relaying the afternoon's events to him, Cath's pregnancy had changed everything for him, He knew he was having second thoughts, Kenny's constant demanding to take Craig's life was getting on his fucking nerves and now he was sat here his mouth running away with him as Craig sat open mouthed, listening intently. Johnny knew he was babbling, he felt like such a fucking prick sitting here contemplating backing out, but he was too far imbedded in this to walk away now unharmed. Kenny would kill him, he was sure of that, but Craig, he scared the living fuck out of Johnny and while they were partners, Craig held all the cards tightly to his chest. Craig shifted in his seat, held his hand up, Johnny instantly stopped talking, and sucking in a breath he paused mid sentence;

"Tomorrow, it happens tomorrow" Craig whispered into the darkness, his voice thick with sadness, heavy with sheer vulnerability and Johnny caught a glimpse for just a second, that Craig was scared. Craig knew he wasn't ready yet, wasn't ready to say goodbye, wasn't ready to leave all of the things he had to say to Jenna unspoken. This wasn't the right time for their plan to get rolling but he couldn't let his friend miss out any more of his unborn child's life than he needed to. If it happened now and he went down for six years, on a guilty charge he would only do three, he'd be out by the time his child was two and a half. He'd still have time to secure his bond with the baby. Craig's world was always either black or white there was no in-between. Logically when he thought about it he saw it as helping Johnny in the long run. Johnny nodded, rose to his feet and left, not saying another word. The pressure and the reality of what was happening had hit them and the next twenty four hours would change their lives. Forever.

Chapter Sixty Three

Present

It had been a long night and Jenna, Claire and Lee sat in comfortable silence in the dimly lit living room, it was six o'clock in the morning and it had been to say the least a night of revelations for them all. They had talked and talked some more, the sadness of the truth etched on all of their faces. So it was out, Kiki Shearan was Craig's daughter, Claire's heart had never ever felt so torn, not even losing her son and now her daughter came close to the grief that had all but consumed her, she was exhausted, emotion had taken her to the depths and it was a bittersweet revelation. Part of her son had been kept alive in the gorgeous little girl who had become part of her world and Claire didn't know whether she felt happy or even further saddened by the harsh reality. The child had been born from a mistake, Craig and Jenna had never even become serious about their relationship, despite Claire's love for Jenna, she obviously hadn't been what her son had wanted in the end. The questions that swam around in Claire's head had all but crushed her relentlessly, merciless in their assault. The morning was breaking and they were all wary about the changes in their relationships within the last twelve hours, Claire was now dubious about Jenna anxious even, she knew their friendship was hanging on the finest thread and another painful revelation and it would snap gloriously in front of all their faces. She stood, said her muffled goodbye and left the flat quietly, leaving Jenna and Lee sitting in an uncomfortable silence. Both drowned in their own thoughts, hazy from the wine and the sheer exhaustion that the night had bought them. He smiled and awkward smile as their eyes caught briefly, both glancing away quickly not wanting to speak through fear of saying the wrong thing. Jenna's eyes were wide, shock set on her stunning face, her curvaceous lips pursed tightly into a grim line, she looked, harder, fearless even and Lee had to admire the girl's courage for standing up to Claire even in Claire's fragile mental state. Lee had to wonder though how the night's events would change Claire in the long run, she was already fragile, unstable, unhinged somewhat and he had to think what the future would hold for Claire if she was pushed any further off the edge.

Chapter Sixty Four

Craig sat at the bar, nursing a large gin and tonic looking and feeling every inch the rich bastard that he was, he looked around the club, at the plush furnishings all black leather and silk red scatter cushions, He had envisaged the place as a red room and had built it around that concept, and now it was a fucking spectacle. Every mans ideal playroom. All the girls who worked here specialised in BDSM, alternative sex was a seller and so many of the dirty fuckers who frequented the place were literally chucking the money his way for a chance to meet one of Craig's girls. He smiled at the thought, not bad for a boy from the streets, he laughed ironically taking another long sip of his drink. His whole demeanour had changed since he had been away, he looked more refined, acted more refined, his clothes dripped high expense, from the Rolex watch, the Gucci suit, the Jimmy Choo's on his feet to the Cartier diamond stud in his left ear. He dripped nothing but money, combined with his bewitching good looks he was a heady drug to any girl who swooned at his well dressed feet. He smiled to himself taking another sip of his drink. He stared at the St George Cross mounted on the wall with its leather cuffs hanging loosely against the dark wood, the chains and shackles that hung from the ceiling, dancing in the subtle glow that came from the dimly lit black diamond chandeliers dripping in crystals that reflected off every surface of the lounge area. The stage lit with heavy red spotlights, the diamante studded dance pole glistening in the glow. The place truly was beautiful, and despite owning six other clubs in and around London this one The Mamma Rouge was his favourite. He glanced over at Dave, who was busy polishing glasses, his floppy black hair folding slightly over his forehead, every now and again Craig noticed he stopped to stare at his reflection in the glasses. He liked Dave, he was a good guy, he had a LOT to learn but he was an all round nice person, trustworthy and honest. Craig knew as long as he was on the payroll he would work hard to please Craig. With power came notoriety and now Craig was swimming in it! He had made a name for himself when he had been away and now he would show everyone just how much of a face he truly was. He raised his glass to the far end of the bar; Dave glanced and nodded back at his boss;

"To us Davey Boy, we run the fucking world!" he chuckled, boyish charm oozing from every single expensive pore of his skin. He was Craig fucking Carter, and he was fucking back! His laughter reverberated infectiously through the empty bar; this was Craig Carter's playground, And play he fucking would. He knocked back the last of his gin and tonic and instantly nodded at Dave to get him a refill. Which of course Dave none too kindly jumped upon. Dominance was something Craig Carter loved within all aspects of his life and he had to laugh at the irony of everyone now jumping to his beat instead of him being the jumper himself. He was his own man now, in business and indeed in pleasure. He had everything, money, notoriety, his little girl who officially owned his heart and his head, Kiki was his everything he would in all honesty go to the ends of the earth for her. She had shown him what true unconditional love was, he knew that the little girl missed her mother, but with each day that passed it got easier, so much easier and Craig wondered whether there would ever be a time where Jenna would be nothing but a distant memory to the little girl, just like he had been. It had broken his heart to leave his life behind, but the Belmonte broke people, made them do things just to survive, drugs, crime and sex were all that lingered over the Belmonte like a deadly mist, it was a place for the broken, in hind sight Craig was glad he no longer had to just be a ball boy in the world of crime just to make a few extra quid. Oh no the tables had well and truly turned. He ran lucrative, efficient businesses, owned various properties abroad and was currently building a fetish club and a chain of fetish boutiques in Hollywood, for the big time S&M market, he was going to bring bondage to the 21st century, make it classy, not the taboo of the sex world. He wanted to allow people to be able to explore their sexual fantasies freely without judgement. He had a vision for the American club, very gothic, leather and Lace, Girls in cages, sex shows after dark the full works, all tastefully done and for display purposes only, he didn't want people starting a fucking orgy in his clubs! He had met with a few girls, professional dominatrix's who were going to run the stage shows and he had been giving a rather mind numbing, intoxicating performance to the song Chandelier by Sia, he revelled in the art of seduction and he relished in the idea of unleashing the possibilities. He knew what he wanted to create and hopefully if it kicked off he could plan to expand. He knew it was a long shot project but all of his British clubs were raking it in, and America was known for its lucrative alternative sex industry and to Craig merging the two would be the ultimate money spinner. Johnny didn't have long left on his sentence and he was going to come out and run the British clubs as his own. Of course Craig's little project was going to take him across the pond; He wanted to control and oversee all of the work over in America. He had already bought himself a fully furnished penthouse above the prestigious Lake Hollywood Knolls. It boasted five bedrooms, huge garden, basement gym and sauna the works! And the view, well the view was simply breathtaking, all palm trees and tropical sunsets. It would be a fresh start for him and Kiki and of course he and Johnny would be fucking rolling in it! He smiled at the thought, he had always had an eye for a niche in the market and here he was to fill it! Craig Carter wanted a slice of the pie so to speak.

Chapter Sixty Five

Dom lay sprawled out naked in his double bed staring at the ceiling, his delicious muscles rippled highlighted by the morning sun that crept through the window his hair floppy, curled sexily on his head and his three day stubble making him look wildly beautiful. His mouth was dry and his head pounded from too much cocaine, he could happily sleep for a week. The last few hours had been a blur and his heart felt heavy in his chest. He knew in his head he had done the right thing telling Claire about Kiki, but his heart told him that he had well and truly fucked things royally with Jenna. He was devastated, he had really invested himself into their relationship and he had completely fallen for her, he was somewhat smitten. He sat up, taking in the scene before him, clothes piled shabbily in a heap on the carpet, coke tipped out all over his bedside cabinet, the empty vodka bottle that lay beside him on the bed, the blankets hanging off bunched in a crumpled pile towards the foot of the bed, his body so sticky with sweat that he literally clung to the crisp sheets, running his fingers through his wild hair he quickly yanked on a pair of boxers from the bedside cabinet, rubbing his eyes as he tried to focus in the dim light, his skin sensitive and he was still buzzing slightly from the drugs, he didn't even know how he had managed to get to bed, what concerned him more was that he didn't know how long he had been there. He stretched out, glancing across on the floor, he stopped dead in his tracks as he noticed the second pair of clothes crumpled on the opposite side of the bed, The silky red bra, matching Lace panties, skinny Jeans and for a second his face lit up as thoughts of Jenna spilled into his head, had she come here last night? Had he finally fucked her? His head felt as though it might implode with sweet anticipation. He could hear the rush of water from the shower and his heart rate escalated as the blood sped through his veins, his whole body was on high alert, his skin hypersensitive with intrigue wanting, needing answers. Had they sorted things out? Did she finally want him? His mind was blown with possibilities. He sat back against the headboard, running his hands through his glossy messy hair, the sweat making it even more unruly than usual and he tried and failed to control it with his fingers alone. He hated to think what it looked like, but he didn't care, just fucked hair suited him. He smiled at the irony, what if she was here; he smiled a genuinely shy nervous smile at the thought. What would he say to her?

The shower went dead and Dom tried his hardest to listen for any movements, he pulled the sheets back onto the bed, spreading them out flatly and frantically he tried to clear up the chaos that was his bedroom. He was just about to shovel the coke rocks on the bedside cabinet back into the small wrap of cling film that lay beside the mess on the table. A shadow caught his eye momentarily and he looked up, his jaw nearly smacked the floor as the realisation of who was stood there in the doorway wrapped seductively in a crisp white towel, hair tumbling over her slim shoulders hit him;

"Hi" she smiled shyly at him, Dom gulped back speechless in his reply;

"Did we" his eyes flitting from her clothes on the floor to the messed up sheets on the bed as words finally found his dry, parched mouth, she smiled coyly, running her fingers through the long dark hair and suddenly Dom felt inferior, the stirring in his boxers evident despite him wishing away the thoughts that invaded his mind. They couldn't have... Could they?

Her head tossed back as she stifled a giggle, her laugh playfully infectious, Dom couldn't help but smile back, nervously, fully aware that her eyes were locked on his. Water droplets snaking down her naked chest glistening in the pale light as they traced seductively between her full breasts.

"I like my men fully alert and responsive thank you Dom, and you were not responsive in the least" she giggled, and silently Dom Breathed an inward sigh of pure relief. She was gorgeous, her body curvy and full, deliciously kissed with water from the shower, and as quick as they entered his head he shook away the thoughts of fucking her immediately.

"Say something, you're making me nervous" she half smiled, detangling her dripping hair with her long skilled fingers.

"I thought you were Jenna" he whispered, regretting the stupid words as soon as they had escaped his mouth. He saw the disgust spread over her pretty face, the sadness in her eyes were not lost on him at his rejection, she distracted herself by picking up her mangled pile of clothes from the carpet, trying to organise her inside out jeans and her creased hoodie. She grappled with her scattered garments, scooping them up into her arms and shunting herself towards the doorway as she saw the sheer confusion etched onto Dom's handsome face

"Lisa, I'm sorry" Dom called out after her, his heart not fully in his limp apology. He didn't attempt to go after her, he didn't even attempt to call her back, when the door slammed violently ten minutes later, he breathed an outwards sigh and slumped none too gently back into bed.

Chapter Sixty Six

Jenna opened the door to a dishevelled and slightly petulant Lisa, her creased lips set into an incredible full beautiful pout, her clothes creased, her hair messed bunched into a tight ponytail, loose tendrils spilling around her face. She was breathless, her eyes ablaze and Jenna was suddenly taken aback by her friends appearance.

"He fucking loves you Jen" she pointed across the hall to Dom's front door, her body constricting with the harshness of her breathing. Jenna pulled her into her wilted embrace, their tired bodies sagged against each other, Jenna cuddled her close, smelling the sweet just washed smell of her friend, and in contrast to her unwashed self she felt inferior. She stepped back admiring Lisa at an angle, she felt like she hadn't seen her in an age, she looked amazing, glamorous even. Even now her hair still dripping wet, her clothes edging on over creased, her eyes still buzzing, dancing around from last night's drugs she still looked beautiful. Outstretched in her arms she looked Lisa up and down;

"What?" she questioned hesitantly, the notes of surprise in Jenna's voice weren't unnoticed by Lisa, who smiled, a full megawatt smile, she truly was gorgeous in that singular moment.

"Dom, he's in love with you, you silly bitch" Lisa laughed, a head tilted back full guttural laugh that invaded the dense space between them. Her fingers pointing to the door in child like admiration. Jenna's face was picture perfect, high eyebrows, wide eyes mouth dipped in sheer confusion. She studied Lisa closely; surely she was still off it. She shook her head, disapproving of Lisa's words. She stepped back; hand on the wall as she backed her way into the comfort of her living room, surrounded by Craig and his all consuming appearance. Love! Dominic! She almost burst out laughing. No she assumed Lisa must definitely have it wrong! She stared into the wide, dancing eyes of her friend and cackled, a high pitched chortle that completely consumed Lisa with confusion surely Jenna didn't think this was a joke; she stared hard, trying to reason with her friend, her laugh reaching a sudden deafening crescendo. Lisa pulled at Jenna's grubby dressing gown, the urge to slap her friends face hard completely overthrew her, and she was laughing with almost hyena like haste, the pitch bordering on lunacy. Lisa just stared into the blank space between them.

"Are you fucking serious?" Jenna quizzed, when words finally managed to make their way out of her mouth without sounding like a hysterical wail. Lisa simply nodded, not even regarding the shock on her friends face as the intensity of Lisa's words hit her like a stinging slap. Jenna found Lisa's crazy eyed gaze and slowly the laughter turned into simple silence as she came down from whatever planet she was currently on, Lisa's face was as straight as a die and Jenna sucked a harsh breath in as she realised Lisa wasn't fucking around.

"How do you know?" Jenna pushed, a hint of subtle jealousy overflowing over her usually velvet tone, shocking her as she spoke the words breathlessly. She stepped back further into the backdrop, surrounded by the face she loved and regarded the most. Craig was her safe place and here was Lisa wading in like the martyr she was, all bed fucked hair and seductive smile. She glanced at her friend for long moments; she saw exactly where this was going! Fuck only last night she had kicked him out and already he was getting under her so called mates. Lisa hovered in the doorway, her eyeballs protruding, bulging from the sockets and Jenna couldn't help the sadistic snarl that crept across her ghost white face. Jenna lunged forward smacking Lisa sharply across her face and all of the last few weeks of pent up anger and frustration exploded the surface and she erupted in fistfuls of hair and resounding slaps to the face, she had never ever been a violent person but she had been pushed to the edge this week! Her daughter was fucking missing, her best friend was dead, his mother had all but abandoned her and now Lisa was fucking her said boyfriend. She was furious, absolutely livid and when the tears unavoidably came she stood back and viewed her handy work completely and utterly spent. She shook her head and walked back inside and slammed the door behind her, what the fuck was she turning into! She couldn't answer herself as she slid down the front door and lay in a heap on the carpet crying harshly to oblivion. Her head was splitting and she honestly felt as though the heart had been ripped from her chest, maybe if she'd fucked him that night maybe he would have stayed she thought ironically clutching her knees to her chest and feeling her whole body letting go of the small amount of sanity that she had left Clinging to her limp frail body she finally let go and surrendered to the weeks of sleepless nights, the weeks of staying strong to please others and she let out an almost animal like howl as the fear and anxiety embraced her, she was all alone, alone and helpless and right at this moment she would give anything to be with Craig, to be safe in his arms one more time.

Previously

Johnny Fenton sat in the communal gardens of the Belmonte smoking his last joint as a free man, the thought unnerved him as much as it excited him, he toked long and hard on his cigarette, the hazy fog making him brave, he had been to see Kenny, told him that the hit was arranged for this morning and as of this afternoon Craig Carter would be lying on a cold slab in the mortuary. Kenny of course had almost come in his pants at the thought and Johnny knew that he had the man's trust implicitly, the funny old cunt. He knew the rewards would outweigh the cons in this scenario, Craig had been setting up the business for months now, they were already worth hundreds of thousands of pounds and they only owned the one club between them, no one knew of course they all thought Craig was off doing English literature in college, in truth he'd turned up at the induction, fucked the tutor and she occasionally sent letters to Craig's mothers saying how well he was doing. It had been an easy camouflage of their clubs, fetish was the new thing and sex was the oldest business in the book and it just made sense to merge the two. Johnny felt the blade siding up against his jacket pocket, the excitement was too much and sucked a harsh breath inward as he took another puff of his joint, he knew Craig wouldn't be long ready, they had staged it perfectly, there were cameras facing towards the gardens so there would be no dragging investigation, in a sense he was being caught red handed. He was pleading guilty as planned and he was looking at a cushy little cell in Strangeways for a short time. Craig had already paid off the judge so he knew that he was only facing three to five years for the act of "manslaughter". Craig would throw the first few inches and they were away. Everyone was on standby, everything carefully planned, months of preparations, months of work, months of acting like Kenny Creepy Kreegan's best mate all boiled down to this. He smiled, on his release he would be a multi millionaire, the thought intoxicated him. He could see himself married to Cath, their little baby running around the gardens of their large manor home, the notoriety, the fame, the sheer power that was to come was the most bewitching cocktail and Johnny couldn't wait to get the ball rolling. He flicked the butt end of his joint to the ground and watched as it fell, fluttering like a willow to the concrete below, he looked up, Craig was in the doorway to his mothers, kissing her his last goodbye, the thought saddened Johnny momentarily, all this to clear a drug debt that Craig could more than afford, the real reason of course was revenge. Revenge on Kenny for treating him like his gofer instead of his equal, the fact that Kenny couldn't kill him outright, he had to use someone else as innocent as Johnny to do his work. The fact that Kenny had hired Craig back into the firm knowing that he had indeed been planning Craig's demise behind his back. Craig hated inferiority, unless of course it was his own. Johnny loved Craig's enthusiasm, he was clever, funny and completely smart, he was a fucking genius when it came to business ideas and he knew what would make money, and of course keep them making money. He also admired Craig for his courage and his mental strength, having to put his whole life on the line just to propel them both into the real business world and of course make his name known. He watched Craig's arms loop around his mothers neck, he kissed her goodbye as she always did, the single moment so precious and for a second Johnny was frozen in time, Craig with his rucksack on his back, smart suit pants and a clean shirt, he looked every inch the model student as Craig turned away from Claire, Johnny breathed an outwards sigh of relief, it was here, it was time.

Craig Groaned as the knife struck his flesh over and over again, the crimson blooms springing up all over the front of his shirt, bursting brilliantly into sheer intense colour. It didn't hurt much; his mind was numb, completely lost in the job at hand. He smiled at Johnny, the boys face was wrung with sheer hate, disgust even. His harsh breaths forced out into the cold air in heavy blows leaving clouds of condensation hanging in the damp air... This cunt could win an Oscar Craig thought; the irony wasn't lost on him at all. He felt his body crumble as he hit the ground with a sickening thud. He gazed up at Johnny who threw the bloody knife down beside Craig, turned and fled. Craig closed his eyes, the sound of blood rushing through his ears broke his silent reverie, this was it, it had finally began, he smiled as the sound of the ambulance rang out in the distance and the petulant screams of his mother sang out across the Belmonte estate, Craig lay back and let the world close in around him, "and the Oscar goes to, Craig fucking Carter he thought as he slipped into cold unconsciousness, the smirk on his face never left him, had it really been that fucking easy?.

Chapter Sixty Eight

In the days that followed Craig spent his time recovering in a private suite with top British and American doctors taking care of his wounds, they stitched him back up, all of the surface wounds were cleaned and he was allowed to rest away the days. Johnny had been arrested and remanded in custody; it had been a pure flawless performance from both sides and now Craig could breathe easy and take his time on his recovery; his focus was solely on getting better and building his business empire into something perfect for when Johnny was eventually released. He really had played a blinder and Craig had never felt so proud in his life. Of course at first guilt had consumed him, he had felt like the ultimate cunt for putting is mother and Jenna through this. But now, looking at it through his rose tinted glasses he realised that unfortunately this had been the only way that he was guaranteed a fresh start. This way he could come back and literally storm the underworld. He had never felt such an intoxicated high as he did now, he was free, free to start again and it was a thought that simply blew his mind. He had never felt so serene, flopping his arm lazily over his eyes, he succumbed to a luxuriously long sleep. Despite being broken, battered and aching, he smiled. It was finally over, the beginning of the next chapter in his young life had just started, he had done it, and he had effectively gotten away with murder.

Chapter Sixty Nine

Present Day

Jenna awoke to a heavy almost needy thumping on the front door; she crept from her sofa to the hallway, her eyes strained against the bright sunlight that burst in through the glass panels. She saw the outline of a body against the glass, running hands through a curly mane and her guts knotted deep inside her as she instinctively knew who the body belonged to. She sighed dejectedly and prepared herself for the onslaught that was about to come. Opening the door slowly, her eyes hesitantly met Dom's and she instantly looked away, this was too much, the heartbreak of his betrayal still fresh in her weary mind. But by God did he look absolutely drop dead gorgeous, his jet black hair wild, floppy and wet from the shower, his stubble so rugged against his smooth cheeks, he was a complete juxtaposition to Craig, but he was still fucking stunning, a complete rugged Adonis. Jenna stared at the floor, her eyes couldn't even contemplate a glance of his handsome face, she could already feel the tears pooling in her eyes despite trying her hardest to hold them back, and she felt a single tear roll down her sallow cheek, hitting the threshold between them.

"What do you want Dom" she whispered, her eyes still fixed on the floor. Her voice painfully strained as she spoke. She felt weak in his presence, she couldn't even dream to think what she looked like right now and she hated the fact that he was looking at her, so low, so desolate. She felt his finger curl under her chin, the nail biting her skin gently with the gentle pressure, tilting it slightly so she was caught between his hot blazing gaze, he had such beautiful eyes. She turned away, her focus now caught on the framework of the front door. Her whole body tense, her stomach tied in delicious knots of anticipation despite her heartache, she loved this man, despite her earlier reservations, and her reactions towards Lisa had confirmed her feelings. She had never in a million years imagined she would find a way to move on from Craig, but here he was, kind, gentle loving Dom. His glassy eyes cut into every inch of her skin with their calculating grey gaze, exploring her as though she was standing there completely naked. The silence between them was infuriating as much as it was exciting, their breaths quickened and both of their hearts were racing it was as though time had stopped around them, Jenna looked up, her eyes finally met his, she swallowed down the urge to vomit such was her anxiety, still he said nothing, his face still devoid of emotion, giving nothing away.

"Why did you do it?" Jenna's words were out of her mouth in a gentle whisper before she could even attempt to revoke them. Her lips faint against her pale face, making her look slightly ill. Dom's face contorted, his eyebrows raised confusion etched on his soft features.

"Did what?" he whispered, leaning into her, dominating her in every single way, his eyes bright captivating despite his obvious confusion at her words. Jenna squirmed beneath him, feeling completely and utterly inferior to this beautiful man.

"Fuck... Lisa" she managed eventually to speak her words filled with embarrassment and her cheeks flushed a dangerous scarlet, Dom wretched back, his look feral, wild, he laughed then a boyish hearty chuckle that consumed him entirely. His face relaxed instantly, Jenna's face mirrored his moments ago, full of confusion. She patiently waited and waited for Dom to come down from his high, euphoric fit of giggles, her face etched into the most serious expression she could manage, despite her exasperation.

"I didn't" he smirked suddenly, his face back immediately to its tranquil calm, his lips curved deliciously he looked like a naughty school boy almost.

"You swear" Jenna protested, arms folded over her ample chest, her lips pouting the perfect cupids bow, fuck she really was beautiful even when she was whinging like a disappointed schoolgirl who'd had her heart broken by the jock. Dom replied with a simple nod of his head and then he was on her, his mouth searching for hers, taking her head in between his long fingers, his tongue exploring her mouth was an almost illicit need, her eyes widened in shock as she responded to his domineering kiss. Her whole body loosened and she was suddenly in his arms pinned against the wall in the hallway, he slammed the front door with his foot, the pictures shaking from the vibration, his hands began trailing her body, feeling every single inch of her slim body, leaving soft kisses down her neck, deep against her collar bone, she threw her head back, her glossy hair tumbling down her back as she gasped loudly. He dug his throbbing erection into her thigh as he trailed his hands down her slender waist, kissing her hard. His fingers found her hair and pulled it gently back so he could nestle his kisses at the base of her bare throat. She moaned softly against his ear, he was completely insatiable, her hands desperately tugging on his short black curly hair, kissing him with sheer lust, this time it felt so right, so perfect. She pulled him in closer swimming in his scent, so different from Craig, he smelled so clean, so fresh, and Jenna was intoxicated. As they continues their raunchy assault He scooped her up into his strong arms spanking her playfully on her backside making her throw her head back, her girlish giggles reverberating around the small space. He bent her down on the bed, pushing her head into the mattress as he ripped off her small g string thong and tossed it aside, and there she was completely naked before him, and the need to simply take her here and now completely enveloped him, quickly he unzipped his fly and wriggled quickly out of his jeans and boxers slinging them in a crumpled heap onto the floor, he sucked a breath inward steadying himself behind her, his hands on her bare behind as he sunk himself deeply into her delicious wetness, she moaned gently beneath him, her hips moving back and forth in perfect sync with his own, his breathing was harsh and laboured as he picked up the pace slightly, her hips reaching his with every sultry stroke, she was so wet for him, her frequent muffled moans into the sheets spurring him on harder and fast until suddenly he came, pouring himself into her, his body shuddering as he found his release, his breathing erratic with lust. He leant over and kissed her neck softly before easing out of her ever so gently. Before pulling her down onto the bed and nestling her into him.

Dom held Jenna's thin body to his own, cuddling her close his nose in her hair as they came back down to normality momentarily from their respective orgasms, he smiled as he gently planted a soft kiss on her sweaty forehead. She arched closer into his naked body breathlessly, brushing her naked backside against him, smiling provocatively as they're gaze finally met.

"Worth the second attempt Miss Shearan?" he smirked as he spoke, planting another delicate kiss on her lips, laying his arm across her flat washboard stomach, holding her so tantalisingly close to him, his long pianist fingers just brushing her breast making her nipples stand ever so expertly to attention. He revelled in her, she truly was the most beautiful woman he had ever seen in his life and now he had finally taken her as his own. The thought made Dom's face split into the biggest most boyish grin he could possibly achieve. She nodded silently; words were more than beyond her as she dropped her head up onto the pillow so that she was staring down at him. His just fucked hair wild on his head, his lips slightly swollen from their hot passionate kiss, his naked body rippled and muscular like something that literally came from a romantic novel. He was stunning to look at, absolutely breathtaking in bed, he was an affectionate lover, her pleasure was tantamount and above all he genuinely did care for her. Love her even. Jenna nuzzled her cheek against the stubble on his chin, kissing his soft lips tentatively before resting her head on his bare chest. What the fuck had she been thinking turning him down the first time? She thought idly as she drifted off into a lazy just fucked slumber.

Chapter Seventy

Craig watched the flat like a hawk ever since he had seen the fancy boy enter but the cunt still hadn't left, this amused Craig almost as much as it made his blood fucking boil. He undid the first few buttons of his shirt and turned on the air con, his eyes never leaving the front door. Kiki hadn't been gone long and already the little slag was getting her kicks with the new bloke opposite. Craig cracked his pale knuckles in fury, he had a good mind to go and knock on the fucking door and pull pretty boy out by his short and fucking curly's. He couldn't wait to take Kiki away from all of this. He knew she missed her mother now, but she was only two, she would adapt, she had to, there was no way Craig was coming back for the slag now. He rolled down the window, barely an inch gap and lit himself a cigarette, puffing gently on the tip, lost deep in uncontrolled thought. He fucking hated this estate; it was the same fucking shit hole it had always been all druggies, unwashed bodies sex and violence. No one here had prospects, no one here even valued their lives, it was a sad realisation for Craig that this was where all of his family were and where he knew all of his family would stay. He couldn't think about that now. Guilt wasn't something that Craig recognised as an emotion anymore, it had all but consumed him at first, but now fuck them, they wanted to mope around this shit hole, leave them crack on, he was taking his daughter and he was off. But first he had the very small matter of Kenny Kreegan to deal with. The smile that played on his lips as he sought revenge was satanic; he couldn't wait to get his hands on Kenny, the jumped old cunt. And when he did there would be murders. He turned to his driver Ronnie and nodded for him to take him home.

Chapter Seventy One

Craig poured himself a stiff drink from the empty bar, the only light came in red bursts from the stage area. He was absolutely shattered and couldn't wait to get home, see Kiki have a shower and get himself to bed; it had been a long uncomfortable day. Intrigue had taken him back to the estate and now he wished with a passion he hadn't bothered. Despite his desperate attempts to hate Jenna, today had shown him two things, one that she had moved on from him, the thought of course ripped him in two. The second was that he was still madly and completely head over heels in love with her. The thought of course killed him. He knocked back his scotch and immediately poured another, pondering over his past was always a hurtful exercise for Craig. He had so many regrets, so many things he wished he had changed; they all of course centred on Jenna fucking Shearan. The thought unnerved him. She was truly the singular most special person he had ever met in his life and he loved her whole heartedly or at least he had done when he was "alive" he had been so scared to tell her, show her in case she rejected him, in case it didn't work and now in the aftermath of it all he knew, that was all he had ever needed to do because she was already in love with him. And for the first time in his life, in the comfort and solace of his empty bar, Craig Carter cried, tears of pure sadness. He had nothing, not really. Money and notoriety were nothing, merely material possessions unless you had someone to share it with. He had even resorted to stealing his own fucking daughter to prove a point to himself, prove he didn't really love Jenna, and prove he didn't care. But all he had realised was that he felt nothing but guilt, he knew Jen was suffering, fuck his people had been watching the poor bitch long enough. He knew she had been taken to hospital, he knew she had literally drunk herself into oblivion, the thought unnerved him. Scared him even. She was his, his only. Pretty boy would find that fact out soon enough, very fucking soon, Craig thought as he sank another glass of scotch, sweat pouring in torrents down his face, his head fuzzy from the strong liquor. He took his phone out of his pocket and plugged it up to the sound system behind the bar, he flicked a few switches and then the sound of Ke$ha filled the empty bar space. Craig's whole body chilled, his spine literally tingled as the memories came flooding back, the drunken nights out getting plastered off of Lambrini, and the drunk dancing her slim body entwined in his, Jenna singing along to the words like she was part of the song itself. The crazy drunken sex that would start when the party ended and end when the morning started. Craig smiled then a genuinely warm, happy smile. He missed her so fucking much, she was his Jenna, they had always been as thick as thieves and Craig had adored her. She was over funny, incredibly flirtatious, kind and empathetic and beneath the false lashes and the killer body she truly was a beautiful person. Craig knew that it would soon be time for Kiki to go home, the police were swarming around and he had been lucky to get this far. The thought daunted him, he dreaded returning the little girl to her mother, but he knew that the life in America wasn't what he wanted for his daughter. Kiki was a mummy's girl. She pined for Jenna and Craig knew that he had already put her through too much in her young life. But as much as his head was telling him that he had done the right thing by taking Kiki, his heart was still playing catch up. He hated how quick his heart beat in his chest when the mere thought of Jenna came to the forefront of his mind. She was like a drug, totally addictive and Craig craved her more than the air he breathed. He saw her in his mind's eye, all thick eyeliner and big glossy hair that tumbled in a waterfall down her lean shapely back. She was stunning; there was nothing more to be said for her. Craig stared at the docking station as the music changed and the sound of UB40's "Kingston Town" filled the bar area, Craig grabbed another large measure of whiskey and went and sat on one of the plush leather sofa's that were scattered around the main lounge of the club, he pulled his tie loose and unbuttoned his crisp linen shirt, just a hint of his bare muscular chest on show, his lush sun kissed tan visible blaring off his soft supple skin. He flung his head back and stared at the ceiling, his whole body was simply numb. His head was all over the place, he had never ever in his life felt so torn. He knew if he were to go back to the estate that the game was up, he would have to expose himself something he wasn't sure he was prepared for. His alcohol fuelled head was hazy, the memories of his past flooded his mind and he couldn't shake them no matter how hard he tried. He ran his long fingers through his short hair, wiping the sweat off his brow and taking another skilled sip from the tumbler that was clenched in his hand. He felt drained, completely and utterly shattered. He glanced at the clock on his phone, it was nearly midnight he paused for a moment taking another sip of his drink he dialled a number on the keypad. Holding the phone to his ear he listened to the monotonous ringing at the end of the line, and for a moment Craig worried he may have changed her number.

"Hello" Jenna's confused voice on the end of the line made his heart skip several beats, sweeter than nectar to his ears. He could hear the tiredness in her tone and for a moment Craig couldn't help but picture her fucking pretty boy earlier. The thought made him hang up automatically and led to him slinging his phone across the bar. The suspense was killing him slowly; he knew that the time was drawing ever so close. He would have to go back, he would have to rectify the situation, he was going to kill Kenny Kreegan and then in his drunken mind, he was going for Pretty boy.......

Chapter Seventy Two

Jenna stared at the phone limply in her hand, she hadn't known the number but there was a strange familiarity in the air, the fragile sounds of UB40 whispering in the background had stopped her dead in her tracks. It had been Craig's funeral song, Dom's soft snoring echoed in her ear as the blood rushed to her head in sheer panic. She hugged herself tighter to Dom's naked body, sucking in his scent as her skin met his; she had never felt so scared in her entire life. She clutched the phone tightly, the front screen picture of her and Kiki glared back at her, her eyes literally popped out of her skin as the number popped up on the screen for the second time. Her hands trembled as she pressed the answer button, nervously; between baited breaths she held the phone closely to her ear, hugging the sheets closer to her naked body.

"hello" she whispered into the receiver, this time she could hear Ke$ha playing in the background, then there was the whistle, the agonisingly painful whistle along to the track, Jenna dropped the phone and leapt back against the headboard, tears rolling down her cheeks, her naked body literally crawling with Goosebumps as she heard the melodic lyrics of "Crazy kids" resonating through her phone speakers. She swallowed hard as she brought the phone to her ear again, the shrill whistling had stopped, there was a harsh breath and then the phone went dead. Instantly she threw it against the wall, as thought the phone had literally burnt holes in her hands. She breathed inwards, literally sucking at her lungs as thought her life depended on it. Dom stirred slightly, turning into her, cuddling her close, she turned away from his gaze, the tears threatening to cripple her. He sat up in the bed, rubbing his tired eyes, his naked flesh highlighted subtly by the dimly lit streetlight outside, his hair sprawled wildly on the top of his head. His face slightly ashen from sheer exhaustion, he leant back against the headboard, stretching out with an almost panther like prowess. His naked buttocks tinted amber from the glow of the outside lights, his dark curly hair shadowed against the light, he truly was handsome. Jenna gasped as he pulled her into his sleepy embrace. His nose instantly in her long dark hair as she succumb to his intoxicating touch, his lips etched into the prefect pout, his muscular arms around her slender waist, his manly hand spread across her tiny stomach pulling her into him. She cried then, really cried, her eyes balmy wet from her tears and Dom hushed her quietly, kissing her smarting lips as they parted to greet his.

"What's Wrong babe?" he groaned sleepily against her lips as their kiss heightened, she needed him now, needed him close. The phone call had scared her out of her wits. She didn't understand it, no one had known about her addiction to Ke$ha like Craig had. No one had known about her fixation with music like Craig had and here it was, UB40 first, Ke$ha a close second, both had come from the same number and Jenna was simply and utterly bewitched by the situation. Surely this couldn't be someone playing a sick fucking joke on her; she had been through enough with losing her daughter and her best friend. Surely no one would want to punish her further? No one knew about her eclectic tastes other than

Craig and that was what had scared her the most, as her breathing hitched in her throat she glared at Dom, her eyes wide, almost doe like as she said;

"It's Craig..... He's here" the words escaped before she could even reconsider them. She sat on the bed completely rigid, her eyes transfixed on the pale painted walls. Dom's face scrunched, etched with horror as he pulled the sheets closer around himself, his semi- erect member deflated almost instantly. What the fuck was she on about now? He thought as he sat himself up, he crossed his legs. He tucked his hands into his legs concealing his slightly flattened manhood, glaring at Jenna. He was fucking livid. There were literally no fucking words for how angry he felt. He tossed the blankets aside, pulling himself up, searching for his boxer shorts in the dim light. He slammed the bedroom door behind him on his escape. Jenna strained to hear him throwing things around downstairs, shouting and screaming to himself like an erratic child. She swallowed hard, flopping back against the headboard, her hands covering her wanting eyes. She could hear him shouting to himself downstairs, she heard glass smash and she knew her photos were being hurled around the living room. Despite her needs, she chose to stay glued to the spot, her ears pricked for the slightest movements. She heard the front door slam, for long moments her eyes were glued to the door. She was completely alone in her hopeless abandon but she couldn't help herself, curiosity got the better of her, she climbed out of bed, her naked body glistening with beads of sweat as she bent down to grab her phone. She glared at the screen; all she could see was her precious daughters face smiling back at her. She went back through her calls and saw the random number that had played her the music. Her finger hovered over the call button, her whole body was shaking, and her heart was palpitating uncontrollably as she pressed the button hard. She turned on the loudspeaker button as the shrill ringing rang out around the apartment. Bathed in silence she sucked in an exasperating breath, she waited, patiently. The first time the phone went to answer phone. Her hands trembled as she pressed redial. Her whole face creased into stressful thick lines. She heard the person on the other side pickup, their breathing was laboured, desperate even and Jenna smiled subtly at her control.

"Craig?" she whispered, barely believing the words as they leapt from her mouth. Her head was spinning wildly, Craig was dead, and this couldn't be him. It was just her head playing tricks on her surely. She glared hopelessly at the blank space before her, her emotions were completely spiralling. This was a dream surely. She tried to pinch herself awake but no this was a hopeless reality, her skin crawled nervously she exhaled a sharp longing breath, her fingers clutching the phone so tightly that she was convinced it would explode in her hand.

Craig stared at the phone in bewildered amusement, how could he have been so thick as to not withhold his number. Her tender voice melted his heart and he could feel her fear radiating in waves around him, he was literally glued to the spot. He bit his lip in mock consternation and felt the unsightly bulge rising in his boxers as he thought of his Jen. He cleared his throat, but his words were all but failing him. He could barely breathe such was his sheer deluded excitement at the situation in hand. He wiped his brow, the sweat trickling down his slim fingertips drenching the open cuffs of his shirt. The silence was comforting and he knew she was just as afraid as he was at the realisation of admitting the truth. He felt the tears choking him as they spilt from his eyes, it had been so long since he had heard her voice, felt her presence so close and Craig was completely bewitched, captivated, lost in his own silent reverie. He could hear her soft, rhythmical erratic breaths down the line and his heart literally leapt into his mouth, the shock of it all absorbing him in its entirety. The shadow of a smile played on his lips; this was it he thought as he opened his mouth to speak, brushing away his tears with the back of his sleeve he sucked in a deep breath, nodding his head as he spoke as though she could see him herself.

"Yeah babe, it's me"   He heard the painful shriek coming from the other end of the phone, Jenna repeating the word NO like a mantra, Craig swiped at his eyes again, he knew this would kill the poor girl. But there was no going back now he had made contact. He could feel her desperation; hear her disbelief rattling in her words. She was howling now a deep angry mournful sound that cut Craig to the core. He swallowed hard his heart raced so fast he thought he would pass out at any given moment. The sweat literally rained from his brow, his shirt clung to his heavy muscular frame highlighting every delicious curve of his abdomen. He tried to regulate his breathing, all the while listening intently to the completely unrestricted moans and sobs that came from an almost carnal Jenna. She was almost primal in her need and her whole voice ached for him to reassure her that he was really alive. He waited patiently for her incandescent wails to subside and for her to regain a little control. He heard her pick up the phone again, her wracking sobs coming in stuttering waves down the line, he shuddered inwardly at the thought of upsetting her anymore than he already had.

"Jen...listen" he soothed, his tone soft as he spoke, she sobbed again, she had never ever felt so stricken in all her life, he was alive, he was fucking alive, she was so stunned that she felt as though someone had smacked her clean across the face. The stab of pain that had been in her heart ever since the day he had left her completely lifted. Her whole body was on high alert, every single sense heightened by her fear. She was completely engrossed by the voice she knew so well on the end of the phone, surely this was a dream. Her whole body quivered acutely every single muscle in her body constricted at the thought of him. She couldn't fucking believe this. The urge to vomit was completely over riding her and she knew if she made the tiniest of movements then she wouldn't be able to control her body any longer. She laughed then, a nervous, slightly over the top laugh that completely consumed her. She threw her head back in complete sensation, revelling in the knowledge that Craig was alive. As much as the thought completely scared the shit out of her, this was so unreal. She bought herself back down from her insatiable high, panic stricken, overwhelmed. She was completely and utterly lost;

"This is a fucking joke isn't it? You sick cunt!" she whispered vehemently into the receiver her heart not really in the effort. She felt as though her head had literally been blasted off her shoulders. Her aching head slumped against the headboard, her naked skin alien against the soft cotton sheets; her whole body covered in puckering Goosebumps, every single inch of her skin tingled in sweet anticipation. He was alive; he was out there somewhere, living, breathing, and the thought made her insatiably nervous.

"Jen you still there" the voice at the end of the line mouthed breathlessly, it was him, there was no denying that now. It was his voice, dripping with his distinguished, slightly more refined than she remembered accent, but it was him. It was Craig.

"Yes I'm here" she whispered in return, her pulse was galloping now, thumping hard against her skeletal chest bones. Her head was still completely drowning, trying to play catch up with her aching body. She suddenly felt overly exhausted. She couldn't even begin to process any of this mess. All she had felt, all she had gone through, all she had endured the past two years had been a lie. The raw emotion that still completely ruined her every time she thought of him being gone, the empty space that he had left in her heart, the thought of him never coming home, never smiling at her with his naughty boy grin, the thought of him never loving her again, it had all but killed her too. Now here he was on the phone, completely absorbing him with his silky voice. She felt her stomach muscles constrict tightly and as much as she tried to stop it, she felt the familiar flush of scarlet on her pale cheeks. How could he have ever done this to her? All of the memories that she held so dearly came flooding back in full crystal clear stunning clarity. She had always submitted herself to him fully; they had been stupidly devoted to one another part of her couldn't accept that this was happening. He couldn't be alive, not after all of this time. She glared at the phone and hung up, taking the sim card out she snapped it in two and tossed the phone to the floor.

No, she rationalised, it couldn't have been her Craig, and Her Craig was dead. Wasn't he?

Chapter Seventy Three

Craig tried to ring Jenna's number back several times over the next few days, but to no avail. He sat in the deserted bowling green with Kiki, her long hair streaming behind her as the wind caught her by surprise. She was giggling to herself chasing a single red balloon that she had been handed by a woman in the market, her floaty pink cotton dress flaring as she tried to catch her treasure. Craig was completely engrossed by her; she was simply fascinating to watch, she was such a beautiful, happy little girl with not a single care in the world. Craig smiled as her beautiful laugh echoed around the park, she was so infectious and Craig could have kicked himself for missing out on her baby years. At almost three years old she had a much older wiser head, she was incredibly clever, incredibly bright and she was daring just like her mother, she had a wild little personality and Craig saw Jenna's spirit mirrored almost identically in their little girl.

"Daddy Look!" Kiki squealed in delight as she finally caught up to her balloon and was waving it around in her pudgy hands like something possessed. Craig giggled a full boyish laugh that revealed his still tender youth. He jumped up from the grass, dusting off the backs of his ripped jeans and proceeded to chase after the little girl who ran away as fast as her little legs would carry her chortling as she was picked up and swung around in Craig's strong arms. Craig hugged her close, holding on, clutching to the last piece of Jenna that he had left. He knew the time was coming where he would have to take her back home, the American club was almost in the finishing end of production and he had to go and oversee the final stages of construction before meeting with his interior designer to go through the last few adjustments of his decor plans. He was filled with anxiety and excitement all at the same time, he didn't want to leave his daughter, he couldn't even comprehend saying goodbye to her. He knew he had to see Jenna first, explain why he had taken their daughter, why he had faked his own death. He didn't know where he would even attempt to begin.

"I Love you Keeks" he whispered, holding his daughter close to his chest, feeling her instantly relax into his embrace, he nuzzled her hair and kissed the top of her head. She truly was perfect.

"Love you daddy" she replied sweetly. Planting a big wet kiss onto his slight stubble ridden cheek Craig's heart melted, how the fuck was he going to leave her go? Would he ever be able to now? The thought tore him to shreds. She was his little girl, his flesh and blood, and she was the only thing that still connected him and Jenna. It was a fucked up situation, but now he had to rectify it. Picking up Kiki's plastic tea set and their picnic rug, sweeping her up into his arms and kissing her tiny forehead one more time he had made his decision and now he knew he had to stick to it........

Part Three

The Return

"Don't forget to remember me... I'll be back... so remember me....
Please keep me in your heart.... if we ever have to part.... Don't
forget to remember me"

T.I Ft Mary J Blige – Remember me

Chapter Seventy Four

It was late, Craig didn't know exactly how late but what he did know was that he was here on the doorstep to Jenna's flat. His nerves were completely shot, his whole body rigid with fear, he was slightly tipsy and at the time coming here seemed like a good idea, now he had arrived he wasn't so sure. He smoothed down his lapels on his navy suit jacket, ran a nervous hand through his hair and took a deep breath inwards, exhaling slowly he reached his hand out and slowly knocked the door, stepping back away from the door he shuddered with unnecessary anxiety, he looked around, checking that he was out of sight, he was almost panting now, his baited breath hitching in his throat as he struggled to maintain his cool composure. He saw movements beyond the glass pane, the hall light went on and then he saw Jenna's curvaceous silhouette against the glass.

"Who is it?" she called out nervously, her voice almost had a sing song tone to it and the corners of Craig's lips twitched into a salacious grin. The smell of lager hung on his breath and he wished now that he had attempted to brush his teeth before coming here.

"Uhhh Dom" he smirked at his cunning attempts of unhinging Jenna, running a slim finger over his bottom lip. He knew as soon as she opened the door that she would put up a fight. So he braced himself, his whole body was tense and expecting, wanting her near him so much that even his pores were on stalks. The sweet anticipation fuelled his drunken high. He turned away slightly as he heard the key slide into the lock, his stomach muscles clenched deep inside him as he saw the crack in the door appear, then their gazes locked instantly and she took in the handsome man before her, her mouth dropping to the floor as she almost leap away from his gaze. Her heart raced in her chest, her eyes were as wide as saucers as she took in the chiselled jaw line, the perfectly straight nose, slightly stubbled chin and the brightest blue eyes she had ever seen in her life. So familiar yet so strange, it was the headiest of potions. She took in the smart navy suit jacket, tight white t shirt that hugged his amazing figure so simply the ripped jeans and pristine converse pumps. He had changed so much, gone were the smart tracksuits and trainers, gone was the teenage boy who stole her heart and in his place was this aged, beautiful, smartly dressed man. He smiled simply at her, a full megawatt smile that made Jenna slightly delirious. She stepped forward, drinking in every single striking feature, the electrical surge between them was still there, and she could feel it drawing her in, sucking her closer to him. She pulled on his jacket and held him in the hardest, most needing embrace she could muster; she was rendered completely speechless as his arms traced her thin back, the air caught in her throat as she struggled to breathe, he was fucking here. Craig was here. She inhaled his intoxicating scent, expensive soap and of course the familiar musky tones of his Joop original. Her fingers traced his face, his skin was so soft, so real, and so warm and then she finally believed it. Her eyes glassed over with unshed tears, he cupped her chin in his hands, staring wildly into her eyes, completely alive with desire as he pushed his way into the hallway, shutting the door behind him.

"Missed me?" he whispered against her earlobe, nibbling it gently as she collapsed into his arms, so much for pretty boy he thought as she clung to him desperately. She groaned against his lips, her eyes searching his for answers, his expression was cool, a playful smile lingered on his gorgeous mouth and she bit her lip in anxiety as her fingers ran down his cheeks, across his neck to his chest. She nestled against him, her lips pressed against the tight cotton of his shirt, he was really here. She had only been able to dream of this moment ever since he had been gone, dream of the way he used to touch her and now here were his hands, in her hair, tugging slightly so her face was looking up at his. Her lips quivered beneath his steely hard gaze, his eyes alive with lust. He kissed her then, his expert tongue exploring her wanting mouth, she returned the kiss, slow at first, his breath hitching as he pushed his tongue deeper into her mouth, biting her bottom lip on his release, their eyes never leaving one another's, Craig thrust his hips against her tiny body, his bulging erection pressed against her thigh. He smiled cheekily at her, kissing her again this time harder, his hands all over her, she had changed she was shy and reserved and her body had become so slim. It didn't suit her Craig shook his head in disapproval. She was almost like a child who sought acceptance and Craig didn't know how to react to her now, would she tell pretty boy? Would she tell his mother? That was the last fucking thing he needed.

"You haven't told anyone about this have you?" his voice gruff as he planted soft kisses against her bare throat, making his way down to her already swollen breasts, her nipples protruding through the barely there material of her nightdress. She glanced at him, her lashes fluttering as she shook her head, he could feel his cock was about to burst out of his fucking trousers, he smiled at her accordingly and yanked the cotton nightdress up over her head to find to his delight that she was completely naked beneath, he groaned as his hands and mouth ravaged her. His lips instantly sought out her stiff hard nipples, his tongue lapping at the left while his fingers expertly squeezed the right, pinning her to the wall whilst pushing his erection against her leg, she moaned softly against his ear, her fingers toying with his hair. He pulled his hands around and caressed her naked buttocks, before giving her a short sharp spank, taking her breath away as he picked her up so her legs were latched around his waist, her lips found his again and they're kiss deepened, her long dark curly hair tumbled down her naked chest slightly concealing her breasts as he carried her into the living room, his skilled mouth never leaving hers as she pushed off his suit jacket, leaving it fall in a heap onto the wooden floor. He lay her down onto the fluffy shagpile living room rug. She sat up leaning against her elbows as she watched him pull off his crisp white shirt, his deeply tanned skin, shone with perspiration, his broad naked chest, his rippled abdomen shaped into the most perfect taught six-pack Jenna had ever laid eye on. He had shaped up so much since she had last seen him; he was so muscular, from his toned shapely torso to his bulging biceps. The only flaw on his perfect skin was the angry purple scars that slashed his torso; Jenna stared at them for long moments with sheer amazement her eyes unable to dodge them despite her wanting need to forget about what had happened. She sensed his obvious embarrassment as his hand flitted to his stomach and she diverted her gaze down to his hips. Jenna tossed her head back; her hair fanning out on the rug, her hands trailing her own body, Craig unbuckled his belt, the crisp white Calvin Klein waistband of his boxers poking through subtly. He kicked off his converse and pulled off his socks and jeans, leaving them in a neat pile on the sofa. He knelt down in front of Jenna and splayed her tiny legs, shuffling in between them he bent down and gave her a swift kiss on the lips, her hands found the waistband of his boxers and with a sense of urgency she yanked them down to his knees, he kicked them off, revealing his huge erection, he licked the end of his fingers and used his fingers to lube her, he slid one finger inside her, biting his lip as he slipped his finger in and out of her soaking wet vagina. She was so fucking ready for him, he positioned himself between her legs and slowly he eased himself into her. She was so so tight, just as he had remembered, yet she was so wet for him. He pulled himself back out of her slowly and desperately slipped back in again, his movements so agonisingly slow Craig could see she was close to coming already. So he pulled out again and started his delicious assault all over again. She squirmed beneath him, her legs instinctively latching around his waist so he leant across so he was practically lying on top of her. His mouth kissing every inch of her baby soft skin as he quickened his pace, his hands tugging her hair hard as she moaned against his ear, a wanting moan that echoed around the living room. His fingers ran down her naked body, until they found her clitoris, he rubbed gently against her, until she fell apart beneath him and she came hard, aching with lust all over his rock hard member. A few thrusts later and he unloaded blissfully inside her, both of them panting and sweating as they reached their climax. She pulled him close, kissing his hair as she held his head against her naked chest. They lay there for hours in comfortable silence surrounded by pictures of themselves. He barely recognised the boy in the photos as himself in any of them. HE looked so fucking young, young and indeed very much in love.

Chapter Seventy Five

Craig lay awake on the sofa, his eyes pinned to the ceiling, his sweat making him stick to the sickly hot leather. Jenna lay naked on top of him both wrapped loosely in a double bed sheet, both hazy from the sex. He held Jenna close to his bare chest, the faint smile that played on his face as he kissed her hair spoke volumes. He felt like he had finally come home. She had fallen asleep and her glossy black hair tickled his bare skin as she nuzzled her head against him. Fuck he had missed her. He knew he would have to leave soon, despite his over whelming urge to stay the night. He knew that Kiki was perfectly safe with her Nanny, Leah. But he knew he couldn't risk being seen in the morning by pretty boy, or even worse his fucking mother. He glanced around the living room, filled with pictures of their perfect little family, Jenna and Kiki, Craig and Jenna, Kiki and Craig. So much had happened and Craig was happy to see that she hadn't forgotten him completely in his absence. He didn't think he would ever regain her trust fully, he knew that in the past he had fucked her about, messed with her head, but he had only done it to test her. To see if she would fuck off with someone else, and she never had. He ran his fingers down the arch of her naked back, trailing, stroking her beautiful pale skin, even in slumber she was completely flawless. Gently he pushed her hair away from her face, her eyes fluttered slightly adjusting to the dimly lit room she leant up and her tired gaze met his own.

"Hi" she whispered trying to stifle her yawn as she stretched out widely against him, her naked ribs digging into him and he winced, his eyes widened slightly as he pulled her closer to him.

"You don't know how much I've missed you" he held back the tears as he kissed her forehead, his nose nestled against her thick mane of hair. Here she was in his arms, the feeling elated Craig, and he finally felt complete. A long time had passed and they were here as though the last two years had never happened. He swallowed hard; he knew it was time for him to tell her the truth about Kiki's whereabouts. He sat up, his skin sucking to the leather as he recoiled away from its sticky embrace pulling Jenna onto his lap he kissed her heard on her swollen lips.

"Jen, about the baby...." his voice went off at the end of the sentence and his heart pained as she almost shot off his lap, her eyes wild, she hadn't expected him to ask about Kiki yet! How the fuck was she to explain that their baby girl was missing? Her body broke out in the coldest of sweats as she tried to control her jangled nerves. This was all too much. First of all her dead best friend turns up on her door completely alive, she had fucked him right here on the wooden floor and now she had to explain that their daughter, the one he hadn't believed to be his own, had been fucking snatched from off the doorstep! She glared at Craig, her eyes almost feral with carnal need. She caught the glimmer of a smile whispering on his lips and she snapped as the whole sorry saga came full circle. He wasn't asking about Kiki at all, he was confessing to taking her! It took Jenna a while to put the pieces together, she shook her head at him, repeating the word "no" as her hand shot to her mouth, the tears exploded down her cheeks, but she couldn't work out if they were tears of relief or tears of sheer madness.

Jenna lunged at him then, her hands hitting out, grasping his naked flesh, she was screaming at the top of her lungs, she clawed at his handsome face, watching as the red grazes popped up on his cheeks and she recoiled in horror as she caught the evil red scars across his torso, she cried then, loud, erratic sobs that rattled her whole body. Her whole body exhausted with these wicked games. He clutched her wrists and glared at her, his steely gaze cutting her skin deep, her lips quivered and she squirmed on his lap, her naked skin shone with a thick film of perspiration. She focused on her breathing, trying to calm herself down. She turned her gaze away from him, he released her wrists, and allowed his hands to trace her waist, her hips, her naked behind, and in one swift movement he pulled her further onto his lap so she was straddling him. His eyes locked on hers as he swiped the tears from her eyes with his skilled fingers, she flinched slightly at his touch. He pulled her into him, the fight literally sucked out of her as she rested her head wearily against his chest, his heart racing almost as quickly as hers. She stilled as their eyes met again, his lips whipped into a salacious grin as he rubbed his erection against her inner thigh, she gasped as she found herself slowly easing herself onto him, and he filled her instantly within one swift push of his hips. She was still wet from their earlier encounters and Craig groaned with pleasure as she started to gently slide herself up and down his throbbing erection. He sat open mouthed, his eyes not leaving hers for a single second, his hands finding their way to her hips and resting themselves there as she slowly continued her passionate illicit torture. Slowly she wound her hips around, grinding on him harder with each delirious thrust. His breathing spiked harshly as she led her lips to his, forcing her tongue in between his sultry soft lips, tasting the sickly sweet bite of his lager breath, a taste she had relished so much in the past and now she was reliving it all over again. She moaned breathlessly against his lips as she took him inside her again, relentlessly he bucked his hips up to meet her agonising thrusts. Each sensational stroke taking her higher and higher until she climaxed against him with a mind blowing convulsion that shook her whole body, he pushed himself deeper and deeper inside her until he unloaded another thick load of his semen inside her. He clung to her desperately as he felt his flaccid member gently slip out from inside her. He planted a soft kiss on her forehead before rolling her off his lap and onto the sofa beside him. He stood up and stretched out wildly, groaning with sheer exhaustion. He picked up his phone from the chair and checked his calls list. His driver had left him a message saying that he was going home to help Leah with the baby and to let him know when he was ready to be collected. Craig smiled, he had known for a while that his Nanny Leah and his Driver Ronnie had been having an affair for a while now, of course he hadn't let on to the two of them that he knew, but it was in the simple glances and the private smiles that the two constantly exchanged on reuniting with one another that they were completely smitten. He hoped against hope that they would soon just give into each other and make it official. He called Ronnie, the monotonous ringing sang in his ears as he waited patiently.

"Ron I'm ready… yeah it went well…. see you in what an hour? Okay Bye" he hung up the phone and tossed it onto the coffee table, He grinned as he pulled on his boxers and jeans. Jenna was half asleep curled up on the leather sofa, she yawned loudly and hugged the sheets closer to her naked body, her face slightly flushed and glowing. He bent over and kissed her lips gently as she finally succumbed to slumber, a snored softly in her sleep. He pulled her into his arms and carried her upstairs, sliding her into bed, he stared at her precious face kissed by the light of the moon outside, and He stared at her for a few moments more before making his leave. He went back downstairs, finished getting dressed and scrawled a little note for her which he left on the coffee table. As he stepped out into the cold night air he smiled a pure boyish grin as he saw his Black Lamborghini parked close to the flats, Ronnie standing by the door with a secret smile painted on his face. He locked the door and pushed the keys back through the letterbox and walked away whistling the eerie tune of Ke$ha's Crazy Kids.

Chapter Seventy Six

Jenna woke up to the rain beating against the windows, the wind swirling litter like confetti in the air, she stretched out in the dim light that peered in through the slit in the curtains. She breathed inwardly, sucking in the scent of her own body and Craig's sex lingering on her. The reminder of their night together instantly lifted her disappointment at him not staying with her. She stood uneasily, her legs completely turned to jelly as she stumbled to the shower, turning on the hot water she basked in the warmth, not wanting to wash away his scent off her naked skin, the intoxicating feeling of knowing that Craig had made love to her last night almost enough to give her a heart attack on the spot. She allowed the hot torrents to rain over her, massaging her aching muscles, her head swimming with the fresh memories from the night before. He had changed so much, he was a much more experienced lover now, and the thought excited Jenna as much as it displeased her. She stepped under the shower head, lathering shampoo into her long tresses, allowing the suds to roll down her body, pooling at her feet. She finished her shower and stepped out onto the cold tiles. Her heart racing as she paced down the stairs, the whole room seemed different somehow, she could still feel him there, as though he had just left, the faint smell of his aftershave hung dense in the stifling air. She glanced over at the coffee table and saw the little white sheet of paper and, was that a business card? She smiled at the irony, Craig Crater with a business card. She flounced over to the coffee table, picking up the note she gazed at the scrawled writing.

Jen,

Thanks for an amazing night, Sorry I couldn't stay but being dead does have its disadvantages, next time you're coming to mine maybe you can show me your dirty tricks in MY bed ;) see you soon... I've missed us babe, text me when you wake up Craig x

Jenna smiled at the little note and picked up the business card from the table;

JAMIE WILLIAMS

C.E.O THE MAMMA ROUGE

NIGHTCLUB&BAR

She turned over the card and noticed he'd scrawled on the back of this too;

Jen'

Jamie doesn't suit me I know. LOL ;) Text me when you wake up wench or I'll come back for you ;) x

She smiled at her little treasures as she fished around for her phone. On finding it she flushed scarlet, she had five missed calls, all from Dom and immediately she felt extremely guilty. She realised suddenly that she was trying to explain to herself why she had slept with Craig, the thought disturbed her. In all the time they had been apart Jenna would have put her life on there being nobody who could ever come close to Craig. Then Dom had came along and despite everything, she had fallen for his simplicity. Craig was complex, hard to keep up with; and he was also supposed to be dead. She had so much she wanted to ask him and she found herself questioning her reasons for allowing him to just walk back in here, fuck her and leave. He had stolen her daughter, left her living in hell all these weeks wondering what the fuck had happened to Kiki and yet she could forgive him in an instant the second his boxers were around his ankles. She held her phone in her hand and typed out a quick text to Dom. She suddenly fancied a night out and she knew just the place to go, If Craig Carter wanted to play games, well let the game begin she thought coyly a sly smile playing on the edge of her elegant mouth.

Jenna resisted the urge to text Craig all day and by the time the night came she was nervous, completely on edge, sweet anticipation hoping that he would come back for her as he had threatened. The other half she found unexpectedly didn't want him to. She lay in bed staring blankly at the ceiling running the last few days over in her head, had she been dreaming? Was the question at the forefront of her mind, she worried about that the most, had she imagined the whole sorry episode, was she really that senile? A lot had happened lately and she hoped against hope that she wasn't finally cracking up! She pulled her arm over her eyes and sighed loudly into the darkness, she felt completely and utterly torn. Craig had been all she had ever wanted, she had spent her whole life dedicated to him, submissive to him, she would have done anything he asked of her, but he had never been willing to commit to her and in the end it had tore them both apart. Then there was Dom, sweet, kind, Beautiful Dom who had made her so happy in such a short time, Dom who had stuck by her in her hour of need. Dom who had loved her so gently, so desperately, she knew he was in love with her, and she loved him, in her own way. Craig was so dangerous, unhinged and Jenna was addicted to him, the thrill of him, he was so obsessive he was like a heady narcotic to Jenna. Her silent reverie broken by the phone vibrating on the bedside cabinet, Jenna shot up rubbing her aching eyes she didn't recognise the number, but she instinctively knew it would be him. She swallowed hard her whole body prickling with anticipation, her stomach muscles knotted tentatively; she stared aimlessly at the bedside table, on the third missed call she picked up; His breathing was erratic and torturous on the other end;

"What the fuck you playing at?" his harsh was whisper barely audible against the loud booming music in the background. Jenna could feel his anger reverberating in waves down the phone, his tone full of malice as he sucked in a harsh breath through his teeth. Jenna shuddered at the thought, this man had her daughter, and she had to play the game very carefully from here on in. He overwhelmed her, scared her even, he was so much more grown up, sophisticated, darker than he had been. He wasn't the same person she had known all her life. He wasn't her best friend anymore. It was as though someone had taken Craig, cut him open and replaced his boyish personality with that of a mad man. But as the basked in the glow of the night before she felt nothing but confusion, it was those tender moments that they shared that made her question her feelings towards him. Maturity had been good to him; he was more than ruggedly handsome, flawless even despite his scars. His eyes bore a steely blue gaze that although at times could be intimidating, burned with a lust so needing and wanting it was the most body crippling combination. He had always been like a drug to Jenna but now, he was completely insatiable, she craved him, his touch, and his potent kiss all over her wanting body. Craig had been her everything for such a long time, but her heart had healed with their separation and she had been convinced she had found love again in Dom. Gorgeous uncomplicated Dom, he was her safe haven.

"Craig I don't know if I can do this...." She stammered down the phone, her breath aching in her chest, she felt so torn between the two but she had to think of her own sanity. Craig was gone, dead and buried and now he was suddenly alive and well, looking so bloody beautiful, dripping in money, smelling of their memories together, suffocating her with the thoughts of the two of them actually making a life together, dangling it in front of her nose. It was cruel of him, but then again he knew that, he thrived on it. He thrived on keeping her hanging loose on a string, keeping her in an almost barbaric suspense. It was how he got his ever so fucked up kicks. She was crying; she felt the saltiness stinging her red raw cheeks as she stared hard at the bedroom wall. The big canvas picture of her and Craig on Kiki's first Christmas hung with pride of place. The three of them dressed in hideous Christmas jumpers, all smiling big fat smiles for the camera, Craig's arm slid around her waist as she gazed lovingly into his gorgeous blue eyes, they looked so carefree, so young. Jenna was saddened at the thought. She realised then that he had hung up; she was tempted to try calling him back, the thought of it expelled immediately as she curled herself into the sheets and cried herself into an uneasy, restless slumber, thoughts of Christmas and Kiki evaded her thoughts, and Craig, as always Craig.

Chapter Seventy Seven

The loud smashing of glass, made Jenna bolt upright in her bed, she sat rigid with fear, ears pricked for any indication of where the intruders were . Her eyes scanned the bedroom for something she could guard herself with. Her tense breathing harsh as the blood thundered through her body, eyes latched onto the door of her bedroom, fear spiking her breath as she tried not to make a single sound. She heard the heavy sound of boots on the stairs, the subtle thud as feet hit each step made her shudder with apprehension. She swallowed hard in the darkness, all she could do now was wait, it seemed like hours when in reality it was mere seconds that rolled by. She sat pinned to the headboard, the quilt bunched up to her chin concealing her semi naked body as she shivered feverently. The thudding stopped, the intruder was out on the landing now, she could here breathing, laboured, chesty, rapid breaths beyond the door, the slight creek of the floorboards beyond the door made Jenna jump literally out of her skin. Whoever it was lingered so desirably close, Jenna's mouth was as dry as the desert, her whole body spine chillingly rigid, completely incapable of movement. She exhaled slowly, pulling the quilt closer to her chin as she was left hanging anxiously in wait. Slowly the door arched open and in the doorway stood a lamented, apprehensive looking Craig, his knuckles streaked with crimson his eyes hollow and sad, his shirt loose from his jeans, the top three buttons undone, Jenna noted that he was wearing no tie, sweat that poured down his brow making him look manic in the darkness. She noted the glare in his steely eyes and for a moment she was afraid of what he was capable of. He just stared at her; his whole expression drew a blank. He ran a hand through his hair inhaling deeply, sucking out his breath on the exhale he was rendered speechless. Jenna released the quilt slightly from her chin, only to release the panic stricken claustrophobia that had enveloped her. She watched him intently, her eyes scanning him, trying to even begin explore what he was thinking; he of course gave away nothing.

"What did you mean you couldn't do this anymore?" he whispered, his voice aching, longing for an answer. His mouth set into a grim line as he sighed sadly. Skimming his fingers through his short hair, he took a step closer and positioned himself gently at the foot of the bed, his eyes never leaving Jenna's as he sat down; taking a swipe at an imaginary spot of dust on the covers dismally his gaze shifted to the sheets, the same sheet that was draped over their naked bodies not even a few hours before. A soft subtle smile played on his lips at the memory. It seemed worlds away now, the pure happiness he had felt, now felt as though someone had slit his throat with a razor. He swallowed hard, as though the silence was physically killing him. He had risked it all to be here, risked his sudden resurrection being exposed for this. He couldn't keep what they had shared away from his thoughts and now here he was, virtually breaking into her bloody house, for what reason he hadn't a clue. He could have just knocked the fucking door. He was like a needy child now as he shifted his position slightly, sucking his bottom lip into his teeth, eyes still locked on Jenna, searching, needing answers.

"Well?" he added, his fingers trailing the cotton hem on the trussed up bedspread. His voice bereft with distinguished emotion. He had never been so scared in all his life. If he lost her now then his whole life would be pointless, the last two years of suffering would have been for nothing. He was stupefied briefly by the thought, his face retorting in consternation as he barely pictured his dreaded existence without Jenna. Ever since they were kids he had been completely and utterly under her spell lost in a pure and endless love of her, compelled in sheer abandon at her beauty. The complex and disastrous lust of her body and mind that he craved almost threatening to control him completely. Craig needed her, wanted her. But more than that he simply wanted her to know just exactly what it was she did to him. He leant in closer, anxiety pinching at every pore of his body as his face inched closer to hers. The bite of his alcohol soaked breath, lingering in his mouth and he felt so unsure of whether he was about to vomit or not. He composed himself momentarily; he could feel the tears stinging his eyes, threatening ever so cruelly to spill free. He glanced up into the eyes he loved so much, their piercing green intoxicating even with their slightly wild, feral stare; they were the eyes he wished to stare into for the rest of his life. He could feel himself flush slightly with the delicious cold sweat that broke out all over his rigid back; he had never known fear like this. The fear of losing something that was so completely precious. His life almost hung in the balance between their hitched breaths and their wanting eyes. Still she said nothing, Craig closed his eyes and flopped onto the mattress, his arm raised over his face to save himself the humiliation.

"I Love you, I've always been head over heels in love with you for as long as I can remember. I can't even begin to imagine my life without you in it" he pulled his wallet from his pocket and took out the wad of photos from the money compartment and lay them out on the bedspread in front of them both. Jenna gasped suddenly as she took in each vivid beautiful picture, one of her at Craig's memorial night singing on the karaoke , her and Kiki sat outside the flat on a picnic blanket playing with her dolls, Pictures of Her and Craig together, and a more recent one, of Craig and Kiki. Both smiling broadly for the camera; Her little girl with her long dark hair in two plaited pig tails and a nineteen fifties polka dotted dress with a huge bowl shaped skirt. Her beautiful smile beaming as Craig held her close. She looked so happy, so carefree and completely and utterly in awe of her father. Who despite his striking pearly white teeth and his over enthusiastic smile looked equally as mesmerised by his beautiful daughter. Jenna smiled sadly at the photograph. Usually Kiki hated photos and the thought that she was posing so freely for Craig hurt Jenna. She was such a beautiful child and tears choked Jenna as she stared so intently at the face that she loved more than anything else in the world. Her beautiful baby girl, the girl who she had never ever expected to have to share with Craig. Craig sat up again, inches away from Jenna now, the thought sobering him.

"You see?" he continued the faint smile that played on his delicious lips didn't go unnoticed. "She's so happy Jen, She loves me, and me her. I could give you both everything now. I could take care of you both properly. Give Kiki her Mammy and Daddy, together" his voice a detrimental plea. His eyes begging her to listen, he drifted up the bed so that he was lying beside her, he took the quilt away from her face and hugged it around him, still fully clothed, kicking his shoes away from his feet as he bunched them under the warm blankets.

"Please babe, Let me try?" he begged, his eyes wide like a child pleading for a toy in the shops. His whole body was shuddering with nerves. Jenna stroked his cheek involuntary, her tiny long fingers brushing his stubble, his body prickling slightly at her silky touch; she smiled wearily as she cupped his handsome face in her hand. He leant into her touch, nuzzling against her fingers desperately. It was then in that plain moment of clarity did it hit Jenna of how young he really was despite his bravado. He had done a lot of growing up in the business world; he had matured in looks and characteristic veneer, but he was really just an emotionally unbalanced boy who she had chased all her life. The thought stilled her as she gazed down into his sad eyes. His pleading resonating in the back of her head as she continued to hold her eyes toward his. Craig had been the person who had made her feel so alive, so free, she breathed deeply in the silence, taking in every beautiful pore on his handsome face, gazing into his eyes with reckless intent. She couldn't dream of hurting him now, he looked so vulnerable, so wanting. She ran her fingers down his face once more;

"Okay" she whimpered, the tears escaping, imploding in bursts from her eyes, cascading down her face as he clutched her tightly towards him. He held her so close to his chest, allowing their breathing to steady as he kissed her gently, his lips shaking against hers. He leant his body against hers and simply held her, both exhausted, both overcome with insatiable emotion. He gazed down softly into her blazing green eyes, her beautiful features were striking in the dim light, and the tears that pooled in her eyes glistened brightly against her emerald iris's. He kissed her temple, taking her into him, her body slid between his legs as she shuffled on to his lap.

"I promise I won't let you down again" He whispered softly, kissing her hair, his nose nuzzling her scalp, his whole body relaxed against Jenna as he held her close . She smiled a small discreet smile that lit up her whole face. She left his embrace gently and stood up, pulling on her jeans and a jumper in the barely lit room, brushing her hair through with her fingers, pulling it into a tight ponytail on her head, skinny tendrils of hair hung loosely around her cheeks, making her look younger than her years. Craig just stared, his eyes taking in the scene before him with wonder, she came across and he allowed her to take his hand, she pulled him gently off the bed ad led him across to the door. She planted a soft kiss on his lips before leading him downstairs. Craig perched himself on the sofa, crossing his legs and running an exasperated hand through his hair.

"Right" He spoke in a melodic voice "Shall we go and see our daughter?" His tone full of laughter as he saw the beaming grin that broke out on Jenna's stunning face as her brain registered his words. Her eyes twinkled as the tears came again, this time though they were tears of absolute joy. She ran into Craig's arms hugging him as tight as she could muster. His body inched into her tight embrace and he could feel her delight bouncing off her in waves.

He knew he had killed her in taking Kiki away, but it had felt like the right thing to do. It gave him an opening to get close, watch her again. HE slid his phone from his pocket, checked the time and yanked her off the sofa.

"Come on Miss Shearan, we don't want to miss our ride" he giggled pulling her against him, pointing for her to get her shoes on and grab whatever she may need. She obeyed with an almost robotic poise. Everything was revolving in slow motion and Jenna didn't know whether she could keep up. She stood by the front door, sucking in a harsh breath before they stepped out into the dark, cold night. This was it, she was finally going to be reunited with her baby. She held Craig's hand tightly in hers and they walked across the car park as though they had no care in the world.

Chapter Seventy Eight

Dom stood in his bedroom window smoking a joint, he hadn't meant to be staring at Jenna's flat be he had found himself unable to do anything else for the last week. Since they had slept together his world had shifted on its axis dramatically. He had never ever in a million years dreamt of finding love in this fucking shit hole but indeed, cupid had struck in the wrong place at the right time. He flicked his ash in an empty beer can that he held in his vice like grip. His black hair wildly untamed on his head, his eyes barely there slits from lack of sleep and too much skunk, he wore nothing apart from a pair of black boxer shorts. His bare body pricked with Goosebumps, his skin puckering and mottled blue from the cold. But he stood frozen to the spot, her lights were on and he was tempted to go and knock, see if she was alright. He stroked his gruff overgrown stubble, his lean brushing the prickly hairs subtly as he took another long drawl of his Joint. He moved the net curtain across slightly, the night was balmy, the air cold but dense, full of mystery Dom thought in his hazy stupor.

He leapt back away from the window as he saw Jenna's door creaking open suddenly, his joint flying through the air, had he gone and got himself fucking spotted!? Was she coming over to see him? The thought pleased him more than it oppressed him. He saw Jenna step out onto the threshold, fully clothed, this time of night? Dom quizzed, his eyes firmly locked on the scene before him, barely able to breathe through baited anxiety. She was looking directly opposite to his; Dom did a little dance inside thinking that she was finally coming to him instead of him having to constantly chase her. He grinned, a huge cat that got the cream smile as he saw her step out into the cold night air, hugging her jacket closer, her eyes not leaving his flat for a second. Dom contemplated opening the window and calling for her to come in such was his confidence at that moment but he kept his rather pointless composure. She would come to him, she was just nervous, he reasoned as he noticed that she hadn't moved since. He turned away, searching for his missing smoke, retrieving it from beside the bed, he lit it up and took a deep toke before returning to his position at the window....

On looking back out he spluttered and literally almost swallowed his joint whole. There was a fucking man coming out of the flat, now standing on Jenna's threshold! Dom caught her face slightly as he coughed harshly as the smoke accidentally and more shockingly hit his lungs. She looked nervous now, her expression barely readable in the dim glow of the Security lights. Dom couldn't fucking believe his eyes. He continued to watch barely allowing himself to blink in case he missed anything. He felt slightly stupefied, his eyes wild, dancing around in their sockets with sheer malice, his breath literally wouldn't release from his body and he felt completely lightheaded all of a sudden. His blood felt as though it had reached boiling point in his veins and for a second his whole world stopped. He stared hard at the man, he couldn't place him at first, but as Dom glared even more, it finally clicked into place. His heart completely broke in that harsh, bitter moment of reality. A single tear strolled down his broken face as he realised who Jenna's mystery man was. It was him, it was Craig Carter!

Chapter Seventy Nine

Jenna clung to Craig as led her out to the car park, Her knees almost gave way as the black Lamborghini parked at the front of the flats suddenly purred to life; the headlights illuminated their shadows against the dark red brick walls. Ronnie nodded to Craig who strutted around the car, he pulled the door open for Jenna and allowed her to slide in, before he nuzzled himself beside her. The plush leather seats clung to Jenna's sweat sodden back. Ronnie fiddled with a few buttons on the dashboard and an eerie voice echoed through the speakers as they pulled away from the flats, away from the Belmonte and out onto the motorway. Jenna snuggled into Craig all the while her ears transfixed on the sultry voice that sung about having one last night. She smiled coyly at the irony before her eyes rested out of the window at the outside world, the lights of the cars ahead illuminating the city, London was so beautiful at night, the world flashing past as the Lamborghini whizzed across the rain soaked road. Craig's hand clasped hers tightly, his eyes too flitting into the night before them, neither saying a word, both transfixed in their own little worlds. Lost in thought.

"What's this song your driver has on repeat?" Jenna asked after the song had looped at least three times, her whisper barely audible in their comfortable silence. Her eyes still transfixed on the road ahead, her fingers brushing against her lips subtly as she spoke.

"you noticed then" Craig replied, his voice equally as quiet " It's a song called One Last Night by a singer called Vaults, Good right?" he smiled, his glance still fixed firmly out of the window beside him, watching softly as the city was swept away and they fell into rolling countryside, the trees and fields merging together in one hazy blur from the speed of the car.

"Not as good as Ke\$ha" Jenna grinned as she replied, winking playfully at him before returning her gaze to the window. The silence crept upon them again and they both sat drowning in the music as Ronnie picked up speed and drove them through to the dusky pink sunrise. The subtle pinks and gold's fighting with the angry purples and black shadows of the night, blending together in a wonderful colour enriched symphony. Jenna's breath literally caught in her throat as she stared in sheer amazement. The rolling black hills and moors the perfect backdrop for this beautiful scene before them. In the distance she spotted a glorious Victorian manor house, all redbrick and stunning white wood, it looked like a palace in the distance, surrounded by a high white fence, she could see a small cottage adjacent to the main house, it looked serene, peaceful and even from here in the car she could tell that the views were spectacular. She felt Craig's fingers tighten around hers and she gazed lovingly up at him, the playful smile that licked against his lips made Jenna shift uneasily;

"Honey we're home." he whispered faintly, an air of joviality in his liquid gold tone. He kissed her hair as he spoke, gauging her reaction with his shy eyes. She gasped hard, a wide grin bursting across her face as her eyes shot back to the manor house, her expression said it all, she was simply bewitched by it. Ronnie turned into the winding pathway that ran from the main road to the roughly half a mile drive to the gates. Jenna held her breath in wonder as they drew closer and closer to the stunning mansion before them, her eyes prickled with tears, shining against the morning sun. She looked back at Craig who sat with a grin that resembled a child at Christmas on his face. He had been waiting for this moment for just over two years and now it was here he could honestly say that he loved this woman before him more than he could have ever thought possible. They drew up outside the wrought gates and Craig got out to type in a code into the access point, suddenly the gates began to crank open, and Ronnie slid into the grounds with exceptional ease and suddenly Jenna could see the pure grandeur that was Craig's beautiful home. The stunning manor was lit up like a beacon with soft globe lights that were planted all over the grounds, like fireflies they danced against the pebble drive. They pulled into the parking bays situated by a gorgeous marble and grey stone fountain that spat water into a gentle pool beneath what appeared to be a large stone fish leaping from the water. Jenna was completely speechless. Craig opened the doors and held out his hand. She took it gently and he eased her out into the warm, dewy morning air. Pulling her in to him he just held her close to his chest, sucking in the scent of her, bathing in her warmth. As he stared out into the early morning sun, the chilly wind blowing eerily around them the reality finally hit Craig with a resonating clarity. He had finally made it; he had finally bought her home.

Chapter Eighty

Dom sat alone in his own silence, his whole head set firmly into overdrive. He glanced around at the upturned furniture, the ripped wallpaper, the smashed glass that littered the floor and the trussed up bedclothes that lay in a heap on the floor. His breath rate soared above a normal pace as he calmed from his tirade. His whole body quivered, rigid with complete reckless abandon, his heart beat like a hammer in his chest as he watched the last of the duck feathers from the pillow settle in the wreckage around him. He stared into the blank space on the wall, the gaping hole in the splintered plasterboard and the blood that smeared his bare knuckles even more evidence of his rampage. Dom's skin was rigid with fear, fear for none other than himself. The salty tears that rolled down his cheeks showing him how scared he really was, he never realised how hard he had fell for Jen, until now of course. Emotion wasn't his forte, he gone through life never having to give a fuck for anyone's thoughts or feelings. Now though he saw in stunning clear cut clarity how dangerous emotion was, he wore his calm cool veneer well. He hadn't had to show his temper for a LONG time, it was the same temper that he had showed his ex wife and admittedly his kids too.

His poor, beautiful wife Ami who had disappeared on Christmas night ten years previously. They had lived in Preston then, both worked long hours for their respective companies; she worked for a publishing company, her head constantly in a book or a manuscript. He had been the owner of a successful recruitment business from the age of seventeen. Both tackling hideous schedules, never seeing one another built an immeasurable amount of pressure in their relationship and she had embarked on an illicit affair with her boss. For months she had crept around behind Dom's back, claiming long hours and overtime. Until one night Dom had picked her up from the office. He could picture her beautiful face so vivid even now, her purple dyed hair which he was forever telling her off for. Her gorgeous laugh and a smile that could light up the whole room even now, Dom completely choked when he thought of it. He had never ever been violent towards her in the past; they had shared a wonderful six years together. She had bore him a little boy, Sam, who would have been thirteen now. It cut Dom to the quick to think of his boy. It had been the night after Dom had found out about her affair, he had beaten her so badly that she had been knocked unconscious. He had left her there on the living room floor, he had been so pissed he had passed out on the bathroom. By some miracle she had come around, packed their things and disappeared into the night. Not a single word, not even a note to say goodbye but the bitch had cleared out their bank account of over a hundred thousand pounds and made her escape. For years Dom had searched for them, even battered her old boss to a pulp to try and find some answers, the cunt had grassed him to the police and he ended up with a three year stretch in prison. On release he spent a few months flitting from hostel to hostel, working in shitty nine to five jobs that bored the living shit out of him and then when it all became too much he was sent here to this fucking shit hole by his probation officer. He still lived in the hope of finding his family, even now he dreamed of rekindling his relationship with Ami and rebuilding their little empire once more. That was of course before he had been cast under the bewitching spell of the stunning Jenna Shearan, and for a short while, Ami hadn't crossed his mind. But it was now, as he bathed in the gentle morning sunlight that crept through the net curtain, he realised he was back to being alone. As he had been ever since that fateful night. The sheer thought was too much for Dom and he emptied his stomach right there on the bedroom floor. The dry heaves bringing up the salty tasting black bile that stung his throat as he began coughing harshly, clutching his stomach as he doubled over. Tears rolling down his sallow cheeks as he painfully struggled to keep the urge from ending it all right there at bay.

Chapter Eighty One

The music blared from the car speakers as Craig took Jenna into his arms and danced with her right there on the drive, sweeping her into his embrace as he sashayed with her deliciously, their bodies entwined as Vaults continued to sing breathlessly about one last night, her voice like liquid silk in the backdrop of the glowing morning sun. Both their faces highlighted by the soft delicate light. Jenna still dressed in her hoodie and jeans feeling simply like a million dollars as she danced in the arms of her best friend. The man despite all of the heartache, despite the sleepless endless nights that she swore she would never get through, she still loved whole heartedly. He had been killed buried and bought back from the brink and Jenna didn't think she could have ever been emotionally fully disconnected from him, not really. He was a ghost, a playful perfect picture of her Craig, but he was different to how her mind had remembered him. Age had bought out this beautiful flawless man, his slightly curved nose, perfect straight jaw line, strong ice blue eyes that pierced Jenna down to her very soul. He was muscular, tall and broad shouldered but above all he exhumed sophistication like it was in his sweat. Everything he did, from his walk to his hand gestures right down to the way he spoke, his etiquette was outstanding. He was no longer the chavvy teenage boy who sumped cans of Stella, smoked weed and partied like it was the fashion. He was now strictly business and fine wine, gone were the tracksuits in their place were the plush Armani suits and the Rolex watches. He was completely compelling now, utterly mysterious and Jenna was caught hook line and sinker over this familiar stranger. It had been as though Craig was a completely different man now, he was romantic, exuberant and self confident. His body language screamed self assured, absorbed in his own allure. Gently he spun around so her back was against his chest, he held one arm out and length, their fingers entwined in one another and his other arm slid across her stomach, his palms flat against her, his nose nuzzled her hair as he continued to sway her gently in time to the music. Not missing a single step in his angelic rhythm. Out of the corner of her eye Jenna noticed Ronnie walking across to the little cottage situated alongside the main house, he was greeted with a stunning megawatt smile from one of the most beautiful young women Jenna had seen in her life. The stranger was dressed in a navy knee length shift dress, sheer tights and a pair of gorgeous suede heels, her stunning blonde hair hung in a loose French plait over her slender shoulders, her face devoid of heavy makeup but Jenna could see a subtle blush on her cheeks and mascara on her deep almond shaped eyes. Suddenly Jenna felt intimidated and surprisingly shy. Especially seemingly as she was dressed so casually, she could feel Craig plant a soft kiss on the top of her head, evidently sensing her discomfort.

"You look beautiful" he soothed gently against her ear, and in that moment Jenna almost swooned ecstatically at his feet. He had never ever been this tentative with her before, it was tantalising and Jenna was almost breathless with sheer excited anticipation of what was to come. Both her hands were on her stomach now, his resting on top of hers gently caressing her knuckles with his fingers, his voice singing along in her ear serenading her privately even under the watchful eye of the Driver and the drop dead Gorgeous blonde on the threshold of the cottage door. In one swift movement they were face to face again as the chorus reached its beautiful crescendo, Craig leant in and kissed her hard on the mouth, his lips guiding hers into a slow relentless rhythm, passionate, gripping as his hand ran down her back, the feeling so brutally sensual and Jenna felt as though she may fall apart at the seams at his mere touch. It was so different with him now, still so complicated, there was still so much she didn't know, but in that moment she didn't think that she wanted to. She was lost in him, drunk on his all absorbing love for her. He was an addiction, a strange, pure delectable addiction and she couldn't help but feel as hard as she was trying not to, like she was falling for him all over again, but this time it didn't feel like it was unrequited.

His delicate finger ran against her cheek, making her whole body quiver with an almost insatiable desire. Her whole stomach was trussed up in perfect knots; she had never felt so wanted in all her life. He Put his hand in his pocket and pulled out a large box, his boyish grin electrifying in its intensity making Jenna almost faint with unadulterated ecstasy. She took the box from him and slowly opened it, inside lay a stunning silver charm bracelet. Jenna gazed at the beautiful silver charms that sparkled in the morning light; she smiled as she inspected the bracelet. a Stella Artois challis charm, a music note, a charm with Ke$ha's name on it in the same writing from her album, a gorgeous purple heart, a tiny pink heart with a picture of Kiki printed in the centre, a tiny lock and key, a C for Craig, a diamond encrusted J for Jenna, and a K for Kiki. It was the most stunning thing Jenna had seen in her life, Craig took the bracelet from the box and gently clasped it around her tiny wrist, the various charms jangling as he released her hand, planting a soft kiss on her knuckles.

"Thank you, its beautiful" Jenna mouthed softly, her voice had suddenly abandoned her.

Jenna noticed suddenly that the music had stopped, Craig grasped her hand and turned towards the cottage, the driver and the blonde were stood grinning like Cheshire cats at them, the drivers hand snaked around her slender waist, her hand resting on his; they looked simply gorgeous together.

"Want to go see your daughter now?" Craig asked, his eye lashes fluttering, he knew that this is what had hurt Jenna the most and he was unsure how she would react. She nodded simply, not even being able to manage the slightest reaction, her face paled slightly as Craig led her towards the small cottage beside the main house. It was a stunning pale brick house surrounded by hanging baskets of purple flowers and small shrubs that concealed a little vegetable garden. It truly was a cute, serene little home. As they approached the door, the gorgeous blonde outstretched her elongated hand to Jenna;

"Hi I'm Leah Warren" She smiled a huge welcome to Jenna "You must be Jenna, I've heard so much about you" She smiled warmly again as she introduced herself, shaking Jenna's hand in a firm yet gentle grip her deep American drawl taking Jenna slightly by surprise. Jenna was dumbfounded and could only manage a nod of the head, this was so fucking surreal. Leah led them into the small living space of the cottage and there sat on the floor, in front of a cosy log fire dressed in a pair of flannel pyjamas, her scraped into a little ponytail on her head was her daughter. Eating a bowl of cereals and chatting away mindlessly to her dolls that were having a tea party with a delicate white floral bone china tea set. Jenna just stood and took in the wonder before her, biting her bottom lip to avoid the tears in her eyes from cascading down her face. She looked so grown up, so beautiful and Jenna could see she was thriving under Leah's attentive care. Jenna felt Craig's hand snake into hers and she clung to his fingers fearlessly as he guided her into the room, Kiki turned from her tea party and took in the four smiling faces before her. Ronnie, Leah, and Daddy and.... No it couldn't be? It was, it was definitely her mummy.

Kiki stood up and ran towards Jenna, her bare feet slapping the hardwood as she bounded towards her mum. Jenna scooped her up into her arms, kissing every inch of her perfect angelic face, holding her in the tightest hug she could muster as the tears spilled from her eyes. Caught in this catastrophic symphony of mixed emotions Joy, fear, relief, happiness and every other possible feeling was rushing through Jenna and at that very moment she was absolutely untouchable. Euphoric off her own elation, dizzy off her own crazy love for her daughter. The almost brutal insanity she felt at finally piecing everything together, her beautiful baby girl had been taken by her own father so that he could give her this amazing, all absorbing life. There was nothing but pure exhausting love in that very moment; Jenna relished the thought of finally having her family back as one despite all of the knocks they had suffered. Jenna's whole body trembled as she just held her baby, soaking in every single inch of her, her baby soft skin so delicately fragranced with talc and Johnson's shampoo, her delicate nails painted a soft pink like a proper little lady of the manor. Their perfect daughter.

Jenna stared through the salty haze, wiping her eyes with her sleeve before holding her daughter out at arm's length, drinking in every perfect feature of her tiny face. Kiki had been her everything for so long and now Jenna felt as though she barely knew the little girl before her. For so long she had been solely Jenna's. Now she was forced to share between Craig and the blonde woman who clearly adored the little girl. The delectable smile that played on her lips as she watched the scene before her was one of sheer all consuming happiness. Jenna retreated, kissing the little girl on her tiny forehead and permitting her to go back to her game. She turned back to her audience and smiled gently, this was the start of a completely different relationship for them both and Jenna didn't want to push Kiki away. She hadn't been there for weeks now and the little girl had become accustom to Craig's ways of living. She had obviously grown close to Leah and Jenna could evidently see that the feeling was mutual. Leah allowed for Jenna to stand and make way for her to go back to playing teatime with Kiki, she nodded courteously at Jenna and returned to her perch on the teal shagpile rug.

Jenna pushed past Craig and Ronnie and made her way out into the fresh air, sucking in cool breaths as though her life depended on it, she realised then that her heart was palpitating loudly in her chest and her forehead was smeared with a cold sweaty film through sheer anxiety. She bent over doubled as she tried to control the sobs that eventually took over, her dry cries echoing out over the driveway and suddenly Jenna had never felt so alone, and so useless in all her life. How the fuck had her life become so complicated? She felt Craig's hand slip across her waist and she didn't fight him as he held her close. She placed her head on his broad shoulders and released all of the weeks pent up frustration and anger out in loud, nonsensical wails. All Craig could do was hold her to his muscular chest and repeat "It'll be ok" like a mantra. His soft soothing voice masking the sadness he really felt at the situation that they had found themselves in. Craig knew this would either make them or break them and he had been so assured that she would be ok now she had seen Kiki, but her reaction had thrown him off balance and he found himself questioning their future together if she couldn't forgive him for taking Kiki. He hoped for both their sakes that she would, or all of this would have been for nothing.

Chapter Eighty Two

Jenna lay sedated in the warmth of the plush silk sheets that were splayed across the elegant four poster bed, her eyes fixed on the silver and black beaded chandelier that hung elegantly from the ceiling, Craig lay sprawled out beside her, snoring softly in his deep restful sleep, his face completely serene with calm as he slept soundly. He looked so young and vulnerable in his sleep, his brow completely devoid of any lines, his subtle crow's feet completely erased and his lip hanging slightly as he slept soundly. He truly was a stunning man; even now as he lay naked beside her. His bare chest rising and falling rhythmically Jenna found herself captivated within his presence. His tanned skin glowing softly in the morning sunlight, the subtle beams leaking through the gap in the grey and black silk curtains kissing his prominent cheekbones as his face rested against the light. Jenna lay back against the plump, heavy goose feather pillows and stretched out languidly, yawning loudly as she did so. She glanced around the massive bedroom in vast amazement, everything in here screamed money. From the black carved furnishings, to the silver accessories, the amazing smashed mirrored ceiling above the bed that made the whole room seem huge, the millions of separate pieces reflecting stunning light displays across the vast master suite. The large framed picture of them both on the bedside table on Craig's side sat pride of place in a diamante encrusted frame amongst his watch, his phone, his car keys and his wallet. It truly was a spectacle of sophistication, graceful and elegant and for a second Jenna felt a pang of jealousy as she wondered whether it had been a woman who had arranged the decor. She shook the thought immediately of course, she had spent her first night in Craig's house and her moment of madness the previous afternoon had all but been forgotten. They had enjoyed a wonderful evening together, Craig had given her a tour of the grounds and his home, which boasted six bedrooms, four bathrooms, spectacular dance hall, gym and sauna and an indoor pool. They had spent the evening drinking Rose and dancing to Craig's eclectic taste in music whilst he bought her up to speed on his death and everything that had happened since he had left the estate. He had done so well for himself and Jenna had never felt so proud of him. Then they had fallen into bed in the early hours and made glorious passionate love to one another until the morning had broken. Jenna felt so elated that she almost thought she may burst, she also considered whether she may be bipolar, the last few days had taught her that emotional balance was completely psychotic. One minute she felt as though she could take on the world and all his friends the next she felt reserved, shy and overbearingly guilty at the thought of Dom and Claire and how her actions would affect them. She had thought about Dom a lot last night, not that she had wanted to of course. But with every laugh and every lingering smile that she and Craig had shared she had thought of Dom. She couldn't even begin to imagine how hurt he would be if he could see her now, stark naked and full of post-sex happiness trussed up in the sheets of the dead Craig Carter. The thought made her blush, she had never acted so slutty in her entire life and the thought embarrassed her slightly. Of course she had never intended to lead the two men on, but it had been so hard to make an immediate choice between them both. Craig was danger, Dom was safety. But Jenna never had been one to play by the rules, her mother had always scolded her free spirit; "It'll be the death of you girl" had been the motto of Jenna's life. Jenna had always known that that had been what had originally attracted her to Craig, his complete abandon on normality, he was dangerous, a risk taker, he was sexy, confident and he made Jenna feel like a princess despite his sometimes copious attitude towards her. They held so many precious memories, some bad, some insatiably good, but they had always, without a single doubt remained a constant within one another's life whether together or miles and miles apart they were always in each other's hearts and they held something that was worth so much more than all the money in the world. They had a true, real, unbreakable friendship.

Jenna glared at her reflection in the millions of pieces of glass above her head and sighed, she couldn't decide whether it was a sigh of contentment or one of sadness but she knew she had to figure it out soon.   She pulled the sheets away from her naked body and slid out of bed being careful not to wake the sleeping beauty beside her. She picked up Craig's shirt from the floor and slipped it over her bare shoulders, her rich cotton soft against her over sensitized skin. She padded across the thick black carpet making her way to the en suite, she took a secretive look back at the bed and grinned, it still bewildered her that he was here in the flesh. His hand, was tentatively tucked against his stomach, the nasty purple scars were clearly visible, and Jenna closed her eyes to block out the awful memory of all she went through that day. The day he was taken away from her. Everything she had been through since all seemed so irrelevant now, he was alive. She turned away and headed for the shower, she needed a clearer head before she even tried to assess the situation. Dom was still in the forefront of her mind. The poor man had done nothing more than love her and this was how she had repaid him, shagging her supposedly dead best friend, the mere thought cut her to the quick. She had been pawn in this vicious love triangle all of her own making and it hurt her to think that in the end, this would be a war. She knew Craig would never ever let Dom be a part of her life now, he had made that clear the previous night when he had admitted to none the less stalking her the past six months. He knew all about Dom and Jenna's relationship, from their first initial meeting to their sexual encounter barely a week ago. Jenna blushed; the idea of even facing of Dom crushed her. She knew he deserved more than an explanation. She could still picture him now, all thick black curly hair and short stubbly beard, his older face and slightly crooked nose, he was full of imperfections but to Jenna he was more than perfect. He was the most idyllic gentleman who would take her at her worst and her best. He was something surreal to Jenna. Something now that was unquestionably forbidden. But Jenna was like eve, the bite of the forbidden fruit was etched on her soul, and she craved with suppressed desire another bite of its delectable sweetness. Dom was something completely surreal, he was simple, he was desirable but above all he wasn't Craig; Craig had been the type of person Jenna had avoided ever since his timeless death and now she had learnt to love something different, the compulsion to love something that was completely alien to her had all but consumed her. The emotional tug between them both had enveloped her heart then had literally split her in two. She had never thought for a second after Craig she would find love again. Especially in someone as different as Dominic Grey and his over indulgent allure. Jenna plugged in her phone to the docking station in the bathroom, the sound of Daughtry enveloped as she turned the shower on. The hot water cascaded down in violent torrents as she stepped into the steam ridden cubicle, the music soothing her as she stood under the almost broiling hot spray. She closed her eyes as she plunged into Chris Daughtry's delicious silky voice. The volume almost deafening in the small enclosed shower space, yet Jenna couldn't help but sing her guts out to the rock fuelled melody. The words reverberating against the expensive tiles, Jenna's voice bouncing as she sang along, her heart set solely on expressing herself through the music. For a second she was completely immobilized, the words stung her slightly, "just like that I'm crawling back to you just like, you said I would"

She almost choked, despite being so irrelevant the words rung true. She was crawling without dignity back to Craig. Despite the lyrics Jenna couldn't help but feel as though she was a pawn in this vicious love triangle, embroiled in a vendetta of two hearts. Despite the fact that the two had never crossed paths Craig despised Dom and she knew that Dom wasn't too keen on Craig either. But Dom thought Craig was dead so he wasn't threatened by him in the slightest, he just had to put up with his face plastered all over the walls of her flat and her constant nonstop chatter about him. Her blush deepened as she thought of how embarrassing she had been towards him. Attempting to kill herself, the scars on her wrists still apparent, drinking herself into oblivion freaking out the first time he had attempted to have sex with her. All for that cretin in the bedroom who had made her feel so guilty about moving on despite his deception of them all. She had genuinely had no idea that he was alive, she had grieved so deeply for him, and saying goodbye to him had been the hardest thing she had ever had to endure. The sheer horror that she had gone through when he had died had been enough to break her, the pain still so raw even after all this time and all that had happened. She stood there under the showerhead for almost an hour, trying to wash away the feelings that ate her up inside. Surely she couldn't be so in love with two men all at once, could she? Surely this wasn't normal for any woman to feel so devoted emotionally to two men who were complete opposites. She knew Craig like the back of her hand, Dom was merely a stranger yet the connection, the chemistry between them made her feel as though she had known him all her life. She finished her shower and stepped out onto the marble effect tiles, wrapping herself in a white fluffy towel and tying one around her head to attempt to stem the water that dripped from her flowing mane of hair. She walked back into the bedroom; Craig was awake, sprawled naked in bed talking on the phone. He gave Jenna a cheeky wink, patting the empty space beside him on the bed. Submissively she went and laid beside him her lithe body snaking into his, his arm slid across her stomach and he pulled her into his vice like grip. He cupped her bare breast in his hand, rolling her nipple between his expert fingers making her throw her head back against the she could feel his cool breath on her neck his touch making her whole body shiver delectably with sweet anticipation. She could picture the smile on his face as he continued his passionate assault, whilst still nattering away on the phone. She had to force a hand to her mouth to stifle her suppressed moans, his hands mercilessly trailed slowly to the hem of the towel, in one swift tug she was laid bare. She tried her hardest not to squirm as their gazes met, steely blue eyes cutting into every inch of her naked skin, his fingers still slowly sauntering across her stomach tickling her softly then in a second breath he was down in between her legs, Jenna gasped as he ran his finger up and down her, she was tantalisingly wet already, Jenna sucked in a harsh breath his face still expressionless as he carried on talking away on his phone. Even as he plunged two fingers deliciously inside her his face stayed a calm reserve only his eyebrow arched slightly as he entered her again. Without hesitation he continued his perilous attack on her body, his eyes never leaving hers as his fingers invaded her, filling her with relentless desire. Jenna's fingers gripped the sheets so hard her knuckles flashed almost deathly white, her head tossed back, her mouth the perfect "o" as her breathing accelerated and her body sang sweetly with fevered exasperation. He shifted slightly so he could glide his fingers deeper into her, his fingers slowly twisted and slipped around inside with ease, lubricated by her own incredible wetness.

"John I've got to go mate, I've got some urgent business to attend to" He smiled cheekily as he spoke saying his goodbyes to whoever was on the other end of the line. He hung up the phone and tossed it aside before leaning over Jenna, his fingers at his lips as he licked the salty taste away teasingly, his eyes still staring strong into hers as he gently positioned himself over her, before slipping his hard erection into her, she almost came right then, as he slowly moved in a crazily slow torturous rhythm. Taking her higher with each tentative agonising stroke he made, his breathing slow, resonating in the silence. He leant in closer and kissed her mouth subtly before drawing out and slamming back into her hard, furiously his rhythm stayed the same, each tantalising thrust tearing Jenna apart as she moaned loudly trapped in an all consuming orgasm that shook her whole body. Craig pushed hard into her before picking up his pace, the change in speed sending Jenna over the edge and quickly she came all over again, her body pulsating sedately beneath him as he finally found his release. He stayed inside her as he leant in to gently plant a bewitching kiss on her forehead. She could barely breathe, his intoxicating smell lingered in her nostrils as she bowed into him, running her fingers across his back as they gazed intently at one another. His playful smile dancing at the corners of his mouth, he tried his hardest to keep a straight face, failing catastrophically as he rolled off her his beaming smile almost melting her.

"Very apt choice of song to fuck too Miss Shearan" he whispered as the end notes of 'only you're the one' by Lifehouse played in the background. Jason Wade's incredible voice filled the room softly with its haunting aura. Jenna hadn't even noticed the song herself; it was one of her favourites, Dom had lent her the album and she had instantly fallen in love with them. She of course kept that shred of information to herself. Puzzled on how Craig knew the band himself, she sat up slightly leaning against the pillows.

"You know these?" she quizzed, nodding towards the bathroom where the music was coming from her eyebrow furrowed slightly at the irony as the song changed to another Lifehouse track.

"Their one of my favourite bands Jen" he laughed, a full boyish laugh to juxtapose his throwaway comment and Jenna was thrown slightly at the revelation, so he and Dom had one thing in common. The thought made her uneasy. Craig shifted away from her slightly sensing her unease; he pulled the blanket around him, the gesture almost childlike as he tried to conceal his modesty. His face twisted slightly, his eyes dejected somewhat.

"What is it?" he whispered, the discontentment in his voice thick with evident annoyance. She shook her head, words failing her and not for the first time lately. Her eyes focused on the vase on the bedside cabinet, anything not to look at him anymore. Her stomach churned like the tide as she tried to mask her discomfort. Her heart beat a tattoo in her chest, her breath escaping in shallow bursts, how could he make her feel so under pressure just with his eyes. She could feel his glare burning her skin deep, her stomach knotted tightly as she turned herself away, not wanting him to know the truth.

"Jen" he pushed, as he grasped her arm;

"Dom, he loves Lifehouse, that's who introduced them to me" she replied, her voice barely audible, strained with embarrassment. And without another word shared between them Craig was up and out of bed, he stormed into the bathroom and the music died within seconds. She heard the mirror smash, the tirade of insults that then spewed from his mouth like venom cut her deeply. She flung herself back against the mattress, trying her hardest to suppress the tears that burnt her eyes. Surely he couldn't be that jealous, he had no reason to be. She was here wasn't that enough for him?

When he returned to the bedroom he was freshly showered and fully dressed in a sharp black suit and a crisp white shirt, unbuttoned slightly at the collar. He looked completely mesmerising, beautiful even in anger. He glanced at her for a second, his face like thunder as he pulled a tie from the cabinet at the far end of the room. The silence and tension that lingered between them was excruciating. Jenna sighed weakly as he left without saying a word, slamming the door behind him. She sagged back against the pillows, emotionally exhausted, her whole body numb, aching from the stress. He was split into two separate personalities Jenna was sure of it. She drenched herself in the comfort of the silky sheets and dozed off into a restless, uncomfortable sleep.

Chapter Eighty Three

Craig stared out at the vast countryside before him, the rolling hills, the pale mottled sky slightly overcast. The silence lingered serene, uncomplicated as he attempted to gather his thoughts. He contemplated all of the possible outcomes of the morning's events; he wouldn't be surprised if he went home to find her gone. The flittered thought disturbed him greatly; he puffed slowly on a joint as he stared out bleakly at the open space, the simplicity of it all was a comfort. It took him away from his daily struggles, the thoughts that ate him up as he swaggered through the days like the mogul he now was. But he was haunted, haunted so deeply by the things he had done, by the things he had seen, by the thing he craved the most in his shallow hostile life. Love. To be loved for not only his money or his power but for his personality, for himself. He didn't want to feel out casted anymore, wealth had bought him nothing more than paranoia and distrust in his peers that he found disturbing to say the least. He had learnt to live in constant alert, in constant fear of someone trying to come and take his hard earned reputation away. He had built himself a high wall, a veneer that he wore to mask his vulnerability. But he could feel himself losing it, losing his poker face, being swept away with his emotional turmoil over a girl he knew he had always loved. Jenna had shaped him as man, made him want to be better, made him want to work hard, without her he would have still been stuck on the Belmonte snorting coke and kicking people's heads in for a lousy twenty quid. He had sacrificed his life, his demeanour, and his relationships with everyone to pave his way in life. He had been away only a short time, but he had changed in every aspect of himself. He was a hard edged, wealthy unbelievably gritty young businessman. He ate, slept and breathed his career, the clubs were his empire and they made him millions. He owned numerous properties and had his fingers stuck in many pies concerning all manners of business. But he knew he would give it all away, just to make his family work. It all meant nothing without Jenna.

His shoulders slumped as he sighed loudly, his expression heavy with sadness, he hoped that he was making the right decisions; he couldn't help but feel disappointed in himself. She had agreed to try, she had agreed to make a go of things and here he was fucking it all up at the first hurdle because some other man had showed her some music! He felt pathetic, but the sheer paranoia that ate away at him over Jenna was nothing but soul absorbing. He couldn't help but feel possessive over her; she was his, his only. He took another deep drawl on his joint, sucking in the empowering smoke, craving the feeling of euphoria as it drowned him, his eyes glassy and semi closed his drug fuelled stupor giving him a somewhat clearer outlook. He knew he had to let it go, try and find a way to move forward without allowing all that had happened since his disappearance. There was no way he could move on until he had his final revenge. And of course revenge was something Craig would relish in completely. Kenny Kreegan would have his balls served to him on a fucking platter Craig was sure of it. His fingers instinctively reached for his heavily scarred stomach, the reality of it all still so fresh in his mind. He had marked himself so traumatically all in the name of revenge, the thick purple scars that evaded his body were a reminder of the risks that he had taken just to get to where he was right now. The money, the power, and the domination it gave him he had sacrificed so much. His sister was dead; his mother had been left with no one. But he still had Jenna; the thought filled him with elation. He couldn't forgive what had happened but he could try and see a future between them. He loved her, completely; he loved her with a passion so strong that it had very nearly killed him. He had done all of this for Jenna and Kiki and their future together. He could see his life with her, had planned everything around the two of them. He didn't think he could handle it if it all fell apart now. At least here they were away from it all, away from that fucking estate and the parasites that occupied it. He sat in silence as he finished off the last of his Joint, he knew what he had to do, and it was just a matter of how and when he did it.

Chapter Eighty Four

Jenna had spent her morning in a state that resembled a rat up a drainpipe, she was agitated, nervously on edge and she couldn't for the life of her fathom why. She clutched her phone in her hand as she paced the length of the full room, her eyes flittering around darting from the large bay window to the door. Her mind fuzzy from over thinking, her mouthy sickly dry, her heart pulsing in her chest Craig had been gone hours and so far not a word, she was beginning to panic. She wasn't sure why, he was a fully grown man. A man on edge, her subconscious reminded her subtly. Jenna would give anything to see him safe right now, safe and sane above all things. Her beautiful mystery, his strange addiction to her was intoxicating despite making her feel so insecure. It was the insecurity that ate her up the most, she felt slightly used being with Craig, as though he had a preconceived notion about how their relationship should be played out. He had been stalking her ever since his apparent death and still she was haunted by him, drawn to him, like a moth to a flame just anticipating to get burnt. Despite being so bad for one another she knew she would never ever let him go again. He was her drug of her choice and boy was he potent, deadly but oh so sensuous. Jenna stilled taking in her vast surroundings, the pure luxury of the plush bedroom suite made her bitter with impending jealousy, he had lied to achieve all this, deceived them all just for notoriety and Jenna couldn't help but feel second bested. He had revelled in the dirtiest of deeds and still came out on top, he had faked his own death and to warrant what? His own self assurance, Jenna could never contemplate what he had been through, but she was sure it wasn't half as bad as what he had put her and Claire through. Her thoughts drifted to Claire for a second, Jenna felt an overwhelming sadness envelope her as she thought of her friend, still mulling in her own grief, still plagued by the sour memory of her children. Jenna thought of Sammy briefly, how she had tumbled into the deepest of depressions after Craig had died, her drug abuse had consumed her and she had become simply nothing. Did Craig know all this? Did he know how his actions had affected his closest friends and family or was he still blinded by this false image of power. This ideology he had created of his life being made easier by having money, by having a sense of security. But as Jenna's mother had always said "It wasn't money that kept you warm at night". Jenna found the opposing war of emotions that invaded her body exhausting, she had wished for Craig for such a long time that she still didn't register the reality of it all. She still couldn't bring herself to admit that he was alive, she lived in the fear that she would suddenly wake up from this humbling dream and realise that the grief was still so raw in her mind's eye. She gazed out of the bedroom window, her face etched with sadness, as she took in the breathtaking view before her. The rolling hills, glistening streams and sweeping blue skies were the perfect backdrop for this elegant palace. For a second Jenna pictured her life here, the standard of life she could give Kiki was so much more plentiful than what she could give her on the estate, it was a selfish thought but maybe she could just grin and bear it, forget all about her lingering feelings for Dom just for the sake of her daughter. It was a risk she would have to take, even if it was for Kiki's sake.

Chapter Eighty Five

"I'm fucking telling you Kenny it was Carter!" Dom slammed his fist on the solid oak table, his eyes pinned to Kenny Kreegan like something possessed, his crazy curly hair a wild mass on his head, the look of a man who hadn't slept in days carved on his handsome face. Dom's stare piercing Kenny as he hitched a sharp breath through his teeth his deep penetrating eyes transfixed on the old decrepit toad. Kenny shuffled slightly in his seat; this man was dangerous he could sense it. Hell hath no fury he thought instantly almost chuckling with nervous disposition. He glanced at the man before him, the film of sweat that ran across his strong cheekbones showing the anxiety, his knotted fingers clasped together on the desk before him. Kenny was sure the boy was on drugs, there was no fucking way he had seen Craig Carter, the boy was fucking dust now. Kenny had gone to the funeral just to make sure the muggy little cunt was six foot in his grave. The stabbing was old news now, there was no need to rake it up now, business was doing well, Rosa had finally popped her fucking clogs so he didn't have the added stress of travelling back and for the funny farm to visit, he had money leaking out of his ears, no, dragging all of this up would be a simple, pointless inconvenience. Kenny sat back in his large leather backed chair stretching out sarcastically attempting to stifle a yawn as he did so.

"Look Mr Grey" he smiled his sweetest smile, showing his slightly off green teeth "Mr Carter was dealt with a very long time ago and I will NOT in the interest of my business debate this issue further; the boy was stabbed very publically by the Fenton boy, there was no chance he survived, and anyway a number of us including myself went to the boys funeral as a mark of respect to his mother" a toothy smile played on Kenny's lips as he bathed in the memory. The solemn faces of the mourners, the luscious floral tributes and Kenny and his goons stood beside the grave in their funeral finest all laughing inside at their audacity. Kenny knew without a doubt that the boy was utterly brown bread. He stood straightening his jacket lapels and with mild mannered sensitivity showed Dom the door, none too kindly forcing him out and reminding him not to venture here with such nonsense again or he may find himself in a similar situation to the dead Craig Carter.

Dom wandered off across the estate, his mind a complete void, he had literally nothing left to give. He had hoped in all sincerity that Kenny would have seen at least a scrap of truth in his vivid story. He had now lost all hope and felt shallow for taking a brutal stab at Jenna's attempt of happiness. Jealousy was a cruel mistress and Dom had never felt so low in his entire life, the act that everything was fine wasn't easy to portray and inside he felt as though he was dying. The vicious weight of the world rested solely on his shoulders and he felt that at any given moment he would break. He felt the acidic bile rise in his throat and instinctively he swallowed down hard as he felt the tears stinging in his eyes. Kenny's rejection had made him doubt himself now, had he really seen Craig? It had been dark after all, he could have been mistaken? He suppressed the thoughts immediately, trusting his own judgement implicitly. Of course it had been Craig Fucking Carter the cocky stuck up bastard. The anger that raged through Dom was beyond words as he stormed across the Belmonte, his eyes burning with humiliation and deceit, his trainers slapping the hard concrete as he paced swiftly through the communal gardens, his hands tucked into his hooded jumper, his walk turned into a gentle jog, he pulled his phone out of his pocket and plugged in his headphones, seconds later the beautiful crescendo of Jason Wade's sultry liquid silk voice filled his space as he ran to the haze filled sounds of Lifehouse. He didn't know where he was headed, not a single clue, but he knew without a doubt he had to clear his head. His over worked head playing tricks in the solace of his own thoughts, his tired eyes refusing sleep, his aching body wary of rest as he continued to pound the paving stones beneath him. His heart was pounding in his chest, his whole body buzzing with adrenaline as Jason Wade belted out the chorus of "flight" in his ears, and the song described his current emotional state to a tee. He placed the song on repeat and he continued with his assault of the kerbstones as he escaped the vicious clutches of the Belmonte and headed for town, he had no idea where his feet were taking him, but he knew that as long as he was running, he wasn't getting into any trouble.

Chapter Eighty Six

Craig glanced out over the Belmonte estate, the whole fucking place was a shit hole he had never noticed it much as a child but now, he could see in stunning clarity the sheer poverty and desolation he had been forced to grow up in. There would be no more hiding after all of this was over, he had a few more things to sort first and then he was coming, coming back for his revenge, coming back to finish the job that he and Johnny had started. He gawped suddenly as the handsome Dominic Grey hurtled past his car, he was so stunned he had to look twice to make sure it was him, by fuck it was. Craig's stomach knotted at the thoughts that evaded him, clenching deliciously at the thought of Jenna and this handsome bastard together. He was so different to himself, the complete opposite to be précised. Now seeing him up close Craig sensed why there had been such a competition between the two for Jenna's affections, a fight he was still trying his hardest to win. Even now dressed in nothing but a Man Up gym wear hoodie and track pants he was still a good looking bastard, Craig recognised the brand, he wore them himself ironically. Craig had never felt threatened in his life, always he had remained comfortable and confident with his own body image. But this guy was something else completely. All floppy black hair, slim built but muscular with killer cheek and jaw bones, slightly crooked nose and rugged stubble on his cheeks; if Craig had been that way inclined he would have probably gone for Dom himself. A smile danced across his thin lips at the thought. He started the car, his grin widening as the engine purred to life, slowly he pulled off the kerb and headed ever so slowly toward his prey, keeping his distance so not for him to feel threatened. Craig unknotted his tie from around his neck and unbuttoned the two top buttons of his shirt, anticipation cursing through his veins as he followed Dom down the narrow street, he knew Dom hadn't noticed him, he was too far away into his running and his music to have even paid a second thought to Craig's car. Craig scuttled along slowly behind Dom, his eyes striking against every single move the man made, he was older than Craig that was evident but he would without a doubt match Craig in strength and stamina Craig was as sure of that as he was his own name. He was guarded suddenly, the thought of this man taking away the love of his life effected him somewhat, weakened him, it was an emotion Craig couldn't even begin to digest. He followed Dom for about a mile up the road, mindlessly taking in every effortless stride the man took, he didn't even seem breathless, and it amazed Craig just briefly. If it had been him he probably wouldn't have made it past the Belmonte, as much as Craig adored fitness, running hadn't ever been his strong point. He made a mental note to try harder next time he attempted it, even if only to stem the growing jealousy that relished deep in the pit of his stomach.

His nerves were starting to jangle as he picked up speed slightly, as he pulled up alongside the familiar stranger, he wound down his window slightly, trying his hardest to keep himself under control, Craig's eyes locked on Dom's as he looked directly at the car beside him, Dom's jog died almost instantly as he stopped in his tracks, staring back at the eyes he had grown to know so well, the sickly feeling that mauled his stomach was enough to make him vomit right there on the pavement but he held it back as he stared back blankly at the man in the car. He bent over doubled, his hands on his knees as his breathing restored haphazardly back to its natural rhythm. He ran a hand through his mop of hair returning his gaze back to Craig the silent barrier between them lingering like tense smog in the air. Craig dropped his gaze for a second,;

"Get in the motor" he hissed, his lip curled into a vicious snarl as he leant back further into his seat, the cool leather against the thin cotton of his shirt sending a slight shiver across his back. Dom just stared at him, almost dumbfounded with suppressed shock, this cunt had brass he could give him that, coming here and trying to throw the orders around. Dom rolled his eyes at Craig sarcastically before making his way confidently around to the passenger seat. He slid in beside Craig and pulled his seatbelt on before slamming the door shut. The tension between the two was electric and Dom could feel it cursing through his veins at an almost catastrophic speed. He glared harshly at Craig, his steely eyes dumb with concentration as he took in every single inch of Craig's face. He was young, twenty five at most, his hair cropped short to his head and he owned the brightest blue eyes that Dom had ever seen in his life. His eyes looked defeated, sad even as Dom glared at him; He was nothing more than a love struck child really. Dom felt a twang of sadness for the boy; in reality they were both in the same boat, they both shared an all consuming love for the same woman. Dom said nothing as Craig pulled away from the kerb and drove them away from the city. The silence hung heavy between the two, and both stared straight ahead, neither breaking their imploring glare as they entered the overcrowded motorway, the traffic heavy and slow moving. It was Craig who spoke first, his eyes still fixed ahead.

"You love her don't you" he whispered, his words almost choking him as they escaped his lips, the admittance of it hurt him more than he cared to think about. He knew he had a very hard decision to make here and his actions would affect him for the rest of his life. He noticed in the corner of his eye the reflection of Dom's dejected face and he knew instantly that it mirrored his own pained expression. He saw the nod of Dom's head and in seconds he was torn, he had never planned it out like this but for a second he felt sympathy for the man before him. He had planned to hurt him, kill him even just to get him out of the picture but now they were sat here together Craig felt all of his control shatter into a million pieces, he knew he wouldn't lay a finger on Dom because then he would lose Jenna and his precious daughter forever.

"Me too" he grinned as he spoke, his voice light with innocent false camaraderie. He knew this would end in a war, but for now he was just trying to find a balance between the two of them. He wanted to map out what Dom was about, and then he would put a plan into action. He could see why Jenna would be attracted to him, he was quiet, reserved and despite probably wanting to rip Craig's head off he was nothing but respectful. He was the complete opposite to how Craig had been in his younger days. This was of course the only memory that Jenna had to go on. He had changed undoubtedly with age but she had yet to see it. Craig sucked in a nervous breath through his teeth, he had been thrown off the mark, and it wasn't a feeling that sat well with him.

"I never wanted to fall for her Dom" he continued, speaking directly into the blank space in front of him "we were friends, just friends for years and years." He smiled subtly at the memory before urging himself to carry on speaking, as though he was in his own little bubble.

"When I made the decision to fake my own death, I thought it would be easy just to forget about her, but it ate me up inside. Even when I threw myself into my businesses, she was always there" His sombre soliloquy breaking the tension slightly. "It was the thought of never seeing her and Kiki again that made me come back" he sighed tragically, it was an over exuberant gesture more than anything. Dom nodded his acceptance; he didn't know how to counteract the young man's speech.

"Fancy a drink?" Craig asked subtly, he couldn't even filter why he was being so nice to this guy but something inside him sensed he could trust him and in reality he needed a fucking drink before he went home. His mouth was starch, paper dry from nervousness. He was walking in unknown territory now and the thought shirked him.

"We're never going to be friends you know that don't you?" Dom chuckled to himself as though basking in a private joke. His finger running across his bottom lip in mock irony as his eyes met Craig's, steely grey exasperating eyes. Craig's eyes widened taking in the man's words smiling devilishly as their banter bounced off one another.

"You fucked in the same room as I did surrounded by my pictures, think that makes us acquaintances don't you?" Craig smirked as Dom's face turned slightly sour at the truth. It was a sobering thought. Even though Dom was sure Craig was taking a jibe at him he couldn't help but be amused. His infectious laugh reverberating around the small confined space as he tossed his head back, releasing some of his pent frustrations and he found himself warming to the brazen fucker beside him slightly.

"You know we're gunna end up killing each other over this don't you?" Dom replied sternly as his laughter subsided, his facial expression back to the ice cold veneer he had on arrival. Craig gulped hard, trying to swallow his apparent fear at the man's words. Suddenly the mood shifted and Craig too found himself lost in his own moody apparition.

"I've died once before Dom, I have the advantage" he smirked, his eyes not leaving the road once. The traffic had practically come to a standstill as the hit the dual carriageway.

"You call being left with nothing having the advantage Craig?" he replied, his voice tight with suppressed anger, his body rigid. He didn't know where this conversation was going and in all honesty he didn't want to. Despite his reservations he knew he couldn't hurt Craig because of his love for Jenna, if it wasn't for her he would be already floating in a river somewhere in the countryside for an aimless dog walker to stumble upon. Even now as they drove silently into the unknown, Dom kept his manly composure. His hostile guard didn't drop for a second. He knew Craig had the means and the credibility to bump him off, but he also knew the young boy wouldn't, it was a fear they shared equally because they both knew if one hurt the other then they would both lose the woman they loved the most. The thought was sobering.

"You know, Kiki doesn't shut up about you" Craig smiled a huge beaming smile at the thought of his beautiful baby girl. His perfect straight white teeth glimmered in his mouth and Dom was tempted to whip out the sunglasses. He smiled sadly in reply, he had missed little Kiki, he digested Craig's words and his head snapped back swiftly as he realised that Craig must have had the little girl all of this time, his calm reserve melted, molten around them both.

"It was fucking you!" his calmness had all but deserted him the venom etched on his face evidence of how livid he was. He cocked his head to one side; taking in the face before him, the arrogant cunt had the cheek to smile! Grinning at him like the fucking Cheshire cat!

"Do you not understand what that did to her?" he whispered, his voice brimming with pent up anger and aggression, his blood literally boiling in his veins as he tried his damn hardest to keep his composure, it took him everything he had not to slap the taste out of the vicious bastards mouth.

"She nearly fucking died Craig" the words cutting Dom as he remembered the night Jenna had cut herself open on the kitchen floor, the drunken rages, the horrific drunken mood swings that Dom had sat and endured just because he knew that he wanted to protect her. Wanted to take all of her pain away, wanted to shelter her from it all. Here was the inflictor of that grief, Dom had never known anger like he felt now. He could feel the sticky sweat running down his back, cool against his gym T shirt, his eyes were wide with malice. His breath was coming out in harsh loud blows as he glared viciously at the boy sat next to him. Craig's face had a slight note of fear in it as Dom stared hard into his eyes, the direct contact of their glare was enough to put a sense of anxiety into Craig.

"You gutless cunt!" Dom shrieked, his fingers looming for Craig's throat, the jumped up little parasite he had taken his own fucking daughter away, Dom's eyes clouded instantly with insatiable anger as he lunged for the driver's seat. His fists pummelling Craig's face, the heavy blows raining down on his head as the pair threw out angry insults at one another. The car swerved along the heavy trafficked road, as the pair continued to fight it out in the small confines of the car, the swarm of cars around them were beeping their horns loudly and swerving to avoid the manic rush of the black Lamborghini that raged through the streets. Craig held his hand up over his head to try and avoid the shocking blows that were being heaped upon him. Dom was shouting and screaming obscenities at him, whilst Craig attempted to steer the car blind with his free hand. The two of them knew that this was probably the worst time they could have gone at it with one another but Dom had never ever felt so angry in all his life. This boy before him had caused him so much hurt and he couldn't even begin to reign in his temper as he pounded the boy's bare flesh. Dom could barely understand the deafening babble that was escaping his mouth but he knew that he had to try and control himself for both their sakes.

He heaved himself off Craig, the bloody mess that sat in front of him gabbling pitifully under his hot glare. Craig pulled himself up into a sitting position trying as best he could to stem the violence and bring back his concentration to the road. He hurtled down the busy road, the car swerving all over the place; Craig's head was pounding from the visceral beating he had endured. He couldn't concentrate on the road properly, everything was blurred, and slightly hallucinating he tried to focus. For a second it was as though he was having an outer body experience, he could hear Dom shouting beside him. He felt Dom's hand gripping the wheel as he tried to swerve the mini bus that they were hurtling towards......

Chapter Eighty Seven

The deafening crash was all that echoed through Craig's mind as he slipped in and out of consciousness. The sound of screaming was blaring loudly in his mind, his eyes trying to piece together the scene before him. His balance seemed out of sync as his eyes rolled around trying to make sense of what had happened. His whole body was completely numb, devoid of any feeling whatsoever. He looked beside him to see Dom pinned to the leather seat, the blood sprayed across the shattered glass that lay splintered across their laps. His eyes were shut tightly and his body seemed limp Craig pulled his hand out and attempted to shake Dom.

"Dom, Dom wake up mate" he whispered breathlessly. Taking in the bloody corpse beside him, the huge gash in Dom's head was still pumping out blood viciously. His gym suit was splattered randomly with crimson spray. His weak chest rose and fell with an incredible effort. Craig's aching body sagged into the cool leather, he coughed harshly as he smelt the bitter exhaust fumes mixed with the heavy scent of petrol as the thick black smoke that emitted from the bonnet flurried up before them. He tried to unclip the seat belts but they were jammed shut, Craig shifted slightly, the jolting pain in his legs whipping his breath away. He looked down and regretted it instantly, his legs were trapped, bloody and mangled where the driving shaft had been shunted inwards by the mini bus. He could see his meaty flesh tearing out of his shredded trouser leg, and the bone splintering through the skin. The vomit rose to his throat, painfully he swallowed it back, not wanting to worsen the humiliation. He looked across to Dom, Craig placed his hand subtly on his, and it was a gesture of friendship this time. Craig had to see this man survive, there was no way he could let him die. Jenna would never ever forgive him. He could see people rushing to the car, trying the handles, peering in through the broken windscreen all of them with the same look on their faces. Craig felt his head spin uncontrollably as his world turned black.....

Epilogue

Three Months Later

Jenna stared absent minded at the little white stick that was clamped between her fingers, her heart completely pounding with anxiety, this was just what she didn't need and the guilt consumed her as she waited the agonising three minutes to find out her answer. It had been twelve weeks since the fatal Crash that had almost taken the lives of Craig and Dom. The news was still bleak; Craig was in a rehabilitation centre unsure of whether he would ever walk again. The damage to his leg had been horrific and he had been touch and go on whether the doctors were going to remove his leg completely. Dom was still unconscious, clinging to his fragile life with every breath he took. Jenna had been his bedside vigil for the last twelve weeks, barely leaving his side all the while talking to him as though he would spring to life at any moment and talk back to her. She had sat, smoothing his soft black hair between her fingers for hours, taking in his scent like it was the most potent drug she had ever known. She had kissed him, held his hand, she had loved him. The guilt she felt at how the whole scenario between them had played out killed her. She loved them both with a love that was almost illegal, they were both so different, yet they both intoxicated her so much.

And now she had this to contend with, her imminent pregnancy that had by no stretch of the imagination been planned. She felt such a fool for sleeping with them both so soon after one another and she wondered momentarily whom the little life inside her belonged to. She patted her barely there stomach and promised herself there and then that despite whoever had fathered her unborn child she would love it no less than unconditionally.....

TO BE CONTINUED......

The Dirty Deeds

The Second Explosive Novel in the Craig Carter Series

Coming 2016

Printed in Great Britain
by Amazon